DIRTY BUSINESS MYSTERY SERIES

DEATH at the UNIVERSITY

A Sonja Hovland Adventure

SUE BERG

LITTLE CREEK PRESS
MINERAL POINT, WISCONSIN

Little Creek Press
5341 Sunny Ridge Road
Mineral Point, WI 53565

Printed in the United States of America

Cataloging-in-Publication Data
Names: Sue Berg, author
Title: Death at the University
Description: Mineral Point, WI Little Creek Press, 2026
Identifiers: ISBN: 978-1-969183-09-6
Classification: FICTION / Mystery & Detective / Women Sleuths
FICTION / Mystery & Detective / Amateur Sleuth
FICTION / Thrillers / Domestic

Book design by Little Creek Press

ACKNOWLEDGMENTS

Thanks again to Little Creek Press for believing in my stories. And of course, thanks to the blue-collar people who keep the world running with their grit, determination, and optimism. To Alan who believed in me from the beginning – thank you!

CHAPTER 1 • KITTY

Hiding in Plain Sight

My name is Kitty Currant, "currant" as in the sweet dried seedless fruit grown mostly in California and used in baking and cooking, not "current," a body of water or air moving in a definite direction. Most people believe I'm dead, but I'm not. Currently (no pun intended), I live in a little suburb of Fort Worth, Texas, known as White Settlement. My house is located on Sierra Mesa Drive, which merges with Arapaho Creek Road to form a two-mile loop through a lovely neighborhood. It's a beautiful, quiet place to live, filled with live oaks and a bubbling brook that winds its way through the residents' yards.

I know most of my neighbors, but I keep a low profile since the police may still be looking for me, even though I've been presumed to be dead for several years. I really don't want to be found. (You might have guessed by now that I live under a false identity of my own invention purchased on the black market many years ago, and you'd be right.) I have worked at Innovative Fabrications (IF) in Fort Worth for almost thirty-five years, making components for the aircraft industry. Over the years, IF has expanded and grown to meet the demands of the aerospace market. It's been a wonderful place to work, and I have experienced great job security and professional success as an employee there.

My neighbors are interesting, kind people. They keep me grounded with my feet squarely planted on Texas soil. Scott Turner, my neighbor to the north and the first house on the loop, is a retired robotics engineer who worked at Lockheed Martin Aeronautics in Fort Worth for over thirty-five years. He's an interesting dude, always fabricating these fantastic metal sculptures in his workshop. Right now, an eight-foot Easter Island head sits in the tiny woods that borders his house. It lights up at night and gives you a creepy feeling when you see it in the dark, making you wonder if we've been invaded by aliens. Scott also made a huge fourteen-foot Jurassic dinosaur by welding hunks of metal together. The black prehistoric monster stalks unchecked across his lawn. I'm surprised it doesn't spew live fire from its mouth. Everyone in the neighborhood watches his place for new works of art. His front yard is like a revolving art exhibit.

The "General," a retired Marine, lives on the loop south of me. His name is Carl Miller, and his lawn is so neat it's hard to believe it unless you see it. Does he vacuum his grass? I don't know, but there's not so much as a blade or leaf out of place. The shrubbery is precisely trimmed. Every rock and piece of bark is meticulously arranged for maximum aesthetic effect. He is usually working outside on his lawn when I go for my walk at six-thirty every morning. He waves to me with something that resembles a salute. Nice man, but very obsessive. His wife, Penny, is charming and friendly, but I have no idea how she handles Carl. How does someone live with such perfectionism and survive? I'm clueless.

Halfway around the loop and heading back up the hill is Walter Oldenberg. He's originally from Iowa and never fails to tell you that when you talk to him. Frankly, I think he lives with his mind in Iowa while his body resides in Texas. Nice man, but somewhat scatterbrained and very nostalgic. His wife died five years ago. He's terribly lonely, a condition I can relate to. Every day on my walk, I see him sitting near his front living room window with a cup of coffee. He waves, and I wave back. Sometimes, if he's outside, I stop and visit, but I walk away after fifteen minutes, or I'd be there for hours listening to him reminisce about his childhood on the farm in Iowa.

Up the hill and across the street from Scott Turner are the Forseths. They're a nice family with a Texas flag waving in the wind near their large, imposing house with its white columns and circle driveway. A few horses graze within the confines of a white corral, and a very friendly Doberman pinscher patrols the perimeter of the fence that surrounds their property.

Next door to Forseths is Ron Anderson, a very successful real estate agent in the area. His house remodel was recently featured on the television show *Texas Renovation*. He divorced his wife four years ago and has tried to date me for the past two years—unsuccessfully, I might add. Although I bought my house from him, he didn't make much commission from the sale since my home is very modest with a small yard out front and a patio out back, which is nestled under a couple of massive live oaks and maples. Other neighbors are scattered along the loop, and I know their names, but I won't bore you with the details.

I live at the bend of the loop. I try to be very predictable in my habits by not drawing attention to myself. I have no pets since I never know when I may have to leave suddenly and disappear. As I mentioned, the police are still looking for me even after all these years. I have two sisters; one lives in Lake Elmo, Minnesota, and the other lives in La Crosse, Wisconsin. They think I've been dead for thirty-five years, but as I told you, I'm very much alive. Believe me when I tell you that people in La Crosse, Wisconsin, still remember my name.

PART 1

"THE PAST IS NEVER WHERE YOU THINK YOU LEFT IT."

Katherine Anne Porter

CHAPTER 2

Unanswered Questions

Sonja Hovland, proprietor of the Dirty Business Cleaning Service, had taken the day off. It was Friday, September 19. The weather was glorious, and when she finished cleaning out her office closet, maybe she and her husband, Trygve (Trig-vee), would head down to their tiny log cabin near Towerville for an overnight camping trip. She glanced out of the window at the rolling hills behind their house on Shilling Court in the township of Barre Mills near La Crosse, Wisconsin. The trees were ablaze with red, orange, and yellow hues, a kaleidoscopic blend of riotous color. Tall, stately evergreens added a punch of dark color and created a sharp contrast to the variegated leaves that floated gently to the ground. Sonny and Cher, the Hovlands' two mules, were happily grazing in the lush pasture next to the iconic red barn, and Sonja's flock of laying hens pecked greedily around the barnyard near the white chicken coop looking for choice bugs, worms, and seeds. Coco, their spoiled black poodle, gnawed on a rubber kangaroo while he sprawled on the carpet in Sonja's office. Watching her owner, the poodle's liquid brown eyes were alive with curiosity, as Sonja sat on the floor with her head stuck in the dark depths of the closet, shining a flashlight at cardboard boxes stacked to the ceiling. Coco eventually tired of watching Sonja and snuffled in boredom, let out a loud sneeze, and went back to chewing on his kangaroo toy.

Since her husband worked four ten-hour days and had every Friday off unless he was plowing snow, Trygve was home today, too. He'd spent the morning sawing, hammering, and pounding in his newly created workshop on the north side of the garage. As much as Sonja hated losing the space in the garage to an array of power tools and benches while her husband's pickup sat outside, she understood Trygve's need for a place to express his newfound creativity.

Since their involvement in the murder investigation of Dr. Tony Diangelo in La Crosse last year, Trygve needed a diversion to relieve the anxiety he'd experienced when Sonja became the target of evil intentions and went missing—if only for a few hours. Although Trygve had discouraged Sonja's involvement in the murder probe, in the end, she had used her blue-collar connections in the La Crosse community to dig up clues and information that eventually helped the police apprehend the perpetrator. Since then, Trygve had been in recovery mode, which explained his new hobby—creating rustic chairs.

It all started when Sonja gave Trygve a book for Christmas called *The Rustic Furniture Companion* by Daniel Mack. Trygve had devoured the book and promptly headed to the woods behind their house in search of twigs, sticks, and branches in various sizes, shapes, and forms, which he used for the arms, stiles, and rails of recycled chairs. After an expensive shopping spree at Home Depot, where he bought drills, planers, jigsaws, hammers, and screwdrivers, he began remodeling and embellishing chairs from discarded ones he'd found in the landfill, thrift shops, or neighborhood garage sales. He'd learned to deconstruct the old chairs, salvage the seats, and add peeled branches and other objects for the arms, back, and legs. He'd even used canoe paddles in a couple of them. As he'd become more experienced, his chair designs became more flamboyant and intricate, abstractions of the natural world.

Trygve sold his first chair to Art Ravenwald, a mobile artist in La Crosse who was also one of Sonja's cleaning service customers. He encouraged Trygve in his construction techniques, introducing him to other people he thought would appreciate his unique perspective on chair aesthetics, people who could give him a few pointers about chair construction. Sonja had to admit that her husband seemed to have a knack for creating one-of-a-kind masterpieces that blended used chairs with the natural inherent beauty of a tree's anatomy. This ethos had attracted the attention of the art-loving community and nature preservationists in the surrounding area. People enjoyed displaying the chairs in their entryways, on their porches, or in their cabins. Since he'd started making his creations, his list of customers had grown, and now there was a six-month waiting list.

Trygve stuck his head around the door frame of Sonja's office. His bushy hair was turning gray at the temples, his face was tanned, and his brown eyes were warm and friendly.

"Hey, honey. Are you going to make lunch?" he asked.

Sonja stood up, pulled a cardboard box out of the closet labeled "The '90s," and set it on her desk. "I was just about to make some sandwiches," she replied. "Then I'm going to go through a few more of these boxes. It'll feel good to get this stuff sorted out."

"Aren't you going to get rid of it?" Trygve asked.

"Yeah, eventually. But some of the stuff I might want to keep."

"Well, you should be good at this. Aren't you always encouraging your clients to get rid of items they don't need anymore?"

Sonja nodded. "Yes, I am. As I always say: simplify, dejunk, declutter, recycle. That's the theme of most of the talks I have with my customers, although very few of them buy into that philosophy. If you haven't used it in the last year, toss it out," she said. "That's the standard rule for clothes closets, and it works for household stuff, too. That's my mantra, and I'm stickin' to it."

"But most people ignore your advice, right?" Trygve asked.

Sonja walked toward the kitchen as her husband followed close behind. "Yes, they frequently ignore my advice, unfortunately," she said over her shoulder, "but that's to their detriment. After all, nagging them about their choices isn't my job."

In the kitchen, she opened the refrigerator and got out the sandwich fixings. They built their sandwiches as they stood by the counter. Sonja had Havarti cheese and ham on wheat, and Trygve had Swiss cheese, salami, pickles, mustard, and mayo on a French baguette. Sonja made a pot of coffee, and the sharp aroma filled the kitchen. Sitting down at the table, they talked quietly, ate their lunch, and enjoyed a cup of hot, fresh brew.

While they ate, Sonja studied her husband's rugged good looks and considered her life with him. He was an interesting man—a blend of Norwegian heritage and traditions and good old-fashioned American values. He'd been a faithful companion who'd held down the same job at the La Crosse City Parks and Streets Department since his graduation from high school. Personalities aside, Trygve sometimes displayed a gruff, impatient demeanor that others found offensive and annoying, but underneath it all, he was kind and gentle. *He would have made a great father,* Sonja thought wistfully. While Sonja had a flashback of her life with Trygve, he sipped his coffee and munched on a krumkake, a buttery Norwegian delicacy his mother had made and dropped off last night.

"What are you doing this afternoon?" Sonja finally asked.

"I'm going to finish that chair for Lester Krantz. It just needs a coat of varnish, and then I can deliver it to him in the next few days. You?"

"The closet is calling my name. I don't take a day off very often, so I've got to make the most of it. What about a trip to the cabin tonight? Can we manage that?" Sonja asked. She brushed her bangs away from her face and took another sip of coffee.

Trygve observed his wife across the table. She was beautiful, at least to him. Her dark hair had a few streaks of gray, her steely eyes were pools of mystery, and she had a wonderful, firm body. They didn't always agree on things, but if you had a dynamic marriage, then differences of opinion were bound to happen. It kept things interesting.

Trygve made a wry face when she suggested a trip to the cabin. "We could probably go later this afternoon. It might be our last trip for a while, though. It's getting colder at night now, and I'm becoming more of a wimp than I want to admit. Be sure to pack the air mattresses. Sleeping on the cold, hard floor of the cabin isn't my idea of a good time."

"Okay," Sonja replied. "I'll pack our stuff and some food. Can we leave about four?"

"Yep, that'll work." Trygve got up, put his plate and cup in the sink, kissed Sonja, and headed back to his garage workshop. While she washed their lunch dishes, Sonja thought some more about their marriage. Although they'd lost three children to miscarriage, Trygve had remained devoted to their relationship despite the hardships they'd been through, giving generously of his time and love to make her feel secure and happy. *What more could a woman ask for?* Sonja thought.

Although Sonja loved her husband fiercely, if she were being honest with herself, she had to admit that lately she'd been secretly waiting for another criminal investigation to rear its head. She thought back to the Diangelo affair late last spring. Finding a dentist dead in his examination chair had been a total fluke and had propelled them into a world that had its own set of rules, a world that seemed to spin wildly under its own power. With little or no evidence about the dentist's demise, Sonja chased down clues around town, talked to her contacts in the blue-collar community, relayed information to Police Chief Tanya Pedretti, and observed the procedures the police employed to catch crooks, thieves, and murderers, which she found fascinating. The whole experience had been completely invigorating, awakening something in her that must have been buried in her subconscious her whole life, even though at times during the investigation she'd been scared out of her wits.

Chief Pedretti encouraged Sonja to consider a career as a detective, but she knew that Trygve would never approve, and his approval was very important to her. Without her husband's respect and admiration, her life would be empty and unsatisfying. His last word on solving another mystery had been stark and to the point: "Where you go, I go." It reminded Sonja of the biblical story of Ruth and Naomi. She knew if she got tangled up in another investigation of some sort, her husband would be there right beside her all the way, just like Ruth had been there for Naomi. There was a certain comfort in that, and it gave Sonja confidence that Trygve would be supportive and sympathetic if she became embroiled in another criminal investigation.

Sonja returned to her office and opened the cardboard flaps of the box labeled "The '90s" that was sitting on her desk. Peering inside, she began perusing the contents. There were several newspaper articles yellow with age including wedding and birth announcements from her Swedish relatives in northern Wisconsin, an informational article about the dedication of a county park in honor of her great uncle Cyrus, a handmade booklet that traced her ancestors back to the Swedish province of Dalarna complete with a family tree and numerous pictures of whiskered gentlemen and exhausted women, and various other items from the *Stickley Swedish Gazette*, most of which she threw in the trash bin. But two stories grabbed Sonja's attention, jogging memories of her childhood and sending her into an uncomfortable state of déjà vu.

The first article was from the *La Crosse Sentinel* dated April 19, 1990. On the front page was a large picture of a pretty twenty-year-old female student from the University of Wisconsin–La Crosse who had died in a kayaking accident on the Mississippi River. Sonja would never forget the day when the police knocked on her parents' door in Stickley on the southern shore of Lake Superior and informed them of their daughter Katherine's accidental drowning in a kayaking accident near Pettibone Park in La Crosse.

Sonja could still hear her mother's screams and sobs as she took refuge in her husband's arms. The days that followed were a nightmare of sadness and grief. After the funeral at the Lund Swedish Lutheran Church in Stickley, Darlene and Sonja tried to resume their lives without their older sister, but there were so many questions about the accident that remained unanswered. Why was her sister kayaking by herself at midnight? Why didn't she tell someone where she was going? Why was her body never found? Did she commit suicide? What happened to her VW bug, which seemed to have disappeared into thin air the night of the accident?

Sonja sat at the desk in her office, her hands shaking, her mouth dry with the remembrance of the horrible event. For just a moment, the present had receded, and she was reliving the very real past of her sister's horrible death. Up until today, she hadn't thought about her sister Katherine's drowning for several months. Occasionally, her sister Darlene would bring up the subject, but Sonja usually tried to distract her and redirect the conversation. Of course, it was a well-known fact in the family that Darlene was a difficult person: headstrong, argumentative, and abrasive. She'd had many shouting matches with Trygve, who made a valiant effort to protect Sonja from Darlene's scathing judgmental rants about societal wrongs and the problems people brought on themselves by their own stupidity and truculence. And when Katherine's death reared its ugly head in passing conversation, Darlene grew livid, blaming the ineptitude of the La Crosse Police Department for failing to fully investigate Katherine's death. No one could cuss out someone like Darlene, and her diatribes about the idiocy of the police were the foremost reason Sonja did everything she could to divert her sister's attention to a more prosaic topic.

Another article from the same newspaper dredged up the other shocking event that had rocked the La Crosse community to its core. Skimming the article, she recalled the details as she read them again. In the early morning hours between three and four o'clock on April 17, 1990, a crude, homemade bomb had gone off in the basement of the McMurphy Science Hall on the University of Wisconsin campus in La Crosse. A professor named Dr. James McClintock was killed in the blast. He'd been working feverishly on a new drug that would help infertile couples increase their chances of conception. Apparently, as the police explained later when their investigation was complete, a group on campus opposed the release of the drug on the market based on their belief that the nations of the world were already overcrowded; countries, including the United States, could not sustain the population explosion at its current rate. Who would feed and house all these people? Why weren't governments advocating birth control and abortion to control the population?

Two of the three students involved in the bombing were eventually caught the day after the tragedy, but a few days later the police discovered that the third participant in the university bombing had been a girl named Katherine Waite who'd drowned the day after the incident. Her death in the Mississippi River closed the tragic chapter of the whole explosive affair on a heartbreaking note.

As Sonja sat by her desk and stared beyond the window at the autumn scenery, she found it hard to believe she had ended up in the same city where her sister had participated in a horrendous crime and then, a day later, lost her life in a drowning accident.

Once again, the questions of the past that had troubled Sonja for years returned to torment her. Was her sister's death an accident, or was it suicide or possibly murder? She wondered if Police Chief Tanya Pedretti would remember the bombing incident and be able to shed some light on it. Perhaps it was time to find out what Pedretti knew about the facts surrounding her sister's case.

Early on Saturday evening, Sonja and Trygve sat by the campfire in front of their small log cabin near Towerville, enjoying the night air after their evening meal. In front of them, the fire crackled and hissed, sending a shower of blazing sparks into the night sky. Sonja sipped her wine, but Trygve noticed her vacant stare into the fire. She'd been awfully quiet on the trip to the cabin, which was unusual for her, especially when they were headed to their favorite spot on earth. Usually, she chattered about all the things that had happened during the previous week, and Trygve enjoyed hearing stories about some of her favorite cleaning clients. He'd tried to engage her in conversation during the evening meal, but she was distracted and distant.

The ten acres of land Trygve had inherited near Towerville from an eccentric bachelor uncle held a special place in their hearts. They'd constructed the cabin during a terrible time of grief and loss almost ten years ago after the miscarriages of their three babies. The hard physical work tired them out and helped them sleep. They labored on the construction of the sturdy log cabin, which they'd made from old, weathered beams and gray shed boards salvaged from a decrepit barn on the property. As they worked, they experienced a rebirth of hope which replaced the despair that had invaded their aching hearts. The cabin became what they needed—a healing place of solace in a beautiful, isolated valley where the bubbling creek sang as it tumbled over the rocks. Surrounded by the rolling hills, flowing water, and abundant wildlife, they experienced a deep sense of peace. *God grant me the serenity to accept the things I cannot change, the courage to change the things I can, and the wisdom to know the difference,* Trygve recited in his mind as he watched the glowing embers of the campfire. The prayer had become the theme of their marriage as they struggled to relinquish their dream of having a family. *How many times have I prayed that prayer?* he wondered. After three failed pregnancies, they had come to a place of acceptance—they would not have children.

"Are you okay, honey?" Trygve asked gently, watching

Sonja's expression. She was sitting cross-legged next to her husband, and when she looked over at him, he noticed the tears in her eyes.

"Not really," she said quietly.

He reached over and grabbed her hand. "I'm here for you. You can tell me anything, you know."

Now Sonja began crying in earnest. Her sobs broke Trygve's heart. He pulled her over to himself, and she nestled her body against his chest while she let out all the emotion of the day. After several moments, Sonja stopped crying.

"So, what did you find in the box that turned you on your head?" Trygve asked, kissing her cheek tenderly.

"I can't hide anything from you, can I?" she asked tearfully, looking into his sympathetic eyes.

"Nope. I have a degree in marriage psychology and the female psyche." He smiled.

"Very funny, bud," Sonja replied softly. Sometimes, though, her husband did amaze her with his astute observations and knowledge of human behavior. He might only have a high school diploma, but he was wise in the ways of the world like few other people she knew. There was plenty going on in that brain of his behind those kind, brown eyes. For several minutes, Sonja remained silent as they sat by the fire and sipped their wine. Trygve didn't hurry her; she would tell him what was bothering her when she was ready.

"While I was rummaging through that box of stuff in my office, I came across the newspaper article about my sister, Katherine," she finally said.

"The one who died?" Trygve commented.

"Yes. April 18, 1990, is a day I will never forget," she said. Trygve waited patiently, nodding his head. "I still remember my mom's sobs and my dad's shocked expression when the policemen came and told them she'd drowned. It was absolutely awful." A few tears slipped down Sonja's cheeks.

"I can't imagine," Trygve said softly, but in some ways, he could identify with the grief of Sonja's parents. The only difference was that his grief was for his children who'd never been born and had the opportunity to live a full life.

"But there's something I never told you about all of that," Sonja said. Suddenly, her voice took on an edge of bitterness. Trygve wondered what she was about to tell him. Leave it to his wife to blow him off his feet with some long-held family secret she suddenly wanted to get off her chest. He cringed at the thought of what might be coming. Hadn't their lives just returned to normal after the disastrous chase around La Crosse trying to find the killer of Dr. Diangelo? Trygve braced himself for what his wife might say. *Calm down. You just told her you'd be here for her, so buck it up,* he thought.

"My sister was involved in that bombing when they blew up the science building on the La Crosse campus in 1990."

"What? Are you serious? I remember that like it was yesterday," Trygve blurted. "You mean she was one of the three kids who planted the bomb that killed the professor?" His eyes widened as he recalled the horrid details of the story.

"Mm-hmm. Somehow she got involved in that, although I can't imagine why. Her participation in the crime and her death the day after the bombing have always left me confused and angry. It's hard for me to believe my sister would do something that would endanger the life of another person. It goes against everything she was taught."

"Well, it's possible the students weren't planning on someone being killed because of their actions," Trygve began.

Sonja gave him a hard look of disbelief.

"Kids do stupid things, honey," he hurried on. "Maybe they were just trying to make a statement and express their beliefs. Isn't that what idealistic college students do sometimes? The bomb went off in the middle of the night, didn't it? I'm sure they never expected a professor to be working in the building at that time of night."

Sonja was surprised at Trygve's defense of the miscreants' actions. "I guess that could be true," Sonja said, "but couldn't they have found a better way of protesting than blowing up a building? It took several months to repair the damage, the drug research was destroyed, and McClintock was killed in the process."

"Yeah, when I think about it now, that was pretty radical, I guess," Trygve said.

"And then there's my sister's drowning. I've never believed that the kayaking incident was accidental. To me, it makes more sense that someone killed her and staged her drowning to keep her from ratting out the rest of them who participated in the bombing."

The light from the cracking fire reflected Trygve's troubled expression. "That's a possibility, but the police were able to identify the perpetrators quickly within a few days. When two of the kids were taken into custody a few days later, they confessed to the whole thing," he explained. "Except your sister, of course. She was nowhere to be found."

Sonja sighed heavily. "Yeah, Katherine went missing and was presumed drowned the day after the bombing when they found her kayak along the river, but her body was never found."

"I'm going to tell you something, and I don't want you to freak out," Trygve warned. His brown eyes flashed with worry at the reaction his wife might have. Sonja wondered what her husband knew. He was not an alarmist or conspiracy theorist, something that was so prevalent in today's world. Shocking others with information or suppositions was not his modus operandi.

"Okay, go ahead. I'm listening," she said. "What do you know?" There was a long pause.

"Not everyone thinks your sister is dead," Trygve said quietly as he stared into the glowing embers of the fire. Sonja slowly turned her head and gazed at her husband.

"What do you mean?" she asked, a chill running up her arms despite the warm, radiant heat from the campfire. When he stayed silent, she grabbed his arm and demanded, "What do you know, Tryg? You've got to tell me."

"Calm down, honey. I don't really know anything other than the rumors that have been kept alive by the gossipers around town for the last thirty-five years. All I know is that lots of people in La Crosse believe she's still alive."

"Based on what?" Sonja asked sharply.

"That's the problem. It's all conjecture and rumor. Nothing more, nothing less," Trygve said, keeping his voice level. "Maybe you should ask your friend, Tanya Pedretti, about all of this. She might be able to share some details with you that will put your mind at ease."

Sonja nodded her head at his suggestion. "Okay, that's a good idea. I'll talk to her." There was a significant pause in the discussion, and then she asked, "Do *you* know anything about my sister, Tryg?"

"I just learned a minute ago from you that she was involved. All you've ever told me was that she died tragically while she was in college in a freak accident. I don't know anything else that would make a difference and ease your sadness and troubled mind. I've just heard a lot of stories filled with innuendos, most of it untrue, I'm sure. I'm sorry," Trygve said softly. Sonja rested her head on her husband's shoulder, and some of the tension seemed to retreat into the shadows. They sat by the fire for several minutes in the descending darkness. The discussion about the gruesome subject seemed to be over, but a hard ball of anxiety had formed in the pit of Trygve's stomach. He knew his wife better than anyone, and he shuddered to think what she might uncover about her sister's death in her search for the truth. Nobody, but nobody, could be as stubborn and persistent as his wife when she was on a mission. Trygve felt a shiver along his spine and silently hoped this was just a passing fancy.

CHAPTER 3

Deep and Wide

MIDNIGHT - APRIL 18, 1990

The April night air was balmy; in fact, it had been in the upper 70s during the day, and now the warmth lingered, hovering above the wideness of the inlet. However, no matter how warm the temperatures had been during the day, the water was still very cold. The river had thawed only recently, and in some places, ice chunks floated on the surface of the water. The trees along the riverbank shifted in a warm breeze, their branches creaking and swaying. Up above in the dark night sky, a crescent moon hung like a bauble on a Christmas tree.

Katherine Waite stood on the bank of the Mississippi River in Pettibone Park and stared into the darkness, listening to the night sounds, reviewing the plan in her mind. She had no idea if it would work, but she'd already unloaded her orange kayak in preparation. She fiddled with the buckle on her life vest, a nervous gesture that indicated her disquiet about this entire fiasco.

At this point in time, her options were limited. After the

bombing at the university, she knew she couldn't stay in La Crosse, or even the state of Wisconsin. Although she'd only driven the getaway van, she had to get out of the area, or she knew she'd end up in prison for a very long time. The police had scoured the campus and city asking questions, knocking on doors in an all-out effort to find out who was responsible for the crime on campus. She shook her head in disbelief. How could a bunch of idealistic, starry-eyed intellectuals determined to change the world decide to carry out such a harebrained plan? Obviously, they were long on enthusiasm and short on foresight. The proof was in the pudding—just look at how everything had turned out. Her two friends were being questioned by the police, and it was only a matter of time before they came knocking on her door. She let out an exasperated sigh, then turned and walked up the bank to the 1978 Ford F-150 pickup she'd bought from a guy over in Chaseburg that afternoon. She hoped the rust bucket was reliable enough to get her out of the state of Wisconsin, but frankly, she was worried. How far could a four-hundred-dollar pickup take you?

Late today, as the sun was sinking below the bluffs, she'd tucked her well-loved 1980 sky-blue Volkswagen Beetle into an old, abandoned tobacco shed north of Viroqua, covered it with an army-green tarp she'd bought at Home Depot, and then biked the back roads to a friend's house outside of Coon Valley, where she'd slept for a few hours. Maybe someday, when things cooled down, she would retrieve the car from its hiding place. She hated to part with it, but she had no choice. Circumstances and her foolhardy decisions had forced her to make some hard choices in the last few hours. Hopefully her plan would keep her from being arrested and ending up in a prison cell.

Katherine grabbed the paddle for the kayak from the back of the pickup and walked down the slope to the shoreline. She shivered with anticipation, imagining the ice-cold current washing over her body. Would the strong swimming skills she'd learned along the shores of Lake Superior be enough to get her out of the predicament she was in? *There's only one way to find out—do it,* she thought.

She dragged the kayak into the water, grabbed the paddle, and got in. Quickly she began expertly steering the kayak in and out among the small coves jutting into the river. In addition to the inlets and bays along the shoreline, there were several islands in the backwaters of the Mississippi, adding to the challenge of maneuvering the river at night. She had a route in mind, one she'd taken many times before, but it was different paddling in the darkness rather than in broad daylight. Silently she passed Houska Park and the municipal boat landing to the south. She steadied her resolve for what she knew would come next.

Ten minutes later, she positioned herself close to shore, backpaddled briefly, and without any more hesitation tipped her kayak over and plunged into the frigid water. The shocking cold of the water sucked the breath out of her and sent a massive alarm throughout her body. Her skin tingled like a thousand electric shocks, and she let out several loud gasps as her head broke through to the surface. Treading water briefly, she began swimming for shore, which was about fifty feet away. She pumped her arms and legs frantically, surprised at the slowness of her reactions. Her body felt clumsy and stiff. "Don't panic! You can do it!" she said to herself. She struggled awkwardly, her natural athleticism vanishing as the cold penetrated her muscles. Finally, her feet hit bottom, and she crawled up onto the muddy shore, panting and breathing hard. She stood up shivering violently, sucking in gulps of the night air. She unbuckled her life vest and, with a mighty effort, flung it far out into the river current. She grabbed one of her shoes and threw it in the river as well. Her paddle was floating somewhere in the water while the kayak moved away from her in the rapid current.

She began walking back to the truck, which was parked along a side road in Pettibone Park. When she reached the dilapidated vehicle, she stripped off her wet clothes and dressed in sweatpants, a warm sweatshirt, and a pair of woolen socks. Katherine leaned against the truck, still shivering, feeling a huge sense of relief that she had survived, but thoughts of her college career and her dreams of entering the business world crashed through to her brain, and the euphoria she'd felt about escaping a brush with death evaporated. She began crying. The very thoughts she'd banished from her mind now came roaring back: She was leaving her family forever—her mother and dad and her two sisters. She tried to imagine their reaction to her death, but everything felt like an illusion, as if she were a magician creating a new life by rubbing a genie bottle and making a wish. Her plan to flee the country seemed radical at best, insane at worst. What would people say at her funeral? Would they remember her because she was bold, daring, and smart, or would she be remembered as a victim of pity because she'd drowned and died at such a young age after participating in an abhorrent crime? What about Sonja and Darlene? How would they cope with the loss of their older sister? What would her family think when they found out she had helped the bombers escape from the scene? Suddenly her confidence sputtered to a halt, and another crying jag came over her.

After several moments, she calmed down, walked around the front of the pickup, got in, and started the truck. Sitting in the vehicle with the heater turned on high, she continued shivering and shaking as the warm air blasted into the cab from the vent on the dashboard. Her thoughts were jumbled and confused, but undergirding them was a hard ball of determination.

I am dead now, and my alternate life has begun, she thought as she drove west into Minnesota in her rattletrap truck. *Whoever I used to be doesn't matter anymore. I have ceased to exist except in people's memories.* Those words provided a certain level of comfort now, but she wondered how she would begin her life again. Years later, the memory of this terrible night would come back to haunt her again when another desperate situation pushed her into new, dangerous territory.

CHAPTER 4 • SONJA

Mama Said There'd Be Days like This

On Sunday evening, I looked across the living room at Trygve, who was sprawled in his favorite La-Z-Boy leather recliner. I was sure what I was about to ask him would set his teeth on edge. I hated to disturb his quiet moment of relaxation with another barrage of difficult questions, but it had to be done. During the afternoon, Trygve had been busy nursing one of our mules who'd developed some kind of stomachache. Our vet. Dr. Owens, drove out to our farm to evaluate Sonny, who'd been moping around the barnyard with his head down and ears back avoiding Cher, his companion. Dr. Owens confirmed Trygve's suspicion—a mild case of colic—and administered a dose of Banamine for pain and dry hay in small amounts until Sonny's stomach straightened out, all to the tune of two hundred dollars. Grudgingly, I paid the bill with cash, which saved me twenty dollars.

The television volume was turned low while Trygve sipped on a Spotted Cow beer. Yesterday at our cabin in Towerville, we'd hashed out the uncomfortable facts of my sister Katherine's death and criminal activity in the spring of 1990, but the comments Trygve made only added to the anxiety I had about the whole situation. I was surprised my husband knew about the bombing at the university since he'd never mentioned anything to me about it. As is common for longtime married couples, we both assumed we had no secrets between us. Still, in all honesty, I had hidden my sister's criminal activities from everyone I knew, including my own husband. After all, that's not something you shout from the rooftops, is it?

When the topic of my sister's involvement in the university bombing on the UW–L campus came up in our conversation yesterday, I thought Trygve had handled the news with his characteristic aplomb and graciousness. Katherine's wrongdoing jogged his memory of the incident, and I was sure Trygve knew more than he was revealing. Whether that was his effort to protect me or he was trying to discourage me from investigating the topic further, I didn't know. Since the subject was out in the open now, my questions seemed appropriate.

"If you know something about my sister and the bombing, Tryg, you need to tell me," I said gently, leaning forward and placing my elbows on my knees. Trygve lounged in a semi-prone position, a wary expression on his face, his hand clasped around his beer bottle. I expected him to try and escape to the garage in search of a chair that needed some loving attention.

"Don't even think about heading to the garage," I cautioned, poking the air with my index finger. "Your chairs can wait." Trygve groaned and studied the ceiling as if some earth-shattering information was written there. He took another swig of beer.

"I told you last night, and I'll repeat it again—I know less than you do," he said gruffly.

"I doubt it," I huffed back. "What I know wouldn't fill a thimble. Remember, I was only ten when this stuff happened, and a ten-year-old can hardly be expected to comprehend the ins and outs of a police investigation about a domestic terrorist event. It wasn't exactly a topic of conversation my parents talked about either, at least not in front of me and Darlene." I lifted my eyebrows and stared at my husband until he squirmed uncomfortably. He sat up, and a scowl darkened his handsome face.

"Well, remember I was all of fifteen in 1990," he responded gruffly, "so just exactly what kind of information do you think I possess that you don't already have?"

"Okay, that's a fair question, I guess," I said, nodding my head in agreement, "but I've thought about this a lot, Tryg. You lived in La Crosse your entire life. Is it possible that later, when you were a little older, you learned some things about the bombing and drowning that I don't know? I didn't arrive in La Crosse until 1998 when I enrolled as a freshman at UW–L," I reminded him. "By that time, the police had closed the case, thinking everything was solved and tied up in a neat little package, and my parents had moved on from their grief and shock."

"And you think there are still unresolved issues? Is that what you're saying?" Trygve asked. His voice had become harsh, and I understood his frustration. I could be as stubborn as an old dog protecting his favorite chewed-up bone. "Just exactly what do you hope to accomplish by asking questions about something that happened over thirty-five years ago?"

I sighed and felt a deep sadness that made tears well up in my eyes. "Please, Tryg, try to understand. I loved my sister. She was smart and funny and had a great desire to be successful. She was driven and ambitious, and I really admired her. She wanted to be the first female executive of a Fortune 500 company in American history, and I think if she'd lived, she might have succeeded in reaching her goal. I still can't believe she participated in such a horrible crime in which an innocent person lost his life. For all the explanations and rationales that have emerged from the investigation into her death, I've never been satisfied with any of them. I have a lot of unanswered questions about the whole affair." I ran a hand through my hair and let my arm flop into my lap. "I know I'm just a bullheaded, stubborn Swede who refuses to believe the skimpy facts that have been fed to me. But maybe, just maybe, it's also possible . . ."

"No. No. Don't say it," Trygve interrupted loudly, waving his hand in midair as if he were trying to hold back a flood. I was surprised at his reaction.

"Don't say what?" I asked innocently.

"Don't say that you think your sister is still alive and living somewhere in South America or Canada . . . that you believe all those stupid rumors that have been kept alive by people around here."

"Well, maybe she's alive somewhere in the United States!" I spouted, my cheeks reddening as my temper fired up.

"Oh, brother," my husband groaned, rolling his eyes. "Haven't you ever heard the saying, "Let sleeping dogs lie"?

"Oh, I've heard it," I said, bristling with annoyance. "I

just don't believe it."

"I was afraid that's what you were gonna say."

"So, are you going to help me or not?" I asked my husband.

"Depends on what you mean by help." Trygve scrunched down in the recliner, his shoulders slumped, and his arms crossed over his broad chest. His face was like granite, all hard angles and lines. For all practical purposes, he had shut down.

I sighed with frustration. "What I mean is this: Help me re-examine the facts and evidence of Katherine's case to determine whether there was a cover-up or a glossing over of her death," I said, although I sounded more confident than I felt. "I just need you to be my sounding board, Tryg, so I can bounce my ideas and information off you." Trygve groaned as if I was torturing him, which I suppose wasn't too far from the truth.

"Are you prepared for what you might discover on this search you're determined to carry out?" he asked gruffly.

"Probably not, but I want some closure, and I want to know the truth," I said with staunch determination.

"Are you sure about that?" Trygve asked softly. "Because sometimes, sweetheart, the truth is a bitter pill to swallow."

We sat staring at each other in silence for several moments while I thought about the commitment it would take to search for and uncover the facts about my sister's death. Was I prepared to be disappointed? Perhaps my sister really was dead. What if her death had been an unfortunate accident, as the police had concluded, and her participation in an infamous crime had been her choice all along? I had to admit my questions made me very uncomfortable.

Maybe I should pause and re-examine my motives. Despite Trygve's misgivings, I knew he would support me as much as possible, but I also knew that without his help, my search would probably fail. However, I had another friend on my side—Police Chief Tanya Pedretti. It was time to find out what she knew.

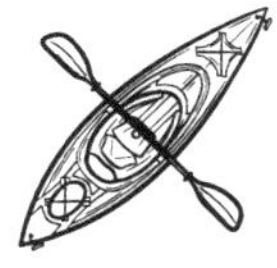

CHAPTER 5

Candle in the Wind

On Monday morning, Police Chief Tanya Pedretti sat at her desk in her office on Ranger Street in La Crosse. As usual, she was impeccably groomed with shining hair and tastefully applied makeup. She wore a dark gray jacket and skirt accentuated with a hot pink silk top. A pair of small gold hoop earrings and a gold necklace completed her outfit, but despite her fashionable clothing, she was in a sour mood. Her husband, Roy, had spent the entire weekend working at La Crosse Landscaping & Design, located at the base of Grandad Bluff, doing the staff payroll and arranging the planting schedule of several shrubs and bushes at a new apartment building over by the university this upcoming week. Their marriage had recently undergone some changes for the better, and Tanya thought things were going well—until this weekend. What had happened to the promises they'd made to each other to prioritize their relationship and spend quality time on the weekends getting reacquainted? It seemed to have disappeared or been forgotten in the hustle of everyday life.

To further add to her frustrations, their daughter Leisel had a boyfriend, Craig Morton. Nice kid, good-looking, a straight-A student, an All-American red-blooded male who was obviously enamored with their daughter. Tanya was trying to find a happy medium in her parenting style—watchful without hovering over the two teenagers. Roy was lenient to a fault, frequently telling Tanya she was hanging around the house too much when the teens were home, and how in the world could they be expected to figure stuff out when all she did was spy on them? When Tanya reminded him of their first few months together and the passion and sexual energy they'd expended, Roy got quiet. Later he confessed he was worried about his daughter's sexual activity, too. Was she having sex? Was she on the pill or using some kind of birth control? What about this Craig kid? How insistent had he been in expressing his physical affection for their daughter?

"You need to talk to her, honey," Roy said one evening when they'd turned out the lights for the night.

"Me? You want me to talk to her?"

"Well, sure. I talked to the boys; you should talk to Leisel."

Tanya was aware of the influence a parent could have on a teen throughout the tumultuous years of high school and college. Despite their denial, most teens appreciated the attempts parents made to communicate about the serious issues they would confront in adulthood. A few nights later an opportunity to talk to Leisel presented itself.

"You think I'm having sex with Craig?" Leisel asked, her eyes wide with alarm.

"I don't know what you're doing. I'm just concerned that you don't get in a situation that you can't handle," Tanya said calmly.

"Mom, really? We've only been dating for a few months. Do you think we're going to jump in bed together and have sex?"

"No, that's not what I think. But you and Craig have a lot of school left ahead of you. You both have dreams and ambitions. And—" Tanya stopped abruptly, weighing her words carefully. "I just know what I did at your age and sex was a temptation. I was curious about what it was like. And I'm assuming you're curious, too," Tanya explained. "Am I wrong?"

Leisel rolled her eyes and let out a long, exasperated sigh. "Mom, Craig and I are just friends at this point. Yeah, we kiss and stuff, but we're both busy with all our clubs and sports and friends and homework, so you don't have to worry," Leisel said.

"Your dad and I just want to make sure you know you can come to us about anything, and we won't be embarrassed or shocked."

"Right, Mom. I got it. Can I go now?"

Tanya gathered her daughter in a hug, kissed her cheek, and said, "Have at it. Just checking in, honey."

"Thanks, Mom. I'm fine. Really."

Tanya's thoughts returned to her marriage. She remembered hiking and biking with Roy during the summer months. Roy had revived his interest in healthy cooking, and they'd enjoyed some good food accompanied by great conversations, and best of all, they'd experienced a rekindling of their love life. Things had been improving steadily until it all crashed this weekend. Tanya sighed loudly. *Patience, Tanya, patience,* she admonished herself. *It's only one weekend. The ship will right itself if you just stay cool and don't have a temper tantrum about Roy's work ethic.*

She leaned forward and placed a manila file folder in the basket on the corner of her desk. Marriage worries aside, she had several pressing items on her agenda, including the presentation of police evidence at the trial of Beck Watson toward the end of this month. However, that would have to wait. She sat back in her office chair, crossed her arms, and studied her friend, Sonja Hovland, who'd appeared at her door shortly after nine o'clock this morning.

Tanya had become quite fond of Sonja since they'd worked together during the investigation into the death of Dr. Tony Diangelo last spring. Tanya preferred to call the experience with Sonja a trial by fire. For someone who'd never had an ounce of law enforcement training, Sonja had proven her mettle and instinctive toughness during the case. Best of all, through her contacts around town and her quick thinking, she'd been instrumental in helping the La Crosse police apprehend the guy who'd murdered a dentist and shot Officer Hank Brousard at point-blank range. It was a win-win for everyone except the perpetrator, Beck Watson, who was languishing in the La Crosse County Jail, and Officer Brousard, who was still in physical therapy for his injuries.

Sonja's latest request was unusual. A hard-headed pragmatist under normal conditions, her unusual plea this morning delved into new territory between the two friends. Her request threw Tanya off her game.

"You want me to do what?" Tanya asked, a frown creasing her forehead. "Run that by me again, will you?"

"I want you to reopen the investigation into the death of

my sister," Sonja said.

"I don't think you've ever shared your sister's name with me, or her history," she said sharply, her patience upended by this surprising development. "I don't know her, do I? I don't think you've ever mentioned her to me, so you're going to have to refresh my memory."

"Her name is Katherine Waite. She died in a kayaking accident on April 18, 1990, over at Pettibone Park." There was a long moment of silence as Tanya wracked her brain trying to remember the incident Sonja was talking about.

Suddenly Tanya pointed a finger at Sonja. "Wait a minute. Wasn't she the one involved in the bombing at the U with the two Ainsworth brothers? Are you telling me that was *your* sister?" Tanya exclaimed. Her eyes widened in surprise as she leaned forward and rested her elbows on top of the desk.

"Yeah, that was her. Do you remember it?"

Tanya nodded. "Of course I remember it, although I wasn't a cop at the time," she explained. She continued staring at Sonja, who remained strangely subdued and guarded.

The chief's coolness under fire was not surprising to Sonja. Pedretti was well-known throughout the city as a tough investigator, fair and honest in her assessment of crime and faithful in her execution of the law. The officers under her command were a high-functioning unit who were devoted to the mission of keeping the citizens of La Crosse safe and informed. As the moments ticked by it was clear by the silence that Sonja had retreated into some kind of reverie.

"Sonja?" Pedretti interrupted, snapping her fingers.

Sonja jerked and looked up. "Yes?" Her eyes refocused,

and her face reddened with embarrassment at her brief daydream. She squirmed uncomfortably under Pedretti's intense scrutiny.

"Are you with me, girl?" Tanya asked, tipping her head to one side.

"Yes. Yes, I am . . . now."

"Good. So, let's go through this again. Explain to me why I should reopen the investigation into your sister's death. Usually that means that new evidence about the case has been discovered that will justify the time and expense needed to reconsider the initial investigation. Is that the case in your situation?" Tanya leaned forward, prepared to listen carefully to Sonja's defense.

"I think the case needs a second look because at the time, the circumstances surrounding her death were suspicious," Sonja said haltingly. Her attempt to defend her request seemed weak at best. "The evidence didn't line up with the observations made by the detectives who worked the case."

"Evidence can be hard to come by sometimes. Who were the detectives assigned to the case?" Tanya asked as she swiveled to her computer and poised her fingers above the keyboard waiting for more information from Sonja. She could do an online search into police archives and solve these issues in short order. A long, uncomfortable silence followed, which Chief Pedretti did not fill with mindless chatter. Somewhere, a few blocks away on Ranger Street, a siren pierced the air. As the seconds ticked by and Sonja remained silent, Tanya leaned back and studied the bluffs and blue sky outside her office window, waiting patiently for a response. If Sonja was going to stonewall her, she'd be waiting a long time.

"Well . . . I don't really know who was assigned to investigate the case," Sonja started to tentatively explain, "but I would like to examine all the files and evidence about the incident involving my sister, if that's possible . . . please," Sonja stammered. More silence. "I deserve to know the truth about what happened to her," she finished softly. "I was only ten at the time, and my parents never talked about it."

Chief Pedretti watched Sonja carefully as she attempted to justify her request. Although Sonja's motives might be faulty, Tanya marveled at the woman's backbone. She had to admit, Sonja had grit. It took a lot of resolve for a cleaning lady to walk into the police chief's office without so much as batting an eye and demand to see the official police records about a crime and drowning that happened thirty-five years ago. But Pedretti shouldn't have been surprised. She was very familiar with her friend's amateur exploits into criminal investigations. Tanya had to admit if it hadn't been for Sonja's contacts around town and the information she'd shared with city police officials during the Diangelo murder investigation last spring, Pedretti's team would have had a much harder time finding the perpetrator and bringing him to justice. Besides, technically, according to the law, Sonja had every right to request the police reports concerning her sister's death.

Those issues aside, Tanya worried about the nature of Sonja's request, which seemed to suggest she deserved some kind of preferential treatment based on her friendship with the chief of police. Pedretti knew that when loyalty and favors became the basis for enforcing the law, the slope became very slippery. Upholding the law went above friendship and mutual affection. In any other circumstance, Tanya would have escorted this woman out of her office in a New York minute and told her to rethink her request and take a few days to reconsider what she was asking her to do. *Who did Sonja think she was to question the methodology of police personnel when she hadn't had an ounce of police training?* Tanya thought.

Relegating their friendship to the sidelines for the moment, Sonja's request made Tanya uncomfortable in other ways. Reopening an old case would leave her vulnerable to criticism and suspicion from the public and press, to say nothing of the effect it might have on her staff. She could already imagine the posts on social media and the editorials in the *La Crosse Sentinel.* In addition, she was short-staffed, and reopening an old criminal investigation would require manpower she didn't have to devote to the case.

Casting aspersions on the detectives who'd investigated Katherine Waite's death was not a popular course of action with the police chief, either, but Tanya understood Sonja's angst and misgivings about the incident. She'd seen this before from family members who had lost someone they loved in a violent act or unfortunate accident. Had the police done everything they could to ensure justice was served? Was there a cover-up or incompetence on the part of the police, as Sonja seemed to be suggesting? Was Katherine murdered, or was it a possible suicide? Another uncomfortable thought wormed its way into Pedretti's mind. Did the girl fake her own death and escape to parts unknown? It was a well-known fact that she had participated in the university bombing, although Tanya was unclear what her exact role had been in the crime. She didn't know the answers to her questions, but the rumor that Katherine was alive and living in some other part of the United States had persisted throughout the community during the years since the drowning incident.

At the time of Katherine's death in 1990, Tanya was in college preparing for a career in law enforcement, but she remembered the shock waves that reverberated throughout the state when the university building was bombed, killing a professor. Then, a day later, the tragic drowning accident followed on the heels of the horrific crime.

"What do you hope to achieve by looking at the police records about your sister's death?" Tanya asked, breaking the uncomfortable silence.

"I . . . I guess I don't know, but I've never believed my sister's drowning was accidental. She learned to kayak on Lake Superior in all kinds of weather. She could turn a kayak on a dime, and more than once I saw her negotiate some very swift rapids and fast currents. She was something of a daredevil, an excellent swimmer, very athletic, and in good physical shape. Her body was never recovered, but I understand her kayak and paddle, her life vest, and one shoe were found. If they found all that stuff, then why couldn't they find her body? How hard is it to recover a body from the Mississippi, anyway?"

"When a river drowning occurs, it's not unusual for a body to never be found," Tanya explained. "Conditions on the Mississippi are complex; the river is huge, as much as two miles across in some places, and strong currents and debris are often concealed below the surface of the water. The murkiness of the river results in low visibility for divers and makes locating a body difficult. In addition, law enforcement must balance the issues of recovery versus safety when they send divers into the river. It's a dangerous and expensive proposition, even though we have the advantage today of technology like sonar systems and wide-angle cameras that can help in recovering human remains." Tanya paused for a moment and then reiterated her original point. "You have to remember, Sonja, that people who are swept away in the river's current are sometimes never found again."

Sonja's shoulders slumped, and her expression reflected her disappointment. "So, what you're saying is I'm wasting my time," she said dejectedly.

"Not necessarily, but I think you should prepare yourself for disappointment," Tanya replied. "In the case of your sister, if my memory is correct, several hours elapsed from the time her kayak overturned until the items you mentioned were found the next afternoon downriver. That elapsed time made the search area larger. The currents in the Mississippi are strong and dangerous, often carrying a body several miles downstream. If you think you're going to beat the current, you'd better think again. Old Man River is nothing to fool with." Seeing the dejection on Sonja's face, Tanya softened her response. "I'm sorry, Sonja. I know you want closure and an ending, but sometimes in cases like your sister's, you make your own closure despite the facts. Remember your sister and what you admired about her. That might be the best you can hope for."

Sonja groaned and stared out of the office window. She felt the pressures of her cleaning jobs intruding on her visit with the police chief. She had three customers on the south side of La Crosse who were waiting for her to show up. She needed to get started, but she also needed the chief's advice. Tanya's phone buzzed, and while she conversed with the caller, Sonja considered the things the chief had told her. Should she just drop the whole messy affair as Tanya had suggested? Could she find peace in honoring her sister's memory without knowing the details of her death or her role in the 1990 bombing incident on campus? She shook her head and squeezed her eyes shut as she contemplated her choices. *I don't think I can live with that,* she thought. Tanya hung up the phone, stood up, and walked around her desk, stopping in front of Sonja.

"Listen, Sonja, you are legally entitled to the records of your sister's drowning and death, but I'm not sure you're really going to find what you think you're looking for. If I thought I could help ease your pain, I would, but frankly, I don't see how dredging up the past with all its horrors and sorrow will do you any good," she said.

Sonja stood, and the two friends embraced briefly. "I understand your position," Sonja said. "And I'll think about all you've told me."

Sonja turned and left the office. Tanya watched her friend walk dejectedly down the hall and step into the elevator. *You'll think about all I've told you, but will you be able to leave well enough alone?* Tanya thought. Somehow, she doubted Sonja would acquiesce and bury the hatchet, but a bigger issue nagged at the edge of Tanya's thoughts. Would Sonja discover another can of worms when she began investigating her sister's involvement in the university bombing? *Only time will tell,* she thought, *but this could end badly.*

SONJA

I rolled up to the Victorian monstrosity on 2690 Cass Street after my visit with Police Chief Pedretti and parked under a couple of large maple trees whose brilliant leaves were floating gently onto the street and sidewalk. It was a beautiful fall day with temperatures in the mid-seventies, ice cream cone clouds floated in powder blue skies overhead, and students from the university walked under the canopy of trees along the street, kicking up loose leaves on their way to class. In the distance, Grandad Bluff soared six hundred feet above the city, the iconic sandstone precipice reflecting the sparkling sunlight.

Dale Devine, a former client of mine who'd lived in this splendid mansion on Cass, passed away suddenly in July. I miss him terribly. In his place, his spinster daughter, Molly Jean, moved in lock, stock, and barrel. She frequently entertains acquaintances at the Cass Street mansion with her afternoon soporific luncheons in which she drones on and on about the latest books she's read, the current movies playing at the Rivoli downtown, or the cutting-edge fashions she's seen in the exclusive shops she recently visited on her tour of Europe. I wasn't sure how Molly Jean had accumulated her wealth, but from what I could tell, nobody cared two hoots about her cultural and social recommendations. Her neighbors attended her luncheons purely out of respect for Dale and Dolly, who were fondly remembered in the neighborhood.

Whenever I cleaned the mansion in the past, I hauled items to the nearest Goodwill after Dale and I sorted and purged our way through a closet or cupboard. Now I spent my visits scrubbing, straightening, and unpacking family treasures which Molly Jean insisted were too good to be stowed away in cardboard boxes in the attic.

"A little more to the left, Sonja," Molly Jean directed, waving her hand at me as I shifted the vase on the carved oak mantel above the massive fireplace. If I could have found a trash bin, I would have thrown the ugly pink and green thing in it and covered it up with potato and carrot peelings.

"Yes, yes, that's better, dear," Molly continued. "There is no reason for these treasures to live upstairs in the dark and dusty attic. They need to be seen to be appreciated, especially when it's a Van Briggle vase like this one," she preached. I nodded briefly, resisted the urge to roll my eyes, and waited for more instructions. In my opinion, the vase was still green and pink, and no name, not even Van Briggle, could erase its genuine ugliness. I guess it really is true that beauty is in the eye of the beholder.

"Now let's get started on these paintings," Molly said, pumping her fist in the air in a gesture of determination. She pulled a large box loaded with medium-sized oil canvases encased in ornate frames across the wool carpet. Not being a connoisseur of paintings, I had no idea of the value of such pieces, but never fear, Molly Jean could quote the appraisal figure for every work of art, whether it was a painting, a piece of pottery, or a rare book. I wasn't impressed in the least, but I followed her directions as she blabbered about the monetary value of each artist's work and their influence in the art world. It was all Greek to me. However, I pasted on a smile and tried to look engaged in the process, although my heart wasn't in it.

While Molly pontificated about the art world, I contemplated what Chief Tanya Pedretti had told me earlier this morning. I rarely called Trygve during the day, but I did this morning after my visit to police headquarters.

"What's wrong, honey?" Trygve answered. He could always read my moods with uncanny accuracy. Did he have some special app on his phone that took the temperature of my mercurial disposition and translated it to his phone, accompanied by an emoji? That's not possible, is it? But then I thought about artificial intelligence and wondered if it could be real. I heard the truck engine rumbling in the background. I felt guilty disturbing my husband's workday with my trivial concerns, but there was no one else I'd rather talk to when I was upset than Tryg.

"Nothing is wrong, except my visit with Tanya did not go well," I said.

"That's too bad, honey, but I'm not surprised. You didn't expect her to jump up and down with joy when you asked about reopening your sister's case, did you?" my husband asked sarcastically. "I'm sure she's not crazy about reopening an investigation into a crime and death that happened thirty-five years ago, and frankly, sweetheart, I can understand her viewpoint."

I could feel my cheeks redden as my temper threatened to boil over. Why was everyone so quick to dismiss my concerns? It's not like there hadn't been police abuses and cover-ups in the past. I was sure almost every municipality had them. So why the vacillation on Tanya's part, and why was my husband taking her side?

"Well, maybe she's reluctant because she knows

something's hinky," I said hotly. "Did you ever think of that, huh?"

When Trygve spoke again after an extended silence, I could hear the layer of authority woven into his voice, and I knew immediately I'd better back off. My husband is an incredibly patient man, but I always know when I've pushed him too far. His voice takes on a tone I could recognize in the dark.

"Sonja, we have to come to some kind of agreement about this, because I don't want to argue every time we have a conversation. I'm calling a truce until I get home tonight. So, think about that. We'll discuss it then, okay?"

I paused before I answered, carefully considering my options. "Okay," I sighed heavily. "You're right, Tryg. I don't want to argue all the time either. Let's figure out something tonight that you and I can both live with."

"Sounds good. See you later at home. I'll cook tonight," Trygve said, and he hung up.

Despite my frustration, which had risen incrementally as the morning wore on, I finished helping Molly Jean with her art revival project and slipped out of the Victorian mansion on Cass Street just before noon. As I drove north through the city, I decided on the spur of the moment to recruit the help of my friend, Collette Tierney, a researcher extraordinaire who worked at the public library. There's something about the atmosphere of a library that invites possibilities, and I needed someone smart and levelheaded in my corner if I was going to start digging into my sister's past.

I parked my car in the lot behind the building and entered the cool, calm environment of the library. As I headed to the checkout desk and asked for my friend, Collette, my confidence in her ability to help me calmed my troubled mind.

Collette was seated at her desk in her office behind a large glass window working at her computer, her hair piled on top of her head, her makeup flawless, and her eyes bright with curiosity. My, she was a beautiful woman. When the assistant began talking to her, she looked up and gave me a friendly wave. I waved back. She pointed to her keyboard and held up one finger in a "wait a minute" gesture. When she finished typing, she pushed herself away from her computer and walked out to the desk where I was impatiently waiting to talk to her.

"Hey, Sonja! What's up? Got a new case you're investigating?" Collette asked with enthusiasm. Of all the people I knew throughout the city, Collette had been the most supportive in my amateur sleuthing career, but I flinched at her reference to my detection activities. The situation I faced concerning my dead sister was formidable and was complicated by my feelings, which were close to the surface. The whole affair seemed to be beyond my poor scope of investigative powers.

"Mmm, it's not really a current case, but I do need to pick your brain about something," I said softly, worried about who might be listening to our conversation. My reputation as a rogue detective in the city had grown exponentially since the Diangelo case had been solved and the perpetrator was incarcerated in the county jail awaiting trial. Collette and I moved to the side of the checkout desk and stood in a small alcove where I briefly explained the history of my sister's infamous involvement in the bombing on the

UW–L campus back in the '90s, as I understood it, and her tragic death on the river. As I talked, Collette's expression changed from optimistic excitement to one of sober single-mindedness.

"So, let me get this straight. You want me to do some research into the explosion at the university in 1990 and the kayak accident on the river, which took your sister's life? Is that right?" Collette asked when I finished.

"Yes. Anything you can find out about the circumstances surrounding my sister's death will be helpful in getting me up to speed—newspaper articles, editorials, court records, or other references to the events. I can do some research, too, but it's going to take more than my measly efforts to find everything that's been written about it. I was only ten when all of this happened, so I really don't know many of the details," I explained. "I've avoided delving into the issue for years. Katherine's death devastated my parents, and as a result, they sheltered my sister and me from the gory details, so I really know very little about it. Now Mom and Dad are dead and gone, and I want to put my doubts to rest. Will you help me?" I watched Collette's face for clues about her feelings, but her expression remained neutral and professional.

"I'll get right on it and call you when I have everything gathered together," Collette promised, squeezing my hand.

I left the library feeling confident that Collette would dig up whatever information was out there in the media about my sister and present it to me on a silver platter. But then another thought wormed its way into my mind. Collette was a lifelong resident of La Crosse. She was a little older than Trygve, but interestingly, during our conversation she never divulged any knowledge she might have had about the bombing and my sister's drowning. I shook my head in doubt. *There's no way that someone as smart, articulate, and well-read as Collette wouldn't already know about this. Why didn't she share what she knew about the incident with me when I asked?* I wondered.

I decided I didn't have time to second-guess myself or Collette. I would have to trust my friend with the burdens of my heart and see where it would take me. Besides, I still had two houses that needed cleaning. From past experience, I knew I couldn't afford to ignore my business to go on some off-the-wall truth-finding mission while neglecting my faithful customers. I sighed, feeling prematurely defeated, but Trygve would have been proud that I recruited Collette to help me.

I guided my Subaru in and out of traffic, working my way toward the bluff side of La Crosse. Proceeding up Bliss Road, I negotiated several hairpin turns on my way to the top of the bluff and drove past the turn-off to the famous Grandad Bluff, the well-known lookout point which gave a panoramic view of the river city below. I continued to wind my way through the countryside above the valley until I came to a housing development called Top of the Hill, where I turned into the driveway at 6578 Prospect Lane. The sprawling ranch home of Dr. Lorenzo Bianchi was situated on an immaculate three-acre lawn in the upscale development. The grounds surrounding the home were manicured to within an inch of perfection, the mature maple and oak trees provided abundant shade, and the shrubbery was pruned weekly to keep the illusion of success and prosperity at the forefront in the affluent neighborhood. Behind the house, a series of raised garden beds provided a beautiful variety of vegetables. I'd kill for a garden like that. The home had five bedrooms, two full baths, and spacious living areas for a large family. The expansive kitchen was the favorite gathering place of Kate Bianchi, my client, who cooked fabulous pasta dishes and created desserts and breads fit for a king. Trygve and I had frequently enjoyed the fabulous baguettes and croissants that Kate sent home for us.

However, nothing could erase the sadness that permeated the house since Lorenzo and Kate had announced their plans to separate. They were traveling down the road to a full-blown divorce, and when they told me about their decision, I wanted to scream at them. I restrained myself from a tirade since I knew taking sides and divulging my opinions would only harm our relationship, but I thought about their four lovely children who carried the Italian traits of their parents: dark eyes, tawny skin, and long, flowing manes of thick curly brown hair. It broke my heart that these wonderful little people would have to stand by helplessly as their loyalty and love were tested. No matter how you sliced and diced it, the children would absorb the oppositional attitudes of their parents, and the division would be bitter and linger for a lifetime. I dreaded the months ahead when the beautiful Bianchi children would endure confusion and sadness over events that were out of their control.

When I entered the home's back door from the garage, I expected the house to be unoccupied. The children were back in school, Kate was working at Fitness Forever, a beauty spa and exercise facility in Onalaska, and Dr.

Lorenzo Bianchi was probably removing cataracts and implanting new lenses in patients at the Mayo Clinic in La Crosse, where he worked as a surgical specialist in the ophthalmology department.

I immediately began my cleaning chores. With four active children displaying their various interests and talents throughout the house in a variety of ways, this home was the ultimate challenge to clean in two hours. I smiled at the drawings displayed on the refrigerator. The youngest Bianchi child, Sophia, had left me a drawing lying on the kitchen island. I treasured the children's creations since I will never have children of my own who can draw their mommy a picture. A tennis racket and a hockey stick were flung on the floor in the hallway leading to the living room. I returned the sporting equipment to the garage, then moved along to the bathrooms where I wiped down the showers, tub, sinks, and toilets, polished the mirrors, and scrubbed the tile floors. I worked up a sweat and continued scouring the kitchen. Fortunately for me, Kate was very conscientious in keeping her cooking pots, pans, and utensils clean and in their correct storage area. I checked the refrigerator where a luscious-looking lasagna was ready to pop in the oven later. The oven had a few globs of crusted material in the bottom. I sprayed the gunk and let it loosen while I mopped the floor. When I finished the floor, I wiped down the stove and oven.

Vacuuming the hallway carpets and dust mopping the wooden floors in the spacious living room was next, after a quick once-over of the furniture. Last week I had wiped down the paintings and pottery pieces that decorated the shelves and walls, so that saved me some time this afternoon.

The bedrooms were straightforward. I replaced the sheets with fresh ones, vacuumed the carpets, and straightened bookshelves and bedside nightstands. I glanced at my watch; it was 2:45. I let out a sigh of relief. One more small job at Mr. Belton's farmhouse on the ridge, and I could go home to Trygve.

I finished my duties, grabbed Sophia's picture from the kitchen island, and left the house the same way I had entered through the garage service door. Parked in the driveway next to my Subaru was a forest green pickup with "La Crosse Landscaping & Design" emblazoned on the side in bright orange letters. The tailgate of the truck was open, and Jack Hanson, one of the company's employees, was removing electric pruning shears from the rack of tools in the back. I walked over to the truck and peeked my head around the vehicle.

"Jack! How you doin'? I haven't seen you in a long time," I said in a friendly voice.

"Hey, Sonja! Nice to see you, too. Any new detective cases on the docket?"

I continued smiling even though inside I was recoiling with panic when I thought about the case of my sister's escapades in La Crosse over thirty years ago. Jack was hardly a day over twenty-five, so I knew he wouldn't have any recollection of my sister's criminal history and mysterious death.

"Nothing exceptional is on my radar right now," I said casually. I want you to know I'm not in the habit of telling outright lies, but to unload my current situation on Jack seemed unnecessary. I believed it would get me nowhere in my search for the facts, but I was uncomfortable with the little white lie I had just told.

"Well, if I ever need an investigator to untangle some sticky problem I've got, I'll give you a call," Jack said as he slammed the tailgate of the truck. He gave me a thumbs-up, revved up the shears, and waved goodbye as he began trimming the shrubbery bordering the front porch. I walked to my Subaru, started the engine, and backed slowly out of the driveway. When I was finally on the road again, my cell phone rang, so I pulled over to the side of the road.

"Sonja Hovland. Can I help you?" I asked politely.

A female voice came over the phone. "Leave your sister's memory alone. Nothing good will come from digging up the past," the voice growled. I stared at my phone and sputtered, "What? Who is this?" Abruptly, the caller hung up.

When I heard the click on the other end and knew the caller had hung up, I still shouted into my cell, "You've got a lot of nerve, whoever you are, calling me up and telling me what to do!" I was left with a queasy mix of fear and suspicion. One thing was clear; whoever the caller was, she was *not* one of my people. My blue-collar contacts around the city were my most treasured assets. We watched out for each other. When one of us had a problem, we pooled our resources and talents and supported each other.

The mysterious phone call left me feeling angry and exposed, and for all practical purposes ruined the anticipation I'd had of spending a quiet evening with Trygve. Our normal routine after a demanding day of cleaning houses and patrolling the streets of La Crosse included a delicious dinner, a brisk walk in the coolness of the evening hours, and a rousing game of Scrabble in which Trygve usually walloped me with his ever-expanding vocabulary. He knew more words that started with "Q" than anybody I knew, and the "q" wasn't always followed by a "u."

The anonymous phone call indicated trouble was brewing on the horizon. Was the caller someone who had known my sister? Or was it someone else who had helped plan and execute the crime who was never arrested? After thirty-five years, the Ainsworth brothers would be out of prison, having served their sentences. I knew I had to tell Tryg about the phone call. But what I couldn't figure out was how someone had found out about the possibility of reopening the investigation into my sister's death. Was it because someone in the city knew she was still alive somewhere? Was someone protecting Katherine? I shook my head, trying to clear the confusion in my mind. I had only shared my concerns about my sister with Trygve, Tanya Pedretti, and Collette Tierney. I decided to call Chief Pedretti.

"Chief Pedretti. How can I help you?"

"Tanya, Sonja here. I just got a crank call of some kind. The person suggested I should leave my sister's memory alone. Do you know anything about that?" I asked.

"Why would I? I haven't said anything to anybody, but you have to realize, Sonja, that half the population of La Crosse is familiar with the facts of your sister's case, or at least they think they know the facts. Someone must have gotten wind of reopening the investigation. Who else did you tell?" Tanya asked.

"The only other person I told was Collette Tierney at the library downtown. I can't believe she would blab to someone what I told her in confidence," I said.

"These kinds of situations are very hard to keep the lid on, Sonja. Rumors are bound to fly around town, and we both know they travel faster than a greased pig at a hog wrestling contest. Just wait 'til it gets on social media. It's something you'll have to deal with if you're determined to open this can of worms again. Be prepared for the gossip mill to chew you up and spit you out."

"Well, there's a word picture for you," I replied sarcastically. "Thanks for the vote of confidence."

"Like I said earlier, be ready for disappointment. It looks like it's already starting," Tanya said.

"I'm sorry I bothered you," I snarled. "I know you're—"

"Busy? Yes, I am," Tanya interrupted calmly, her voice softening as she continued, "but I'm never too busy for a friend—especially one who helped jumpstart my failing marriage." We chatted for a few minutes, I cooled off, and we both began to feel the crunch of time. "Stay in touch," Tanya said, "and watch your back." Like I've said before, it's hard to put Tanya off her game. I guess that's why she's the chief of police.

I disconnected and pulled out onto County Road F, turned north, and skirted the perimeter of Hixon Forest Park until I came to County B. Traveling down the road a few miles to Longview Court, I rolled up to a small, compact farmhouse that was one of the original dwellings on the prairie. A clump of red roses climbed up a stone wall near the front door and clung tenaciously to the frame around the window. Every time I cleaned here, I thought the place looked like a fairy-tale house somewhere on the moors of Ireland. Dean Belton, my final client of the day, met me at the door.

"Sonja! It's good to see you. Come on in," he exclaimed as he stepped aside and held the door open for me.

Dean's enthusiastic greeting cheered me. Despite my normal upbeat attitude, I needed a shot in the arm this afternoon, and Dean was just the guy to deliver it. Short but powerfully built from his regimen of weight training, his silver hair, which he wore in a bowl cut, reflected his love for the Beatles, and his bright green eyes belied the difficult circumstances he faced each day. Known to older residents in the surrounding La Crosse area as "Mr. Memory," his phenomenal photographic memory had served him well as a radio disc jockey on a local station known simply as LAX98. Retired from his position now as a radio personality, he was still a beloved figure in the cultural life of the La Crosse community, and he frequently played trivia at many of the local taverns and bars throughout the city, wowing others with his phenomenal recall. He had the trophies to prove it, too.

"How's Mary Margaret today?" I asked as I clasped his hand in mine and gave him a peck on his whiskered cheek.

His green eyes seemed to darken with sadness as if a shade had been pulled over them, and he looked at the floor for several moments. When he lifted his head, his eyes were brimming with tears. "It's just a matter of days now, Sonja. The cancer has spread to her liver, but her smile is still intact. I told her you were coming, and she's looking forward to seeing you. Go on in," Dean said, pointing to her bedroom door while making a shooing gesture with his hand. "Go on. I'll make a pot of your favorite peppermint tea with honey."

I walked down the narrow hallway and went into the

bedroom. Mary Margaret was lying on the bed propped up by several pillows, which supported her emaciated frame. To me, it seemed she had lost several more pounds since my last visit three weeks ago. Frankly, I was surprised she was still alive. Her body had become a shell that housed her indomitable spirit within. Obviously, the cancer was winning. I walked to her bedside and tenderly held her hand. Her eyes fluttered open, and she smiled weakly.

"Hey, how are you doing, Mary Margaret?" I asked gently.

"I'm going home to see Jesus any day now. I'm ready to go, although I don't think Dean wants me to leave. He hates being alone," she whispered. Even that simple declaration left her breathless.

"Is there anything I can do for you?" I asked and waited several moments.

"Yes, take care of Dean for me," she said, and then she closed her eyes in exhaustion.

I leaned over the frail woman and placed a tender kiss on her wrinkled forehead. "I'll take care of him, I promise, Mary Margaret. I'll make sure he's okay," I said as tears filled my eyes. I quietly tiptoed from the room, had a quick cup of tea with Dean in the kitchen, and brought in my cleaning supplies. The house was small, and since Dean was something of a neat freak, my cleaning duties took less than an hour. Before I left, he pulled me aside.

"There's some scuttlebutt circulating around town that you're looking into your sister's death." He gazed into the distance for a moment, then turned to me and said, "April 18, 1990, right?"

I'm sure my mouth must have fallen open in amazement,

but when I thought about it, Dean would have known about my sister's death from his days of reporting the news on the local radio station. His prodigious recollection was on display as he dredged up the horrible facts of my sister's drowning from the depths of his memory. "A Wednesday? Correct?" he asked, lifting his eyebrows. "A little after midnight?" His eyes had a piercing quality to them. I nodded my head. "A kayak accident, if my memory serves me right," he continued.

"That's right, but how did you know she was my sister?" I asked, dumbfounded.

"The case interested me, and I did some research. I happened to come upon her birth certificate in my investigation, and I noticed Stickley was listed as her birthplace. For some reason, I remembered you mentioning your hometown when we first hired you to clean, and then I discovered your maiden name when I looked up your wedding license." When I did a double take, Dean explained, "All in the public records if you care to look, my dear." Dean shrugged his shoulders. "I just put two and two together. And of course, there's a strong family resemblance."

So much for anonymity, I thought.

Dean continued. "So back to my original question: Why are you looking into your sister's death now? The police explained what they thought happened to her after they found her belongings in the river. Are you second-guessing their findings because they didn't recover her body?"

"Honestly, I haven't seen the report yet. Chief Pedretti is assisting me, but she hasn't been very happy about my request."

"You are entitled to see the report of your sister's death," Dean stated firmly. "Don't let anyone buffalo you into thinking you're asking for something out of the ordinary."

"Do you know something else about my sister?" I asked. Dean's face remained impassive, his jaw set with firm determination. He seemed hesitant to share anything he knew with me. After several moments in which I'm sure he was debating the wisdom of revealing his information, Dean said something that shocked me.

"A man living in Chaseburg down the street from the Tippy Toe Inn sold an old pickup to a young girl on the afternoon of April 17, 1990. She paid cash and drove off without giving him a name. He described her as being athletic with brown hair, rather petite, and very closed-mouthed. When he asked her why she was buying an old, broken-down pickup, she said she needed something to haul a kayak. Sound familiar?" Dean asked.

My eyes widened in amazement. "Oh, my gosh! That sounds just like my sister. Do you know this guy?"

"Oh yeah, I knew him. He was my brother."

"Was?"

"He died last spring, but he claimed the story was true," Dean said, shrugging his shoulders nonchalantly, "and I have no reason to doubt him."

"Oh, wow! It could've been my sister. I never knew this. Wait 'til I tell Tryg."

"Sonja . . . be careful." The serious undertone in Dean's voice sent a chill up my arms. "Things may not be as simple as you think."

I wondered what he meant by such a statement, but it was getting late, and I knew Trygve would be waiting for me. I was anxious to see my husband and relay everything I'd learned about Katherine. I leaned over and gave Dean a hug. "Take care of Mary Margaret. She loves you so. If you need anything, you call me, you hear?" I asked.

"I will, but the hospice nurse is here during the night now, so I can get some sleep. Thanks for cleaning. You're the best, Sonja. Take care," he said as he handed me my check and quietly shut the door.

Despite all that had transpired since I left the Bianchi home this afternoon, including the threatening phone call, I felt the tension evaporate as I drove through the hills and valleys of Barre Mills. The rolling vistas were layered with sandstone bluffs, and the hardwoods were blazing with the colors of autumn that I loved so much. The peaceful surroundings, iconic dairy farms, and grazing cows juxtaposed against the fall color were the perfect antidote for my frayed nerves. It soothed me to know that life here continued undisturbed despite the chaotic news reports on television and the internet. Politics, sexual scandals, natural disasters, school shootings, the highs and lows of an unsettled stock market, and sensational crimes filled the television screen each night. Trygve and I tried to limit our intake of the muck to half an hour in the evening and morning. It was all we could absorb and still stay upbeat and optimistic.

I swung into the driveway and parked my Subaru in the garage. Trygve promised to cook dinner tonight, and since he was proficient in the kitchen and I was very hungry, I couldn't wait to see what he had decided to concoct.

When I stepped out of my car, I was greeted by Coco, our little black poodle, who yipped and snuffled around my feet, barking incessantly until I picked him up and we cuddled for several minutes.

Trygve heard the dog, looked up from his band saw, and yelled, "Hi, honey. I'm in here working on a chair."

I walked into the shop portion of our garage and noticed Trygve's latest creation. He'd taken a solid oak chair seat and added peeled oak branches for the legs and back of the chair. Some of the branches extended beyond the normal structure of a chair in swooping curves and jutting angles, but after all, this was a Trygve chair, and rules were meant to be broken. I was sure the interesting proportions and curvy silhouettes of the peeled wooden arrangement were sure to please Trygve's latest customer.

My husband turned off his saw, walked over to me, and kissed me. His expression gave away none of the irritation he'd expressed earlier in the day. I was glad to see him. We'd said some cross words to each other the last few days, and frankly, I was ready for reconciliation. It was never a good idea to engage in verbal judo with Trygve. You were bound to lose, and besides, my husband has blessed my life more than I could ever explain. Why would I want to jeopardize it with jabs, innuendos, and critical barbs?

"How was your day, honey?" I asked, brushing sawdust from his hair and shoulders.

"Okay," he said, making a wry face. "Same old same old. I've got everything ready for stir fry. Let's go in the house," he suggested. He kissed me again on the cheek, grabbed my hand, and led me into the kitchen.

Bowls of veggies were prepped and waiting on the kitchen island, and a pot of steaming rice was on the back burner. Trygve washed his hands and began heating the wok while he cut chicken thighs into bite size pieces and seasoned them with his secret blend of spices. I set the table, cracked open a nice Moscato wine, and poured it into our glasses. Ten minutes later, we enjoyed chicken and vegetable stir fry over white rice.

After dinner, we walked along the country road next to our farm in the deepening blush of the evening. It was a beautiful fall night, crisp and quiet. A luminous moon was rising in the southern night sky, and the pine trees cut a crisp silhouette along the horizon. As we walked, I decided I needed to apologize.

"I'm sorry about today, Tryg. I shouldn't have called you and bothered you."

"Shh, shh, shh. Isn't that what I'm here for? You're my wife. I love you even though sometimes I don't agree with the stuff you do."

"What are we going to do about Katherine?" I asked, feeling tears well up in my eyes.

Trygve sighed, then grabbed my hand. "I don't know if we're going to do anything right now. I guess we'll figure it out as we go. That seemed to work before, and I'm guessing it'll work again."

"That's the plan, then?" I asked.

"Yep, that's the plan, baby. Be flexible and deal with things as they come."

"But there are a couple of things I need to tell you about. Is that okay?" I asked, clasping his hand tightly in mine.

"Let's hear it," he said brusquely.

I told him about my efforts to enlist the help of my friend, Collette Tierney, the research guru at the La Crosse Public Library. He approved. Then I told him about Katherine's purchase of a broken-down pickup from a guy in Chaseburg the day before her drowning. This news stopped Trygve in his tracks. He stared into space, thinking hard as he stood by the side of the road.

"I don't like the sound of that," he said gruffly.

"Why? What do you think it means?" I asked.

"Did she buy it to escape from the area? What kind of car did she drive when she was attending the university?"

"Oh, she had a beautiful robin's egg blue VW bug. I think I have a picture of it somewhere. She'd saved all her high school lifeguard money to buy it. It was a real beauty," I explained. We started walking back to our house again.

"What happened to the VW bug?" Trygve asked.

When Tryg asked his question, it was my turn to stop abruptly along the road. "Well, I guess I don't know," I said. "Maybe Mom and Dad sold it after her death, but they never said anything about it to Darlene or me. I haven't thought about that car in years."

"So, nobody really knows where it went. It just disappeared. Is that right?" Trygve asked. The man could be persistent sometimes.

"Yes, that's right," I answered. "I don't think anybody knows where the little bug went."

"That could be a problem," Trygve said again, grabbing my hand as he began walking back to our farm. I didn't understand how a VW bug that disappeared thirty-five years ago could be a problem for us right now, but I trusted my husband. His mind worked in mysterious ways, totally different than mine. He could ruminate about the slightest detail for days while those same details slipped by me and my pea-sized brain in a matter of minutes.

"There's one other thing, Tryg," I said hesitantly.

"What's that?"

"Someone called me and warned me off my investigation into Katherine's death."

Trygve groaned loudly. "Here we go again. Well, I guess I should be thankful that at least we're not being run down on the highway by someone who's trying to kill us. Do you know who this person was who called you?"

"It was a female voice, but she didn't identify herself. She just said nothing good would come from digging up the past."

"Well, I tend to agree with her on that point," Trygve said. I started to protest, but Trygve held up his hand in a stop gesture. His brown eyes changed from soft and friendly to hard and uncompromising. "I know a little anonymous phone call is not going to stop you from digging into this thing, but I want you to be careful. Keep your cell phone with you all the time, and if someone threatens you, call me or Tanya. Okay?"

"Got it, honey. I'll be careful. Don't worry."

Tryg made a wry face. "I've heard that before."

Little did I know that in the next few days, the things I had believed for years about my dead sister would be shattered into a million pieces. Things were about to get very rough.

CHAPTER 6 • KITTY

You Can Run, but You Can't Hide

On Monday morning, September 22, I arrived at Innovative Fabrications for my regular shift and pushed my security badge through the card reader. The door to the plant clicked softly, and I turned the knob and entered the building. The size and scope of the place where I work is amazing. Even at the early hour of seven o'clock, the plant is humming with energy. There's a liveliness within its walls that fuels my desire to perform at a high level. IF isn't just where I work; it defines my life and has led to my success and job satisfaction in the aerospace industry. This company gives me a place to exercise my creativity and leadership ability, and I love it here.

Located on seventy-five acres of flat land near a maze of other factories and industrial complexes on the outskirts of Fort Worth, IF is filled with machinery used to assemble and produce aircraft and space vehicle components that are constructed with the latest machining, welding, and fabrication methods. The equipment at the facility produced a sense of awe and pride as I walked through the building and headed to my workstation in Section H. My attention to detail and suggestions on how to reduce downtime and encourage creativity, efficiency, and safety within our department were well received over the years by upper management, and as a result, I was promoted to a supervisory role within our department five years ago. Our electrical department won numerous in-house awards, and several of our team members were awarded patents on machinery and electrical components they designed themselves. Managing highly skilled workers is much more interesting than assembling and welding electrical wiring into conductors, which was my former position. Since my promotion, I have been responsible for quality control of our electrical components. Advancing through the ranks, my pay increased substantially, and I now enjoy the freedom to move throughout our department troubleshooting problems, doing visual inspections of our products, and encouraging coworkers to practice more efficient methods of assembly. I am proud of the products our team makes, which are crucial to the aerospace industry.

I arrived at my desk and began my morning routines. Jerry Dunn, a member of my team, strolled by my station on the way to his workbench.

I looked up from my cart, where I was organizing my paperwork, laptop, and other paraphernalia I used in my job. I enjoyed the relationships I'd developed with the people in my department. We all had our quirks, but generally, we got along, and there was a mutual camaraderie as we worked together to achieve our goals.

"Mornin', boss," Jerry chirped cheerfully.

"Hey, how ya doin', Jerry?"

“I’m just fine,” Jerry said, waving his hand in a friendly gesture, “but I’ll be a whole lot better when my divorce is final this week.”

“Divorce? So you’re saying divorce is a good thing?” I said, frowning at the incongruency of his statement.

“Ya darn right,” Jerry yelled over his shoulder as he moved down the aisle to his station. “It’s a great day in the neighborhood, and it’ll be even better when I get rid of my wife!”

I shook my head and shrugged off his odd comment. I’ve never been married, so I had no personal experience to explain his attitude about his impending divorce, so I went back to my preparations for the day.

Gwen Delaruso, another worker in my section of the plant, tapped me on the shoulder five minutes later. I enjoyed Gwen’s company. We’d become friends and occasionally went out for tacos and a beer on Friday nights after our shift. Our section of the company was in the throes of reorganizing the assembly of an important electrical transformer for the new F35 supersonic fighter jet, which was made a couple of miles down the road at Lockheed Martin Aeronautics. I was confident we’d break through the rough spots this week to achieve a better product in less time once we streamlined the process. That was the team’s goal, anyway.

“You still trying to figure out a better way to assemble that new transformer?” Gwen asked, stopping for a quick chat as if she could read my thoughts.

“Yeah, I think I’ve got the kinks out. We’ll give it a trial run this week to see how it goes. How was your weekend?” I asked, continuing the amiable chitchat.

"We drove over to Austin to take in a car show, ate some good food, and got back late yesterday afternoon. The kids enjoyed the muscle cars, and I enjoyed looking at some muscle, if you know what I mean." She smiled and winked at me.

"Doesn't Tom get jealous when you drool over some twenty-year-old hunk?" I asked. I smiled as an image popped into my head of Gwen salivating over some dude dressed in a wife-beater tank top with muscles that bulged and rippled and a skinny little butt stuffed in a pair of tight blue jeans.

"Nah. Tom's secure in the knowledge that it's all just a dumb little game I play to tease him," Gwen explained. "He knows where my heart is, but ya gotta keep 'em interested, ya know."

"More power to ya," I commented nonchalantly, adopting her easy Texas slang. "Whatever floats your boat, honey."

"What about you? Do anything exciting over the weekend?" Gwen drawled.

I shook my head. "Nope. Just cleaned my house and did some shopping. Bought some new clothes. Next weekend I need to clean my garage."

Gwen turned up her nose in disgust. "It sounds like you need to get a life, Kitty. A good-lookin' gal like you should not be wasting her time cleaning and shopping. I could hook you up with someone—"

I waved my hand in front of her. "No, no, no," I warned sternly. "We've already had this discussion, remember?"

Gwen clicked her tongue in frustration. "I know, but girl, you have a lot to offer a man. You're smart and pretty—"

I interrupted her again before she could get on a soapbox about the state of my personal life. "Forget it, Gwen. It's not going to happen," I said curtly.

Gwen's shoulders momentarily slumped in defeat. Then she turned and walked toward her station. "I'm tellin' ya, there's somebody out there for you—somebody who'd love to meet you and get to know you," she said over her shoulder.

"I doubt it," I yelled at her as she walked away, but her statement caused a ripple of sadness inside of me. *After all these years, I'd love to see my two sisters again, but they'd probably die of shock if they knew I was still alive,* I thought. *After all, in their world, I've been dead for thirty-five years. But that will never happen, so don't even go there.*

The morning buzzed by in a flurry of technical activity. Joey had trouble with his soldering gun and had to send it off for repair. Several of my coworkers asked questions about our new welding and wiring procedures. I checked in with each member of my team, inspected a few conductors for quality control, discussed a wiring harness with one of the welders, and filled out my morning report. I decided to have lunch at my station, where my make-shift desk was piled with work orders and parts catalogs. I pushed the piles aside to make room for my lunchbox when, suddenly, I heard several quick, sharp cracks of gunfire followed by yelling and shouting.

I jumped up from my swivel stool and ran out into the aisle. People were swarming from their workstations like a horde of angry bees, hollering and pointing down the line where Jerry Dunn had collapsed on the cement floor in a heap. A redheaded woman stood over him with a small pistol gripped in her fist. She wore a look of shock. When I pushed my way through the crowd of employees and cautiously approached her, I saw hatred gleaming in her eyes and a look of triumphant satisfaction plastered on her face as she stared at Jerry, who'd collapsed on the cement floor.

I slowly approached her and held out my hand. "Excuse me, ma'am, but I'll take the gun, please," I said calmly, despite the raw fear that was pulsating through the core of my body. *Is she going to shoot me, too?* I wondered. The redhead looked at me, the shock of the moment finally hitting her hard. Her eyes filled with tears, and they spilled onto her cheeks. She looked down again at Jerry, who was bleeding profusely from several chest wounds, his shirt soaked in blood, the light in his eyes fading rapidly.

"I . . . I don't want a divorce," she blurted. "Why did he file for a divorce?" She met my gaze as if I had an answer to her question. Then, docile and meek as a little lamb, she laid the pistol in my upturned palm. I breathed a huge sigh of relief as if a cement block had been lifted from my chest. "Someone call 911 and get an ambulance over here—stat!" I ordered in a loud voice.

I heard people scurrying around me, attending to Jerry's wounds. I led the woman shooter, whom I presumed to be Jerry's wife, to a chair about fifteen feet away, laid the pistol on a nearby workbench, and stood next to her as I watched the chaos unfold around me. The acrid smoke from the pistol lingered in the air and stung my eyes. One of my coworkers pumped his fists on Jerry's chest, applying CPR in a desperate attempt to save his life, but I could see from where I stood that he was gone. His eyes were dull, his body a lifeless blob. The blood continued to slowly seep from his wounds onto the cement. I felt nauseous. I looked around and located a trash container, then walked over to it and puked into the black depths of the garbage can. In the distance, I heard the shrill blare of an ambulance siren followed by the loud whine of police squad cars arriving at the scene. In what seemed like less than a minute, cops flooded the building, where they took the woman into custody and placed her in a squad car. EMTs attended to Jerry, but they soon realized he was dead, and they loaded him onto a gurney, covering his lifeless body with a white sheet.

Things began swirling in front of me, and everything seemed out of focus. I felt like I was on a merry-go-round that was spinning out of control. Dizzy and disoriented, I limped to a chair, sat down, and rested my head in my upturned palms. My mouth was sour from vomiting, and I thought I might puke again.

"Kitty? Are you alright?" Gwen asked, kneeling next to my chair.

I shook my head in disbelief at everything that had happened in the last five minutes. *How could my world have changed so drastically in such a short amount of time?* I thought. *What am I gonna do now?*

Gwen grabbed my hands. "Kitty? Talk to me, girl," she said.

"I've got to get out of here," I said softly. I pulled my hands from Gwen's grip. "I'm going home. If anyone asks about me, just tell them I went home." I got up from the chair and felt a wave of vertigo pass through me. I grasped the edge of my desk to steady myself.

"You shouldn't drive. Let me take you home," Gwen said, taking hold of my arm to support me.

"No. No, I'm fine," I insisted, pushing her away. "I just need to get out of here and lie down for a while."

"Are you sure?" Gwen asked. "I can take you home and stay with you for a while." I could see the concern in her kind, green eyes.

"No, no. I'll be fine, I'm sure," I said, patting her arm.

"I'll call you later to check up on you, okay?"

"Yes, that's fine. You do that," I said. I walked to my desk, grabbed my purse and lunchbox, and exited the building. I was about to get into my car when more police roared up to the facility and ran into the plant. A CSI van arrived in the parking lot, and personnel began gathering their tools from the van to begin the arduous job of collecting evidence.

I drove out of the parking lot and took a side street to the ramp that led to the freeway. So far, I had escaped the attention of the police. Sooner or later, though, I knew someone would tell the cops about my actions at the scene of the shooting when the woman relinquished her firearm to me. Since I was involved in the aftermath of the crime, I was sure the police would eventually contact me for a statement. I could not risk being interviewed by a cop.

With sickening finality, I realized the day I hoped would never come had now arrived. The shooting at IF had moved the dial to an inevitable conclusion. I had prepared for this moment, though, so nothing was left to chance. Over the years, I contemplated every contingency and scenario that could happen—anything that might require my immediate departure from the area. I realized with a sinking feeling that my future plans had been shoved into the present when the shooting at the plant occurred. Somehow, this situation reminded me of the moment I had stood on the bank of the Mississippi River in La Crosse, Wisconsin, with my kayak so many years ago, when I'd decided to fake my own death. Now I was right back where I'd started. *It's escape or be found out,* I thought. *It's leave now or risk being arrested for my crimes in Wisconsin. I've got to get out of here right now.* With true sorrow and a deep sense of loss, I knew what I had to do next.

I drove my van to a quiet residential street on the north side of Fort Worth. The storage facility where I kept my pickup was packed with everything necessary to make a rapid, discreet getaway: clothing, fifty thousand dollars in cash, a medical bag, my important documents, a few tools in case of a breakdown on the road, and a small box of pictures and mementos of my life in Texas. I left my car parked under a small sycamore tree, threw the keys into a weed-infested lot next to the storage unit, and climbed into the old truck, which fortunately roared to life when I turned the key. I drove under the overpass a couple of blocks away and then merged into traffic on the freeway.

Looking to my left, I saw Lake Worth and the buildings of the city etched against the brilliant blue of the afternoon sky in the distance. I shook off my regret, aimed the truck north, and prayed my vehicle was roadworthy enough to get me through Oklahoma and into Kansas by nightfall.

CHAPTER 7

Just the Facts, Ma'am

Collette Tierney ran a hand through her long hair. Since Sonja had spoken to her yesterday, she'd been hunched over her computer, locating every reference she could find about the bombing of McMurphy Science Hall on April 17, 1990. She looked at the clock and was surprised that three hours had whizzed by since she'd plopped herself at her desk. In that time, she'd read magazine articles, newspaper reports, gleaned reactions and opinions from eyewitness testimonies recorded by several personnel from the police department and reporters, and generally refamiliarized herself with the horrendous event that had shaken the La Crosse community to its Midwest core.

Stretching her arms upward while leaning back in her chair, Collette stared at the ceiling, thinking about her friend, Sonja. For several moments she rotated her shoulders and moved her neck in circles, then she straightened up, leaned forward, and continued reviewing the details of the bombing from an article she'd found in the *La Crosse Sentinel.* The reporter who'd written the piece was Dwight

LeGrand. Collette knew Dwight. She recalled his instinctive ability to find people who'd been at the scene of a particular accident or crime and extract their eyewitness testimonies. Those riveting accounts were what made his articles stand out from other run-of-the-mill reporters. She jotted his name in a notebook near her computer. He could be a good source to help her clarify the details about Katherine Waite's role in the crime. She'd check later to see if he was still alive and living in the area.

The basic facts of the bombing were listed in the article: location, date, target building, type of attack, description of the bomb, the death that resulted from the bombing, the perpetrators, and the motive. Collette shook her head. She could still remember where she'd been when she found out about the incident—doing an all-nighter with her boyfriend to prepare for a statistics exam the next day. She smiled wistfully. Statistics class had been such a bore, but it was a course every sophomore on campus had to endure. Professor Dettweiler did nothing to add interest to the mind-numbing content, so preparing for his exams was a brutal test of the will. Professor Dettweiler's haughty arrogance and statistical knowledge pitted against the lowly, undeveloped minds of college sophomores who lacked ambition, focus, and the ability to think. Collette recalled her grade in the class and felt a rush of pride. Her studying had paid off; she was one of the few who'd aced the test and passed the course with flying colors.

She remembered the morning after the bombing when the news spread like wildfire throughout the small college town. What? A bomb? Someone was protesting. Protesting what? A professor was dead? That can't be. Who would do such a thing? It seemed unbelievable. UW–La Crosse was a relatively peaceful campus. Occasionally, a group of students would gather on the concourse in front of the administration building to protest some social issue or one of the university's changes in policy, but that seemed minor compared to what happened on other well-known college campuses throughout the country.

Collette read on, familiarizing herself with the construction of the homemade bomb, which had been effective and deadly in achieving the aim of the perpetrators. The bomb had been contained in a large Samsonite suitcase and was known as an ANFO (ammonium nitrate-fuel oil). When a remote-control device detonated it, the basement wall collapsed, and part of the ceiling and outer wall above it on the first floor blew outward, scattering debris for several hundred yards across campus. Bricks were found almost a block away, and a favorite maple tree near the science building sustained significant damage, blowing away part of the trunk and several of the lower branches. Classes had been canceled for several days after the bombing happened.

Collette slowly shook her head back and forth as she scanned the photos contained in the article. The pictures jogged a deep sadness within Collette that had lain dormant for many years. The damage to the building had been tremendous, but it was the photo of Dr. James McClintock covered in a white sheet being loaded into the city morgue van that caused a wellspring of emotion in her. She was surprised to feel tears filling her eyes and a lump forming in her throat when she recalled the death of the popular professor. Her emotions were understandable, though, since McClintock was her uncle.

She moved on, studying the aftermath of the incident. The college campus was shut down while investigators combed through the wreckage and moved throughout the campus, interviewing hundreds of students. Within twelve hours, the police zeroed in on two brothers, Jed and Collin Ainsworth, part-time students at the university who also had a reputation as agitators over many divisive issues, including abortion, race relations, specifically the Black Power Movement, immigration, and population control. They regularly attended meetings of the Communist Party. This small but active group met at various locations throughout the city. The third person of the trio was identified as Katherine Waite, a quiet, top-notch student, who drove the getaway van from the scene of the crime. It didn't take long for investigators to track down the two men who had foolishly bragged about their knowledge of explosives at a downtown bar called Spanky's. Eighteen hours after the bombing, they were arrested without incident in the apartment they shared on Badger Street. When asked why they did it, Jed, the older brother, commented calmly, "It seemed like the only effective way to get people to listen."

At the time the paper went to press, police had not found Katherine despite several leads as to her whereabouts and a thorough search of her apartment and neighborhood, but by the next day, the *Sentinel's* front-page article included the specific facts about Katherine's tragic kayak accident in the Mississippi River. For all practical purposes, her death put a period at the end of the whole terrible chapter at the university. The Ainsworth brothers were in custody after admitting to the dastardly deed, and the third member of the trio, Katherine, had drowned.

Collette studied the photo of the pretty coed and wondered what had caused her to throw her fate to the wind and become involved in the bombing as the driver of the getaway van. Didn't she know what they'd planned to do? Did she adhere to the radical principles the two brothers espoused, or was she buffaloed by their charm and machismo? *Someone somewhere must know how all this came to be,* Collette thought. *I'll call Hatchet; he might know something and be able to help.*

She hesitated a moment when she thought about Hank Brousard. He was a La Crosse police officer, good-looking in his own way, friendly, but reserved, who was committed in his service to the community and attended mass occasionally. That was really all she knew.

Well, you've got to start somewhere, she thought. *Maybe pizza? A beer or glass of wine downtown? A cup of coffee? That might work as a starting place to pick his brain and find out what he knows about the incident. His access to police files would be helpful as well.*

Collette thought briefly about her plan, picked up her phone, and began texting.

Hank (Hatchet) Brousard had just walked into his apartment on the south side of La Crosse at four o'clock after an eight-hour shift at his desk as a detective at the city police department. He was still on light duty after being shot in the chest during the investigation of murder victim Tony Diangelo last spring. His cell phone dinged. He briefly fumbled for his phone in his back pocket, glancing at the screen. A text: "Hey, Hank. Short notice but wondering if you're up for a homemade pizza and a beer. My place tonight? 7ish? Collette"

Hatchet stood rooted to his kitchen floor, stock still. Why was Collette texting him? They barely knew each other, except for his infrequent attendance at mass at St. Joseph the Workman on Main Street in La Crosse. He knew she worked at the La Crosse library, but he rarely went there. No, he *never* went there. He looked off into the distance and visualized Collette in his mind: long, flowing auburn hair, dark eyes, slim body attractively arranged, fashion-conscious. What's not to love? She was gorgeous and smart and seemed to have a lovely personality. Then his doubts kicked in. There had to be some flaws, didn't there? To be fair, we all had them, of course, but didn't a lot of women cover up their bad character traits by making themselves physically attractive? He knew all of this was just a smoke screen for his insecurities with women, but he couldn't help himself. After his disastrous relationship with Tanya Pedretti, the chief of police, years ago, he didn't know if he had the tenacity and grit to engage in another romance.

Collette was waiting for a response, the little icon blinking at him—blink, blink, blink. He felt the pressure, but then he chuckled to himself. Don't be so stupid and bullheaded. If there was one thing he'd learned after being shot point-blank in the chest last spring while on duty, it was this: Life is short and can end at any moment. Don't waste the opportunities that arrive on your doorstep.

He turned his attention back to his phone and rapidly texted a message: "I'll be there @ 7. Hatchet"

His thumb hovered over the send button for a long moment, and then he tapped it. *There. It's a done deal,* he thought. *I'm having pizza tonight with a gorgeous woman. Don't overthink this.*

By six o'clock Tuesday evening, Collette was gathering the ingredients for her veggie pizza. She cut up an assortment of peppers, onions, and mushrooms, made her pizza dough, and reached into the cupboard for a can of pizza sauce, which she perked up with different herbs and spices. Next, she grated a combination of mozzarella and Parmesan cheese. She set everything aside on the counter, then hurriedly walked through her small bungalow on 24th Avenue near the marsh just off Losey Boulevard. Everything was in order thanks to Sonja, who had recently cleaned. The wine and beer were chilling in the refrigerator, and the kitchen table was simply and beautifully set with sparkling wine glasses, luncheon plates from her grandmother's collection, and a lovely bouquet of mums, zinnias, and sunflowers from her garden.

To be truthful, Collette was nervous. This was unusual for her. She was a confident woman with a position at the library whose patrons valued her indispensable skills and knowledge. Her importance to the reading community had grown over the years as she demonstrated her encyclopedic knowledge of several subjects and regularly helped patrons with challenging research and reference questions. But all of that seemed irrelevant this evening. Her fact-finding skills didn't really apply to entertaining a single man, did they? Suddenly, the rock-solid confidence she had in her abilities was shaken. What were Hatchet's expectations for the evening? She hadn't really given much thought about that when she called him, but now his approval loomed large in her evening plans and seemed important in the scheme of things. Would he resent her for using this little get-together as a ruse for collecting information about the 1990 bombing and death of Katherine Waite? Was she wrong to assume Hatchet might possibly be attracted to her but had always been too shy to step forward and ask her on a date?

Collette shook her head vigorously. *You're getting all worked up over nothing,* she thought. *Just have some pizza and a beer and talk. You'll be fine. Keep it simple.*

She stepped in front of the hallway mirror and took one final glance at her reflection: blue jeans, a white lacy blouse, a pair of large silver hoop earrings, and strappy sandals. Makeup? Flawless. Her long, flowing locks were curled and hung loosely over her shoulders. She smiled at herself. Teeth! She'd forgotten to brush her teeth. She ran into the bathroom and hastily brushed, then gargled some mouthwash. The doorbell rang.

H*ere goes nothing,* she thought as she walked to the front entrance. She opened the door and smiled. Hatchet stood on the porch, and when the door opened, he grinned shyly. Collette noticed his ramrod posture and massive shoulders. He seemed nervous, but she was good at putting people at ease.

"Hey, how's it goin'?" he said.

"It's going fine. Just fine," Collette said, smiling widely. "Come on in." She turned, and Hatchett followed her into the kitchen. "I thought you might help me put the pizza together. I've got everything ready."

"Sounds great. I like to cook, but I don't always have time," Hatchet explained.

As they assembled the pizza, their conversation flowed

easily. While the pizza baked, Collette poured wine for herself and got a beer for Hatchet. He talked about his recovery from the shooting he'd experienced late last spring. During the meal, the conversation rambled through some family history, the demands of their jobs, and friends they had in common.

"I didn't realize you knew Tanya and Roy Pedretti so well," Hatchet commented. They had retreated to Collette's screened porch overlooking the marsh after devouring the pizza. It was cool, the air crisp with a hint of burning leaves. A moth made little pinging sounds as it bounced off the screen in the autumn air.

"Well, I met them at church, and I've been to a few of their patio parties up on the bluff. They have a beautiful place," Collette said. She crossed her legs and leaned back in the patio chair, watching Hatchet closely.

"I've known Tanya my whole life," Hatchet said with a wistful smile. "We used to go down to the marsh and catch frogs and toads when we were kids. Back then, we rode our bikes all over town. We didn't worry about abductions and stuff like that. Looking back, it seems those times were so innocent and happy."

"Well, in some ways they were innocent. But kids can still be independent today and have a lot of freedom to explore their ideas—to be happy, as you say. La Crosse isn't that big of a town. It's a great place to raise a family, I think," Collette commented.

"Yeah, I guess."

Collette still had not broached the topic of the bombing, so when the conversation slowed down, she took the opportunity to bring it up for discussion.

"I was talking to Sonja Hovland the other day, and the 1990 bombing at the university came up. Do you remember that?" she asked.

"Do I ever. Anybody who lived in La Crosse at the time has some memory of that event. Me, I was about twelve. I was thinking about being a cop, so I guess I was more interested in it than a lot of other kids my age."

"What do you remember about it?" Collette asked.

For several minutes, Hatchet reviewed the parameters of the crime. Then he said something about Katherine Waite, and Collette sat up straight, listening carefully. "You know the girl who drove the getaway van drowned in the Mississippi the day after the bombing," he said.

"Yes, I'm aware of that. But did you know she was Sonja Hovland's sister?" Collette asked.

Hatchet's eyes widened in surprise. He leaned forward and gave Collette an intense, wide-eyed stare. "What? Are you kidding? Wow! I never knew that. That's brand-new information for me."

Collette continued her explanation. "She's trying to find out more about the bombing and her sister's death. I guess she doesn't believe the police did a thorough job of investigating her drowning."

Immediately Hatchet became agitated. "What's her beef with the police? Why does everyone always believe the worst about cops?" Collette noticed his voice had risen in volume. He leaned forward in his chair, and his index finger wagged up and down. His cheeks were flushed, and his eyes flashed with impatience.

Collette waved her hands in front of him, trying to stem an argument that would ruin the evening. "Whoa,

whoa! I don't think she meant to be adversarial. She was just a kid when it happened, and her parents shielded her from finding out the real facts surrounding the case. She wants some closure, so she asked Tanya to reopen the investigation."

"Reopen the case? You're kidding. Really? You have to have a pretty good reason to do that. That's pretty gutsy for someone who's got an unbelievable network of friends around town. Why doesn't she just ask some of them what they know about it?" Hatchet said sarcastically. "They could probably tell her as much or more than police records could. She seems to have a knack for digging up information without the help of the police department."

Collette picked up on the negativity, wondering about Hatchet's attitude. "You sound like you've got a beef against her."

"No, I don't, not really. Sorry. I didn't mean to give that impression, but the bombing made national news. When I joined the force ten years later, lots of the guys on the force were still talking about it. Investigating a crime of national significance is something you don't forget as a cop."

"The FBI was called in, I remember," Collette said.

"How do you know that?"

"My uncle was James McClintock, the professor who was killed. He was my mom's older brother," Collette said. "The FBI came to our house and interviewed my mom and dad."

"I didn't know that, either. I need to come over here more often. I've found out more about this whole affair in the last fifteen minutes than I knew my whole lifetime. So, what's your interest in the case other than your uncle's death?"

"Curiosity, I suppose," Collette said modestly. "Sonja's

questions triggered a lot of memories for me. If you don't mind, I have one more question." She raised her eyebrows, waiting for Hatchet's approval. He nodded and she continued. "Have you ever heard rumors around town that Katherine staged her own death and escaped to parts unknown and is still alive?"

Hatchet leaned back in his chair and stared off into the marsh. He was silent for several moments. "Occasionally someone will bring that up. There are people who believe it, but I doubt it. My professional opinion is that she drowned. I know her body was never found, but that's not unusual for a powerful river like the Mississippi."

"Is there anything else you can tell me about Katherine Waite?"

"Wait a minute. You aren't fishing for information for Sonja Hovland, are you?" Hatchet seemed to bristle again.

Collette blushed and shifted in her chair. "Well, truthfully, she asked me to do some investigation into the basic details of the crime. I spent this afternoon doing that, but then I thought of you and wondered what you knew about the case."

"Well, obviously I don't know as much as you do."

"I'm sorry. I didn't want the evening to be ruined because you felt I'd taken advantage of your position as a cop in town," Collette apologized.

Hatchet smiled. "Don't worry. I'm not offended. When you've been punched, spit at, sworn at, shot, and made the butt of donut jokes, you develop a pretty tough skin, so your questions don't bother me. But I know Sonja can be persistent, kinda like a dog with a favorite bone. You know?"

"Do I ever," Collette said, laughing. Hatchet noticed the musical quality of her voice. It was a sound he missed having in his life. As he evaluated the evening, he realized how isolated he'd become from the rhythms of everyday life with a woman. He enjoyed being with Collette. She was smart, funny, and he was so relaxed as if he was in the presence of an old friend.

They drank more beer and wine until a wave of yawning came over them both. Collette stood.

"Work tomorrow, so I'd better get some sleep, but this has been wonderful," she said softly.

"Yeah, it has been. Hey, how about dinner on Saturday night? Maybe go to the Freighthouse or to Waterfront?" Hatchet asked.

"That would be lovely," Collette said as she opened the front door.

"I'll call you, okay?" he said.

"Sure," Collette said.

Before Hatchet left, he leaned over and gave Collette a tender kiss on the cheek. She smiled shyly. He turned and walked to his car parked on the street, waving briefly when he got in. Collette stood on the threshold for a minute, touched her cheek briefly, and watched Hatchet drive away.

CHAPTER 8

Business as Usual

The Fort Worth Police Department was always hectic, and today was no different from any other day, with robberies, assaults, domestic disputes, car accidents, DUIs, and a few murders thrown in for good measure. Police Chief Jason Allbaugh stared at the two detectives standing in front of him. He'd taken numerous calls this morning from officers who were interviewing employees at Innovative Fabrications about the shooting at the plant early Monday afternoon. No one could find the woman who had disarmed the shooter and then left the plant unnoticed. For all practical purposes, she seemed to have disappeared from the face of the earth.

"So, you're telling me that this woman—Kitty Currant—who worked at the plant and disarmed the shooter has disappeared? You can't locate her anywhere?" Allbaugh glanced at a sticky note the officers had handed him,

"That's right, sir. We called and texted her cell, and we visited her place in White Settlement at least five times since the shooting at Innovative Fabrications on Monday.

We canvassed her neighborhood as well, but her vehicle is gone, her house looks unoccupied, and her neighbors say she hasn't been seen since she left for work on Monday morning. That was two days ago. They say that's very unusual for her. Apparently, she's meticulous about her schedule—very predictable," Officer Jason Dreves reported. "She leaves for work and comes home at the same time every day."

"There's more, Chief," Officer Ken Stanton interrupted. His bald head glowed in the harsh glare of the fluorescent lights overhead. His suit was rumpled, and he looked exhausted, but what cop didn't? The chief had heard through the police grapevine that Stanton's marriage was in trouble. Marriage difficulties weren't surprising either, especially among the ranks of police officers. In that respect, Stanton was no different than many of his law enforcement colleagues.

"Let's hear what you found out then," the chief growled. He leaned back, his office chair creaking ominously under his large frame. His bulging belly strained the buttons of his uniform shirt. He laid his huge hands across his stomach in what he hoped was a gesture of open-mindedness, goodwill, and patience, but he could tell from the expression on the detectives' faces that the friendly vibes he was trying to send weren't having the desired effect he'd hoped for. He tried to reassure his officers. "I'm all ears, guys, so have at it. Tell me what's goin' on."

"We talked to one of Kitty's friends, a gal named Gwen Delaruso," Dreves continued. "She's known Kitty for over twenty years and worked with her at IF. She told us that Kitty doesn't talk about her family and has very few close friends, kind of a loner. She's very careful about the people she allows into her circle, if you get my meaning."

"Yeah, I get it," Allbaugh replied. "You think she's got something to hide. This Kitty gal knows the murder at the plant will put a spotlight on her, so she's taken off for places unknown. Is that what you're saying?" he asked gruffly. "She avoids close relationships in which her past might come to light. You think she's committed some kind of crime, and she's been hiding out in Fort Worth. Is that the gist of it?"

As the chief talked, the expression on his face had subtly changed from boredom to curiosity. Despite his skeptical attitude and dismissive stance, Allbaugh thought this situation *was* getting interesting. He sat up and leaned forward. "Have you followed up on her? Did you dig into her history?"

"We did, sir," Stanton said, nodding his head. "Her history seems too sterile to be true. Frankly, there's not enough information out there about Kitty Currant to write a postcard. We're wondering if she created a false narrative about herself and had fake documents made to back up her story. When we talked to the HR people at the IF plant, they showed us Kitty's documents, but they seemed contrived and looked fake. We got curious, so we checked through the national police database for women of her age and description who might have disappeared thirty years ago or so. We got two hundred thirty-seven hits for women who disappeared around 1990 and have never been found."

Chief Allbaugh's scowl deepened as he calculated the time the detectives had spent combing through the records, ignoring other pressing matters, namely pounding the turf in Fort Worth to locate this woman. From his thirty years on the force, he knew how difficult it was to fake your own death and hide in plain sight. *It's all very hard to believe,* he thought. *Meanwhile, the criminals are getting ahead of us while these guys build air castles in the sky.*

Stanton shifted on his feet as he watched the chief's reaction to their efforts. The big guy didn't miss anything. Stanton could almost see the numbers hovering above Chief Allbaugh's head as he estimated the hours and wages they'd been paid to investigate a vague hunch. Incurring the chief's disapproval was never a good idea, and Stanton got the feeling Chief Allbaugh was not impressed with their efforts in the least, and he was even less impressed by what they'd found, which amounted to nothing.

"How much time have you spent on this?" the chief asked brusquely, seeming to read Stanton's mind.

"Two days. We read and sorted through the records, specifically looking for someone who disappeared about thirty years ago. There are only three women who have never been found and are presumed to be dead who even come close to matching Currant's physical description."

"And?"

"And of those three, we zeroed in on a bombing incident in 1990 at the University of Wisconsin in a small town called La Crosse. It's on the Mississippi River," Dreves said.

"Why'd you pick the case from Wisconsin?" Allbaugh asked.

Dreves cocked his head to one side and saw his chance to redeem himself and his partner. He began to explain. "This Delaruso woman says Kitty has a definite Midwest accent. She says she pronounces certain words with a "Wisconsin" twang, so we went with it when we looked at the information that popped up. We believe the woman called Kitty Currant is the same woman who participated in the bombing of a university building in La Crosse back in 1990, which killed a professor. We compared a photo of her then and now. Her face shape and features, her hairstyle and color, and body type haven't really changed over the years. Supposedly, according to police records, this Kitty woman drowned in the Mississippi River in a kayaking accident the day after the bombing, but her body was never recovered."

"Supposedly drowned? What's hard to believe about that?" Allbaugh asked rudely. "I'm sure people drown in the Mississippi River all the time—some are found, some aren't." The chief stared at the two detectives for a moment, daring them to come up with a rebuttal, but Dreves and Stanton stayed silent. "Okay. I'll play along," Allbaugh continued. "So, tell me what makes you think this Kitty person is the missing woman from La Crosse? Let's hear this, and it better be good, cause I think this is a long shot and you're grasping at straws, trying to come up with some justification for all the time you spent on this, coming up with nada! Zilch? A big fat zero!" The two detectives grimaced when Allbaugh's big fist hit the top of the desk with a bang.

Undeterred, Stanton began his explanation. "The drowning happened on April 18. Katherine Waite's body was never recovered from the river, although they found her kayak and some other stuff in the Mississippi the next day. People in the area believe she may have staged her own death and is still alive somewhere in the U.S. We think she changed her name and identity and then began her job at IF on April 28, ten days after the accident. She bought her house a year later after renting an apartment in White Settlement. She's been here ever since. She's very quiet, never mentions family or other acquaintances. Polite, but aloof. Keeps her head down, never goes on a vacation, keeps her nose to the grindstone. She's an attractive woman but has never dated anyone—no long-term relationships, no affairs, no love life of any kind. None of her family has ever visited her."

Police Chief Allbaugh shook his head. "Maybe she's gay and stays in the closet?" The two detectives stared at the chief, skepticism written all over their boss's face.

"Gay people today have relationships, sir," Dreves said quietly, "out in the open."

"Well, I don't know," Allbaugh snarled, running his hand across the top of his head, offended that his opinions were considered out of touch with reality. "You're taking some pretty big leaps of faith to get to your conclusion. Have you called the police department in La Crosse yet?"

"We were about to. We'll let you know what we find out," Dreves said.

"Keep me in the loop, but I think you're barkin' up the wrong tree. If Kitty shows up in La Crosse in the next few weeks, you'll make a believer out of me, but until that happens, don't spend too much time on this. We've got other cases to solve that don't need a leap of blind faith," Allbaugh said sarcastically. "What I really need are a couple of detectives with boots on the ground pounding the pavement puttin' two and two together to find the woman who witnessed a murder and disarmed the assailant and then disappeared. She's gotta be here somewhere! Get my meaning?" he snarled.

"We got it, sir," Dreves said. "That's what we're trying to do."

Chief Allbaugh dismissed them with a wave of his hand. The two detectives turned and walked out of the office while Allbaugh stared at them plodding down the hallway.

"There's always a couple of bleeding hearts in every crowd," the chief muttered under his breath. "People believe she's still alive . . . blah, blah, blah. Jeez, two hundred thirty-seven cases? What a waste of time! Give me a break!"

On Wednesday morning, after a soft, steady rainfall that lasted most of the night, the sun broke over Grandad Bluff in La Crosse, revealing shades of peach and orange beneath gray, empty rain clouds. Fingers of fog lingered briefly, floating in wisps along the bluffs until the sky finally cleared and soft golden light sifted through the sheer curtains in Tanya and Roy's bedroom. Tanya had cuddled up to Roy's back. She gradually became aware of the morning sounds and the light in the room. She opened her eyes and smiled. Mourning doves cooed softly from the trees near the garage, and Tanya reveled in her memories of last night.

Roy rolled over, kissed her lightly on the lips, and said, "Mornin', darlin'." He thought about how beautiful she was lying next to him with nothing on. He remembered the warmth of her breath next to his skin after their lovemaking when she'd whispered, "That was wonderful." He felt a shiver along his spine just recalling her tender sentiment. "You are a sight to behold, sweetheart," he whispered, kissing her gently on the cheek, "and I am one lucky man."

"Mmm, really? That's nice to hear," Tanya said as she gently ran her fingers through Roy's hair. "Do I have to go to work this morning? Can't we just stay in bed all day and do what we did last night?"

Roy chuckled. "We haven't stayed in bed all morning since the first year we were married. Besides, we'll both get fired if we don't show up for work, and Leisel might barge in looking for us when we don't come downstairs for our morning coffee." His brown eyes twinkled at the thought. "Might be worth it, though." He grinned wickedly and kissed her again.

"Mmm, it'd be worth it," Tanya murmured in a husky voice. "Of course, without jobs and paychecks, we'd be poor and destitute, but even so, you can't put a price on love, can you?" she said, rolling over on her back.

"Oooh, we're poetic this morning," Roy said, staring up at the ceiling. "That's a nice sentiment, honey, but stayin' in bed all morning is not gonna happen."

"Yeah, I know. You're right. The real world is calling. We've got to fess up and face the music," Tanya said as she swept her arm in an arc over the bed. She sat up, stepped out of bed, and walked to the bathroom to start the shower. She looked over her shoulder. "But . . . you could join me in the shower," she suggested.

Roy jumped up and followed her into the bathroom. "Can't say no to that."

Later at the breakfast table, their conversation turned to Sonja Hovland's recent crusade to learn more about her long-lost deceased sister. Roy had his own opinions about the whole hullabaloo, but he was careful to keep his remarks to himself. Tanya could be persnickety when he inserted his opinions into discussions about ongoing police investigations, even though he was confident she respected his thoughts as a private citizen and his occasional suggestions about difficult cases.

"What do you think about Sonja's latest request to re-investigate the 1990 bombing at the U and the death of Katherine Waite?" Tanya asked, taking a bite of toast. She scanned the *La Crosse Sentinel's* opinion page as she drank her coffee.

"Sonja always seems to have a bee in her bonnet," Roy said carefully, skirting the issue. Honestly, he thought reopening the investigation into Katherine Waite's death was preposterous. That some woman had staged her own demise in the frozen Mississippi and survived to escape to parts unknown wasn't even worth considering, in his opinion. He supposed crazy things like that happened somewhere in the world, but they were very rare. Like only in the world of the CIA or MI5. *Things like that don't happen in La Crosse, Wisconsin,* he thought sourly. *I'd bet a six-pack of beer on it.*

"You didn't answer my question," Tanya persisted.

"I'm still thinking," Roy said quietly.

Balking at his wife's request, Roy sipped his coffee while he composed a response in his head. What he really hoped was that Tanya would forget this whole affair and move on. Usually nothing good came from sharing his opinion about police cases, especially about a situation as controversial as this one. In fact, his suggestions would probably end in an argument with his wife, and he didn't want to ruin the intimacy they'd enjoyed last night at the expense of some long-forgotten person who had drowned in the river over thirty years ago.

After several moments, Tanya leaned over the table and, with her hand, slowly lowered the newspaper Roy held in front of him. "Enough of the hiding behind the paper. I'm waiting. What are your thoughts?"

"Why is my opinion so important to you?" Roy asked, gazing directly into Tanya's hazel eyes.

Tanya shrugged. "I need your guidance, and I value what you think . . . most of the time." She looked over her reading glasses at him.

Roy harrumphed and said, "I've heard that before. But for argument's sake, go ahead and tell me why you value my opinion. I'd like to hear this."

"Well, you're outside the police system."

"So?" Roy said.

"So, you're a member of the general public. It's important for me to keep my thumb on the heartbeat of the community."

Roy sputtered impolitely. "Ya right," he mumbled. "I hardly think I have my finger on the pulse of the community, honey."

Tanya scowled at him. "That was meant to be a compliment," she said.

Roy hung his head and apologized. "Oh. Sorry. Go on."

"You usually think of things that don't occur to me. If I do reopen this case, I'll probably get blasted by the press and social media," Tanya continued, "and you might hear some nasty stuff around town about me. I'm going to need your moral support."

"You mean like the moral support I gave you last night?"

Roy grinned. "If that's the support you're talkin'about, then I'm all in," he teased as he gave a weak salute. "I'm at your service, my lady. Anytime."

"Very funny." Despite the lighthearted attempt at diversion, Tanya persevered. "But seriously, what do you think about reopening the case?"

Roy sighed with frustration. "Before I answer that, let me clarify one thing: I've never let nasty rumors about you bother me before, and it won't bother me now," he said grumpily. "As for reopening the case, all I'll say is this: Don't make a decision based on your friendship with Sonja. Keep it professional. Whatever you decide might affect your relationship temporarily, but if you are truly friends, then the firestorm you're predicting will rock your boat, but it won't sink it."

Tanya nodded and smiled. "Well said, my love. You are a wellspring of wisdom." She clucked her tongue, but her smile disappeared quickly as she thought about the situation some more. "I hope you're right about my friendship with Sonja. Having a row with her would be unpleasant, and I'm sure I'd come out on the losing end of the stick."

Leisel breezed into the kitchen, went to the cupboard for a cereal bowl and a box of Cheerios. With a gallon of milk from the refrigerator, she sat down at the table. She poured the cereal and milk into the bowl and began chewing noisily.

"Mornin', kiddo," Roy said casually, unfolding his newspaper. He studied his daughter: her dark hair, brown eyes, and tawny skin. *She is a beauty,* he thought. *Just like her mother.*

Leisel hunched over her bowl and grunted something

that was supposed to pass as a greeting. Roy watched Tanya over his coffee cup. *Uh-oh,* he thought. He noticed her flashing eyes and a particular tightness around her mouth. *She's irritated about something.* Was she upset about his advice or upset by Leisel's rude morning brush-off?

"Excuse me?" Tanya interrupted, staring at Leisel. "Your father greeted you, young lady. Grunting is not an acceptable form of communication unless you're a caveman," she reprimanded.

Leisel stopped eating, her spoon held midair. "Caveperson."

"What?"

"You used the masculine form—caveman. It should be caveperson. That's gender neutral, Mom," Leisel lectured. "Or you could have used cavewoman."

"Whatever," Tanya said sarcastically. "Greet your dad properly," she said pointing at Roy.

"Good morning, Dad. How ya doin'?" Leisel said obligingly.

"I've never been better. In fact—"

"Let's just leave it at that," Tanya said with a sudden glowing smile. Roy winked at her and grinned.

"What is it with you two?" Leisel snipped. "Why are you acting so weird lately?"

"We're just two people in love," Roy said, still smiling.

"OMG! Could I just eat my cereal in peace," Leisel whined, "minus the love talk and the drama?"

"Got something against love, sweetie?" Tanya asked.

Leisel slammed her spoon on the table. "I've got nothing against love. I just don't wanna watch my parents give each other 'the look' at seven in the morning."

"Well, we're happy, and you're just going to have to deal with it," Roy said as he snapped his newspaper open.

"Whatever," Leisel grumbled under her breath. After a lengthy silence in which the only sound in the kitchen was the crunching of cereal, Tanya rose from the table, placed her coffee cup in the kitchen sink, and turned, kissing Roy and then Leisel.

"I'll see you tonight," she said nonchalantly. "Make it a good day."

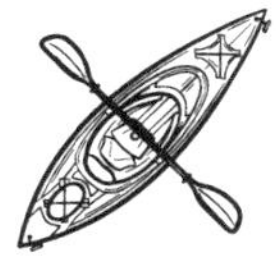

CHAPTER 9 • KITTY

On the Road Again

The tires of my old jalopy whined loudly as I headed north, pounding the highway through Kansas. My destination was still up for grabs, but I had a vague longing to return home to Wisconsin, to the place of my birth along the shores of Lake Superior. I know what you're probably thinking: Criminals always return to the scene of the crime, but that's a bunch of hooey. Truthfully, I was very saddened to leave my home of thirty-five years in White Settlement. Abandoning everything you're familiar with at the age of fifty-five was proving to be more difficult than I anticipated, but what's a girl to do? My choices were very limited. In the last few hours, I found myself driving without a specific destination in mind, drifting aimlessly, desperately trying to get my bearings and calm my racing thoughts.

After I fled the scene at the IF plant and retrieved my pickup from the storage shed, I traveled nonstop for six hours. I was shocked down to the soles of my boots by the shooting of my coworker, Jerry Dunn. Exhausted and strung out from the chaos I'd witnessed, I kept seeing Jerry's lifeless eyes staring at the ceiling as he lay bleeding on the cold cement floor. My eyes were red and swollen from crying, and I felt emotionally adrift, lost and alone. I couldn't tell you the towns I had gone through, or even the names of the highways I'd driven. I was just bobbing and weaving through the flat, hot countryside, trying to come up with a plan, trying to figure out what I should do next.

The sun was sinking toward the horizon when I came upon a nice mom-and-pop motel just at the edge of town along the highway on the north side of Wichita. I stopped, went into the motel office, and asked to look at the rooms. They were clean and comfortable, nothing fancy. I rented a room, parked my old truck in the lot, and got my overnight bag from the back seat. I settled myself on the comfortable bed and ordered a pizza from a place the owners had recommended. In a matter of minutes, I fell asleep. A sharp rap on the door a half hour later startled me, and for a moment, I forgot where I was. I jumped up from the bed, calmed my racing heart, and opened the door.

"That'll be $16.85, ma'am," the pizza guy said.

I turned and grabbed my purse from the bed, giving the delivery guy a twenty. "Keep the change," I said with a shy smile.

"Thanks," he said, handing me the box.

I closed the door and hooked the security chain. Opening the box, the smell of oregano, sausage, and tomato sauce fired up my appetite. I was famished; I hadn't eaten anything since noon. The pizza was delicious. I wolfed down several slices as I flipped through the channels on the TV. Imagine my surprise when I saw my photo splashed on the screen. I turned up the volume.

"Fort Worth police are searching for this woman who was involved in the aftermath of a shooting today at the Innovative Fabrications plant on the outskirts of Fort Worth. The woman whose name is Kitty Currant may be traveling north, possibly to Wisconsin, where it is believed she has relatives. If you see her, please call the Fort Worth Police Department. Miss Currant was responsible for disarming the shooter, preventing others from being harmed."

I turned down the volume on the TV, still staring at the screen in disbelief. Relatives in Wisconsin? How'd they find that out? If they knew that, then they probably knew about the bombing at the university thirty years ago. My cover had been blown.

Acting on impulse, I grabbed my cell phone and called the number flashing along the bottom of the television screen.

"Fort Worth Police Department. How can I help you?" a female voice intoned.

"That woman you'all are lookin' for? Have you found her yet?" I asked in a twangy southern drawl. "The report on channel 5 said her name is Kitty Currant."

"No, we haven't located her. Do you have information to share, ma'am?"

"Well, I live across the street from a small motel called Finally Home in Stillwater, Oklahoma, and I think she's holed up there," I said. "It's on the east side of town."

"Can you describe this woman?"

"Yeah. She's white, with blonde hair. She's about five feet, five inches tall, and she's drivin' a dark blue Dodge Ram pickup with Texas license plates TX8934."

"Just a minute, ma'am. I'd like you to speak to my

supervisor," the woman said.

I immediately hung up. Whether my attempt at distraction would buy me more time, I didn't know, but it was worth a try.

I took a shower, then set my cell phone alarm for three o'clock in the morning. Rubbing my eyes, I yawned widely while checking my phone for text messages. There was one from Gwen back in Fort Worth wondering where I'd gone. That was all. I rolled over on my side and closed my eyes. If I was going to escape from the police who were trying to find me, I needed to get an early start.

By eight o'clock Wednesday morning, Chief Tanya Pedretti was sitting at her desk, discussing a carjacking on Hager Street just off Copeland Avenue. During the incident, an elderly man had been jerked out of his car and thrown onto the nearest curb. The victim was being treated at Mayo Hospital over by the university for head injuries and a possible brain bleed. The perpetrator who stole the car led police on a high-speed chase through the city out past the mall on Highway 16, where he'd escaped into the rolling hills and country roads between Barre Mills and West Salem. A full-blown manhunt was shaping up, and several nearby local police departments were sending men to the scene to help with the search.

"Check in with Mike Leland and see how the search for the carjacker is going," Tanya said to Lt. Chad Hepple. "Get over to the hospital and take a statement from the elderly gentleman who was injured and get a description of the perpetrator out to all the local police stations in the area as soon as possible." Chad was typing furiously on his iPad. Tanya continued. "Tony called in and said a homeowner near the scene has a video of the actual assault taken from a surveillance camera mounted on his garage. The alley has a view of Hager Street, where the assault took place. Here's the guy's address," Tanya said handing Chad a note. "Send someone over there right away to talk to the guy and get the video."

"Right. I'll do that, ma'am," Hepple said. He remained calm as the chief fired off several directives. It was one of the things he greatly admired about Pedretti. She had a no-pie-in-the-sky approach to crime, believing that organization, efficiency, and feet on the street could prevent and solve criminal activity within the city. The politics of her position as police chief was something she downplayed. She stayed under the radar by solving crimes in a timely manner. In addition, she had developed strong, trusting relationships with citizens, especially the mayor and city council, who believed in her mission. So far, it had worked. The mayor, city council, and business leaders had frequently applauded the actions of the police, citing Chief Pedretti's efforts to lead her team as exemplary, balanced, and fair.

"Before you leave, tell me about the assault case on campus involving the Frawley girl? What's the status on that?" Tanya continued.

"The girl is unclear about the identity of the perpetrator. It was dark, and he dragged her into the shadow of the building and assaulted her there. Her description is rather vague and doesn't give us much to work with," Hepple informed the chief. "When we catch the guy, she'll have to decide if she wants to press charges, but that's for the DA and her to decide. We have some leads we're investigating, and we're still interviewing students who were in the dorm where Frawley lived and who were in the general vicinity of Bekkum Hall that night. I'll keep you updated on that," Chad said.

A staccato knock on the door interrupted their conversation. Lt. Hank (Hatchet) Brousard opened the door and stuck his head around the door frame. Tanya waved him in. She walked around her desk and watched while Hatchet strolled across the floor and took a seat next to her desk. It was rewarding to see him back on his feet at desk duty after the shooting, which had threatened his life for several days last spring.

"Good to see you. How are you doing?" she asked with genuine concern.

"I'm better," Hatchet said simply. "Getting stronger."

"Still attending your counseling sessions with Doc Jensen?"

"Yep. She's very good," Hatchet replied.

"Yes, she is. So, what brings you upstairs?" Tanya asked briskly.

"Don't worry. I'm not looking for my old job back," Hatchet said with a tentative smile, flashing a nervous glance toward Hepple.

"That's good because you're probably not ready for that yet," Tanya said. Chad stood up and asked, "Anything else, Chief?"

"No, not right now, Chad. Let's meet about one o'clock and see where we're at."

Lt. Hepple departed to begin his list of duties, and when Tanya and Hatchet were alone, the office became quiet, the mood subdued. "How's Chad doing?" Hatchet asked, breaking the awkward silence.

"Well, nobody can replace you, Hatchet, if that's what you mean," Tanya said, looking into his green eyes, "but I couldn't have asked for a more competent person to fill your position given the circumstances we were dealt. Chad doesn't have your sense of humor, which I miss sometimes, but we make it work."

"Good. I'm glad it's working for you," Hatchet replied, "but the real reason I'm here is to talk to you about something else."

"Sure. Tell me about it," Tanya said as she walked behind her desk and sat down. She began straightening the files she had dug out from the archives about the bombing, which she'd placed on her desk in a somewhat slapdash manner.

"Are you going to reopen the investigation into the 1990 bombing case and Katherine Waite's death?" Hatchet asked.

Tanya stopped tidying her desk and laid her hand on top of the files. "How did you find out about that? I didn't think anyone on staff even knew it was being considered."

"The walls have eyes and ears, Tanya. You know how things go around here," Hatchet said. "Let's just say I have a friend who knows a friend who talked to a friend, etcetera, etcetera."

Tanya shrugged and held up her hand. "I know, I know. Truthfully, I'm struggling with what to do about it. The person who requested it—"

"Sonja Hovland?" Hatchet inserted.

Tanya nodded. "Yes, your sources must be very good."

Hatchet stared into the distance remembering his evening with Collette Tierney. "They are," he said curtly.

"Collette Tierney?" Tanya ventured, raising her eyebrows and tilting her head.

"Checkmate, Chief," Hatchet said with a smile. "Apparently, Sonja asked Collette for help to fill in the blanks about the original crime and her sister's death at Pettibone."

"I'm not sure all of this is going to give Sonja the closure she's looking for. We discussed the whole thing at length, but she wasn't satisfied. She wanted to know more," Tanya explained. "I don't think that's a good move, but—" Her phone rang. "Let me get this," she said.

"Tanya Pedretti. May I help you?" she asked. She listened for several minutes, nodding and giving single-word responses. Suddenly a quizzical expression crossed her face, she sat up tall, and her eyes grew wide with disbelief. "Wait a minute. Are you telling me you believe this Kitty woman is Katherine Waite?"

At the mention of Katherine Waite's name, Hatchet stood up and moved closer to Tanya's desk while the chief listened intently, nodding her head now and then.

"You believe she's left the Fort Worth area and is on the run?" Tanya repeated, looking up at Hatchet, who was standing in front of her desk. "Why do you think she's headed to Wisconsin, specifically La Crosse?" Tanya listened for several more minutes while she jotted down some notes, names, and phone numbers. "Yes, she does have family here in the city," Tanya said. More listening.

Finally, Tanya said, "Thanks for the call. We'll be in touch." She hung up, laid her phone on the desk, leaned back in her chair, and stared upward at the ceiling.

"Who was that?" Hatchet asked, not sure he wanted to

hear the answer.

"The Fort Worth police," she said flatly.

"As in Texas?" Hatchet said.

She nodded. "Yes, as in Fort Worth, Texas." Her expression darkened, reflecting the serious nature of the phone call. She quit staring at the ceiling, sat up straight, and focused her attention on Hatchet while she filled him in on the shooting at the Innovative Fabrications plant and Kitty Currant's role in disarming the shooter.

"What else did they say?" he asked.

"A couple of detectives down there checked out Kitty Currant's background after the shooting incident at the plant in Fort Worth. They believe she's actually Katherine Waite, and she's been hiding in plain sight in White Settlement for the past thirty-five years after reinventing herself as Kitty Currant. Since the shooting on Monday, Kitty seems to have disappeared, and the two detectives believe she's heading our way."

"Holy Mother of Mary, pray for us in the hour of need," Hatchet whispered with reverence.

"I'll second that," Tanya said. "Wait until Sonja hears this one."

CHAPTER 10 • SONJA

The Long and Winding Road...

On Wednesday evening, after our walk, I volunteered to check on the mules and the chickens while Trygve did a little chair work in his shop. I filled an empty ice cream pail with some apples and strolled through the pasture to the barn. Opening the heavy door, I walked up to the gate of the pen where our mules, Sonny and Cher, were waiting impatiently, their ears perked and their eyes bright with the anticipation of a treat. Most people who knew we had a pair of mules couldn't understand our attraction to these two gentle animals. They were unaware of their intelligence and their cautious nature. Although we rarely rode them, Sonny and Cher had often proven useful pulling wagons loaded with wood when Trygve needed to clear brush or cut trees on the steep slopes of our farm behind the house. Tonight, I fed them apples for no particular reason except that I loved listening to them crunch on the fruit with their big teeth. I thought about the conversation I'd had with Collette earlier in the day.

We'd met for lunch at a sandwich shop downtown near the library. The place was bustling, the smell of pickles, onions, and freshly baked bread permeating the atmosphere. We got in line, ordered sandwiches, and found a booth.

"So, let's hear what you found out," I said. I'm sure I must have sounded like a kid in a candy store. I began to eat my sandwich when I noticed the serious expression on Collette's face as she watched me.

"I enlisted the help of Hatchet," she said. I did a double take and laid my sandwich on the table in front of me. This was unexpected. I had hoped to keep the circle of people who knew about my investigation small until I knew the direction it would take.

"You talked to Hatchet about my sister?" I asked. Collette carefully unwrapped her sandwich, then nervously replaced the vegetables that had fallen out on the paper. When my eyes met hers, she squirmed uncomfortably.

"Well, I've been wanting to talk with him anyway . . . to get to know him a little better," she said, blushing with embarrassment at her obvious ulterior motives. "So, I called him and invited him over to my place for pizza. Eventually, I steered the conversation to the subject of your dead sister."

I bristled and leaned forward over the table. "Oh, I get it. You used my sister's death to spark a conversation with a guy you wanted a date with?" Collette winced at my comment as if I'd slapped her. I've always had difficulty controlling my biting sarcasm, and now my temper flared. I could feel heat coloring my cheeks, and thoughts of betrayal raced through my mind. I stared at Collette and wondered why I had entrusted her with my traumatic family history when it seemed she was only interested in filling her social calendar with a hot date.

"When you put it like that, it does sound pretty deceptive . . . and selfish," Collette said apologetically, "but remember you asked me for information. I know a lot of people around town, and I thought there was nothing wrong with gleaning information from a policeman who might know something I hadn't uncovered in my research."

I tilted my head, thinking. "So, you're telling me you screwed up? Was that some kind of apology?"

"Yeah, I screwed up, and I admit I used the situation to my advantage. I'm sorry."

I leaned back in my chair and studied Collette. Was I really going to get all bent out of shape because my friend had solicited help from an outside source in the hopes of gaining additional knowledge about my sister's history? The fact that she garnered attention from a policeman for her own personal advantage raised my hackles, but I decided to calm down and be rational. Trygve would have been so proud of me.

Human nature certainly was mysterious. We were all capable of amazing feats at times, yet we were still prone to despicable self-interest. There was no doubt I had carried out acts motivated by my own selfishness and greed in the past, so Collette's actions shouldn't have come as a surprise. If you don't believe me, just ask Trygve. He'd tell you it was true. A small voice whispered in my ear, accusing me. *You've done some stuff to get information, too. Some might even say you strongarmed people into telling you things,* the little voice said. I shook my head, but in my heart, I knew it was true.

"Well, I guess you did what you had to do to get the

information I asked for," I commented, tamping down my desire to read Collette the riot act. "We're all flawed," I continued, trying to quiet the voice that reminded me of my own shortcomings, "and we all have our weak moments." Collette dipped her head in agreement. We sat in silence for a moment, but I couldn't wait any longer. My impatience trumped my moral outrage. "So, what did you find out from Hatchet? Let's hear the dirt. Anything new?"

"The basic parameters of the crime, as you know them, haven't changed, but, before we go any further, if we're being honest, I should tell you that Professor McClintock was my uncle—my mom's brother."

"Oh, my. I'm so sorry," I said. It seemed the more I found out about the bombing, the more amazed I was at the widening circle of people whose lives had been changed by what had happened that day at the university over thirty-five years ago. "I didn't realize you had such a personal connection to the bombing."

"Yes, unfortunately, it was a very sad ending for my uncle, who was so dedicated to his profession and his research, but I wanted you to know about it up front, so we can have an honest exchange."

"Absolutely, I agree. I don't know what to say, Collette. I'm sorry I jumped all over you. To think that—"

"Hey, it is what it is," she interrupted impatiently, holding up her hand. "We can't go back and change things. Facts are facts. Besides, you had nothing to do with that whole mess, so let's move on to what I found out when I searched the archives online and in the library."

Collette handed me a thick file of articles and other paper paraphernalia related to the bombing. "I copied what I found so you can take all of this with you," she said, patting the file, "and go through it when you have time. Hatchet and I discussed the possibility that your sister is still alive somewhere, but he doesn't believe those rumors are true. He thinks she really did drown in the Mississippi that night. He said back in the day, the bodies of drowning victims weren't always recovered."

"Yeah, that's what Tanya told me, too." My eyes shifted to the thick file. "I guess I have some reading to do," I said.

Seeing the disappointment on my face, she apologized. "I'm sorry, Sonja, but nothing jumped out at me when I went through all of the information."

"Hey, like you said, we can't change the past; facts are facts. Chief Pedretti warned me I might be disappointed in my search for the truth. I guess she was right," I said dejectedly.

Collette's face brightened. "I do have a suggestion for you, though. Hatchet knows some of the older guys who worked on the case. Most of them are retired now, but you might want to talk to him and get the names of those detectives. They might be able to fill in some of the blanks for you."

"Yeah, I'll do that," I said softly.

Now, standing in the warmth of the barn in the gathering dusk rethinking the discussion with Collette, I was comforted by the sights and smells of familiar surroundings: the pungent, drying bales of hay stored overhead in the hayloft, the dusk falling across our beautiful valley like a soothing blanket, and the peaceful presence of our faithful mules who were always glad to see me. I stroked Sonny's velvety ears as he bumped my hand looking for more treats. I left the barn and strolled to the chicken coop. My flashlight illuminated the dark interior where my twenty-five chickens were roosting above their laying boxes, their heads tucked in their feathers, ready for a night of rest.

Walking to the house, I entered the patio door on the back deck. Immediately, I noticed Trygve standing by the kitchen sink running water over his hand. Then I saw the trail of blood from the garage into the kitchen, and I rushed over to the sink.

"What happened?" I asked sharply.

Trygve lifted his hand, and I noticed a deep gash on his right index finger. "Caught my finger in the chop saw. I can't believe I did something so stupid. I could've cut the damn thing off."

"It needs stitches," I said as I watched blood pour out of his finger.

"I figured that."

I grabbed a kitchen towel from the drawer and wrapped his finger tightly in it. "Come on, let's get in the car. We're going to the ER. Just keep pressure on it so the bleeding slows down."

I drove to the Urgent Care entrance at Mayo Hospital near the university and walked Trygve into the ER. Eventually, a nurse led us to an exam room. Fifteen minutes later, a physician's assistant who looked like a teenager strolled into the room. Her bright red hair fell in cascades of curls around her face. Red freckles were scattered across her high cheekbones and aristocratic nose. A pair of inquisitive blue eyes examined Trygve's finger. She looked up at him and said, "Unfortunately, saw blades always win, don't they? Looks like you'll need some stitches."

"I figured," Trygve said forlornly.

The young assistant named Megan O'Reilly bustled around the room gathering supplies. She expertly flicked her finger against a syringe of Lidocaine, grabbed Trygve's finger, and shot the numbing agent directly into the deep cut. Trygve flinched but remained stoic. A half an hour later, fifteen neat, precise stitches marched along Trygve's thick finger. She cleaned the wound thoroughly, neatly bandaged it, and declared, "It'll be as good as new. Be careful with those power tools."

On the way home, I told Trygve about my conversation with Collette, but he was distracted by the pain in his finger, and I don't think he was really tuned into our conversation. I gave him a couple of Tylenol with codeine and tucked him into bed. Then I returned to the living room and picked up the thick file of information Collette had given me earlier in the day. I hesitated before I opened it, thinking, *Do I really want to know what's in here?* I felt like I was opening Pandora's box, and there was no turning back once the secrets it contained were let loose.

I read until after midnight, but nothing really surprised me. Facts are facts, I guess, and so far, all that I'd read lined up with what I had learned on my own about my sister's death. Collette mentioned Dwight LeGrand in passing, and I read the article he'd written in the *La Crosse Sentinel* in which he'd interviewed several college students who lived in the dorms near the science building when it exploded. *Maybe he would be a good person to talk to,* I thought.

I yawned widely, then massaged my neck. I was tired. The trip to the ER and a full day of cleaning had physically worn me out. I laid the file aside, went through the house and shut off the lights, then crawled into bed next to

Trygve. Lying in the darkness listening to my husband's soft snoring, I wondered how our lives would change if I found out some piece of explosive information. Little did I know that things were about to change in ways I couldn't even imagine. I was about to discover that the secrets of the dead never really die.

CHAPTER 11

Ramblin' Man

Collin Ainsworth lived in a small three-room timber frame cabin near Mount Sterling, Wisconsin, about an hour south of La Crosse on a township gravel road called Roller Coaster Lane. The road, aptly named, wound its way up, down, and through the Driftless hills and bluffs, but this area of the Driftless region was best known for its apple orchards. In fact, Collin worked at the Freeman Family Orchard just down the road during the fall, picking apples and doing general orchard cleanup in preparation for the long, snowy winter months ahead. On rainy days, he packed apples in cardboard boxes at the orchard's facility for shipment to local grocery retailers. He had few friends and rarely socialized in public, although when he worked at the orchard, he chatted amiably with several of the seasonal Latino workers.

After Collin's conviction for his role in the university bombing on the campus of UW–La Crosse in 1990, he spent four years in Green Bay Correctional Institution, an adult male facility located in Allouez, Wisconsin. While in prison, he kept his nose clean, attended classes to improve his skills, including a writing class and a class on the works of Shakespeare, and occasionally he attended a Bible study. His ten-year sentence was commuted in 1995, and he was released in January 1996. Another ten years of probation ensued, and then he was technically free of the burden of incarceration, but his years in prison had changed him significantly. He had become painfully shy and wary of people in general, especially anyone who showed him kindness. He avoided gatherings in the community where he might have to answer questions about his background.

Few, if any, of the residents of Mount Sterling were aware of his criminal history, but he supposed they could find out easily enough if they went on the Wisconsin Court System's website and looked him up. He was careful not to provide anyone with a reason to be suspicious of him, but it also helped that he knew how to keep his mouth shut. After serving his prison sentence and fulfilling the terms of his probation, he wandered around the state for a while working odd jobs and living hand to mouth. He traveled west and even lived for a short time on a ranch at the foothills of the Bitterroot Mountain range outside of Missoula, Montana, but the towering mountains and open expanse of sky left him feeling insecure and lonely, so he came back to Wisconsin.

He met Jack Walenski at a little hole-in-the-wall bar in Rising Sun called Owl's Roost one night in April 2004. They struck up a conversation, and before Collin left the tavern that night, he bought two acres of wooded land, sight unseen, just off Roller Coaster Lane. When he went to view the land he'd purchased from Jack, he was pleasantly surprised. It was relatively flat and had a good stand of oak, maple, and birch. A few huge white pine trees were scattered throughout the property, with an open area big enough for a cabin. Initially, after buying the land, Collin lived in an abandoned camper while several Amish assembled his small log dwelling. He picked up a functional wood-burning stove from a farmer nearby and had a well and septic system installed, all paid for with insurance money he'd inherited from his brother Jed, who passed away from colon cancer in the Waupun State Prison in 1994. Collin scrounged his furniture from garage sales, auctions, and castoffs that people had discarded along the side of the road. He was adept with hand tools, repairing and painting the furniture he found for his cabin. The furnishings weren't fancy, but they were simple and functional.

Collin's parents were rough around the edges. His alcoholic father lived with his mom, but their relationship was complicated by addiction, poverty, and domestic violence. They lived on a lonely road in the Chequamegon-Nicolet National Forest near Park Falls in northern Wisconsin, where his dad worked in the paper pulp industry. Collin had not seen his parents for over twenty years; he wasn't even sure if they were still alive.

On Thursday morning, September 25, Collin was busy in the orchard picking apples and driving trailer loads of fruit into the pole shed where the apples were washed, sorted, and bagged. The morning was crisp and sunny, but by eleven o'clock, thunder clouds had formed in the western sky, and soon showers began to fall. Collin found work to do inside the building while the rain beat against the pole shed, falling in cascading streams off the edges of the roof.

By noon, the rain had not abated, so Collin grabbed his lunchbox and sat on an upended apple crate while he ate a bologna sandwich. Another guy who worked with Collin grabbed a crate, and soon several workers formed a circle sitting on crates while they ate their lunches and talked quietly. The subject matter of their conversations each day varied but generally included their families and people in the community: what they were doing, who was sick, who'd had a car accident, funny anecdotal stories, and sometimes tidbits someone had heard recently in the news. Suddenly, one of the men announced something that shocked Collin to his core.

"Anybody heard about the woman from La Crosse who was supposedly dead, but was found alive in Fort Worth, Texas, a few days ago?" Barry asked.

"What are you talkin' about? Where'd you hear about this?" Stanley asked.

"It was all over the internet last night, on YouTube, Facebook, and Snapchat. I guess she was involved in that bombing at the college in La Crosse back in the '90s. She supposedly drowned in the Mississippi the night after the bombing. Do any of you remember that?" Barry asked, glancing at the other guys sitting in the circle. Collin stared at the floor, staying quiet.

"Nah, I was just a kid when that happened," Marty said. "Besides, you can't believe everything you read on the internet. Half that stuff is just made-up crap by somebody who wants attention."

"Well, they say she disappeared Monday from Fort Worth, where she's been livin' for the last thirty years or so. Had a good job, and then she just disappeared after a shooting at the plant where she worked. They think she's on the run. Maybe she'll show up here in Wisconsin again. Wouldn't that be something?" Barry said with a goofy grin.

"You can say that again. It'd be stupid for her to come back here; they'll be watching for her now. Besides, that'll never happen, so don't hold your breath or spend any more time worrying about what *they* say," Marty said, putting finger quotes around the word *they*. "Besides, it's probably not even true. There's so much BS on the internet you can't believe half of what you read."

Barry shrugged and took another bite of his sandwich. Collin remained aloof as usual, staying silent, but his stomach was churning. The woman Barry described sounded like Katherine Waite, the girl who'd driven the pickup after the bombing escapade in La Crosse. *Was that possible?* he thought. *Could Katy have escaped? Was she still alive?*

At the time of his arrest for the bombing, he was so preoccupied with the police and his lawyers that he hadn't really given much thought to Katy's plight. And then he heard she'd drowned, and although he was terribly saddened by her death, he put her out of his mind. To be truthful, he hadn't really thought about her much since then. After all, she was dead. Now he learned she could still be alive. He shook his head at the unthinkable. He'd spent several years incarcerated while Katherine Waite lived it up in Texas, free as a bird. But then he thought some more. The chance that Katherine faked her own death and got away with it for this long was highly unlikely. He decided to exert some patience and see if anything else developed over the next few days. Maybe the story would prove to be true, but he doubted it.

The rainy day at the orchard whizzed by in a flurry of harvest activity, and that evening when Collin got home, he fired up his iPad to see what was being said online about the mysterious Katherine Waite. He searched various sites and found some references—a few interviews from her neighbors in White Settlement—but they were vague. Several other people who posted online were wildly inaccurate when it came to the facts of the bombing, more opinion and imagination than truth. No one had encountered Katherine on the road or had seen her since Monday. She was missing from her home, and she hadn't reported to work, but Collin thought there could be several other explanations for her behavior.

Lying in bed in his cozy loft that night, Collin glanced out the window. The sky had cleared, and stars were twinkling overhead. *Katherine*, he thought. He had loved her once, but that had all ended with the bombing. Now his memory of Katy, as he had once called her, sat at the edge of his mind like the Disney character Tinkerbell, flitting here and there, teasing him with memories he thought he had erased years ago. Collin thought long and hard about the news that Katy could be alive. *Katy, lovely Katy. All of those wasted years sittin' in prison while she was livin' in Texas.* He tossed and turned, agitated by the memories of the bombing and his years of incarceration until finally, near midnight, he fell into a deep sleep.

CHAPTER 12

The Smartest One in the Room

Thursday morning in Barre Mills dawned with the promise of a cool, sunny September day. The nearby hills and sandstone bluffs were blazing with the brilliant colors of autumn, and the air smelled crisp and clean. Across the road from the Hovlands' small farm, Holstein cows were grazing in lush green pastures after the morning milking. A dog barked several times somewhere nearby, and a bluejay answered with a series of loud caws. Sonja woke slowly and wandered lazily into the kitchen in her bathrobe and slippers. Trygve was making coffee and stirring up buttermilk pancakes.

"Mornin', honey," Trygve said. He poured boiling water into the French press coffeepot, his bandaged finger sticking out conspicuously as he pressed the plunger down.

"How's the wounded warrior?" Sonja asked, sitting down at the table.

"Feeling sorry for myself, but what can you expect when you almost cut off your finger? I still can't believe I did that," Trygve said. He seemed particularly disgusted with his carelessness.

"Maybe your mind was on other things," Sonja commented. "Will you bring me a cup of coffee?"

Trygve poured a cup of coffee, carried it to the table, and set it in front of Sonja. He bent down and kissed her tenderly on the top of her head. "What's the news from Collette?" he asked. "What did she find out?"

"Nothing I didn't already know," Sonja sighed. "I'm beginning to think you're right, Tryg. Maybe I should just throw in the towel and forget about my sister. She's dead and gone. Trying to uncover the facts of her death was a bad idea all around."

Trygve poured batter onto the hot griddle. "I'm sorry, honey, but I tried to tell you that."

"Yeah, I know you did." Sonja was silent for a few minutes. "But one good thing came out of it, I guess."

"What's that?" Trygve asked.

"Collette invited Hatchet over for pizza, and they hit it off."

"You mean the police officer, Hank Brousard?" Trygve asked, turning and looking at Sonja.

"Yeah. Collette thought she'd pick his brain about the bombing and Katherine's drowning, but he didn't know anything new or earth-shattering, although he suggested I talk to some of the detectives from back in the day who investigated the crime and her death."

"If they're still alive and don't have dementia," Trygve mumbled.

Several minutes later, Sonja retreated to the bedroom

and dressed in her work clothes. While she went through her morning routine, she thought about the detectives in the whodunit novels sitting on her bookshelves, the ones who were always one step ahead of the killers and the crooks. The ones who had an innate ability to suck up clues like a vacuum cleaner and then come up with razor-edged deductions that led to some new suspect who'd been overlooked in the chaos of an investigation or the ones who'd discovered a startling new motivation that defied reason or justification but made perfect sense in explaining their criminal activity—a conversation, a piece of evidence, a text message, an emotional outburst. Everyday things led to extraordinary insights. The fictional detectives frequently seemed to be just plain lucky, but she supposed that many times in real investigations, luck did have something to do with solving a case.

Sonja's experience last spring trying to find a killer taught her the fundamentals every detective is familiar with: the bedlam and disarray that comes with the initial discovery of the crime, the motives and suspects who begin to surface during the investigation, and the collection of physical evidence and other clues found at the scene. Those things provided a skeletal framework in which various theories could be tested, rearranged, discussed, and tested again.

Sonja certainly was not a detective with any prerequisite skills or training; she'd learned on-the-job, so to speak. However, she had shown an aptitude coupled with dogged determination in uncovering information from her blue-collar acquaintances around town when she'd helped the police during the Diangelo investigation. She wasn't a total greenhorn, although she had to admit her experience in criminal investigations was quite limited.

However, the facts surrounding her sister's death defied any simplistic explanation. Too many unanswered questions still existed in Sonja's mind to give up on her own flesh and blood. The circumstances surrounding her sister's demise seemed to fly in the face of logic and reasoning. Was it possible that the emotional ties she had for her sister Katherine were hampering her ability to accept the truth of the situation—to see things as they really were?

Sonja stepped back from the mirror. Her dark hair was streaked with a few strands of gray, but her simple hairstyle made her appear younger than she really was. She applied blush to her high cheekbones and pale eyeshadow and eyeliner to her deep-set gray eyes. Adding some pink gloss over her full lips completed her morning routine. Coco sniffed her feet, and Sonja leaned down and picked him up, cuddling the little poodle to her chest for a minute before she went to work.

Trygve yelled from the kitchen, "I'm leaving, honey. I'll see you tonight."

Sonja leaned around the frame of the bathroom door. "Sounds good. See you later. Love you."

In the quiet of the house after Trygve left, she prepared a sandwich, grabbed a bag of chips, and tossed an apple and bottled water into an insulated lunch bag. She walked to the garage and backed her Subaru out on the driveway, reviewing her cleaning schedule as she maneuvered the car onto the road. Her cleaning duties today included two houses on the south side, a psychiatrist's office on French Island near the airport, and a dejunking session with a retired teacher on the north side of La Crosse. Somehow, she hoped she could also find time during the day to stop by Art Ravenwald's studio on Apple Blossom Lane to pick his brain about her dilemma. But if anybody else suggested she should toss her investigation onto the scrap heap and go back to her placid life as a cleaning lady, she planned to have a full-blown temper tantrum, complete with tears and yelling—the whole nine yards. Nobody understood the agony of not knowing the fate of her sister, not even her beloved husband.

She hadn't gotten very far down the road when her cell rang. She pulled over on the shoulder, fumbling in her bag for the phone.

"Sonja Hovland."

"Sonja, Tanya here. I have some news. Are you sitting down?" she asked.

"If sitting in the car counts, then I'm sitting down."

"Are you driving?"

"Nope. I'm parked along the side of the road," Sonja said.

"Good. Stay there, don't move, and listen carefully." Tanya began her explanation. "I got a call from the Fort Worth Police Department yesterday afternoon. There was a shooting at a manufacturing firm on the outskirts of the city on Monday, and one of the workers from the factory disappeared and hasn't been seen since. Her name is Kitty Currant, but the police seem to think, based on evidence they dug up on her, that she's your sister, Katherine Waite."

The silence that followed was profound and deep. For several moments, Sonja stared through her windshield while the surroundings melted into smudged silhouettes of muted colors and shapes. Her brain froze. Rational thinking ceased to exist, everything in the present stood still, and her mind raced backward to a time when she was standing on the shores of Lake Superior watching Katherine push her kayak into the dark blue waters. Picking up her paddle, her sister turned around, smiled, and began paddling rapidly farther and farther toward the horizon, her strokes strong and easy until she was just a speck in the distance.

"Sonja? Are you there?" Tanya asked. The silence dragged on. "Sonja? Answer me!"

Finally, Sonja answered, her voice weak and breathy. "Yeah, I went away for a little bit." She leaned back in the seat, slowly coming back to the present, the image of her sister fading rapidly from her mind. She took several huge, deep breaths.

"Did you understand what I just said?" Tanya asked.

"I think so. You're telling me that Katherine might still be alive?"

"Yeah, maybe, but don't get your hopes up. Just remember, this is the theory of a couple of detectives at the Fort Worth Police Department. They haven't been able to locate Katherine, so they won't know for sure if they're right until someone actually finds her, but the possibility of that happening is slim. These two detectives are on her trail right now. They believe she's traveling north, possibly to Wisconsin, but they're not sure. They're trying to track her movements as we speak. Somebody called the Fort Worth police and reported they'd seen her in Oklahoma, but that turned out to be a bust. They now believe the call actually came from Kitty, who was trying to throw the police off her tracks. From what they've told me about her, she's very smart, flexible, and creative—qualities that make tracking her movements difficult. I'll give her credit; she's going to be one hell of a challenge to find."

"She always was the smartest one in the room," Sonja responded.

"I wanted you to know in case Kitty—Katherine—tries to contact you."

"To be honest, I'm having a hard time believing all this," Sonja confessed.

"Hey, I understand that. It is pretty unbelievable," Tanya admitted.

"I just have one question."

"Sure. Go ahead. I'll try to answer it," Tanya said.

"This shooting at the plant? Was Katherine involved?" Sonja asked.

"According to eyewitnesses, Kitty calmly walked up to the shooter, asked her for the gun, and the shooter handed it over. I don't have the details, but somehow, your sister managed to convince her to surrender the weapon to her without incident. She must have some kind of magnetic personality or an authoritative presence. Maybe both. Afterward, Kitty walked away, got in her car, and nobody has seen her since."

"The shooter was a female?"

"Yep. She walked into the plant and killed her husband because he asked for a divorce."

"Wow! That's crazy," Sonja said.

"Crazy, but not uncommon," Tanya answered. "Domestic disputes are very dangerous situations, especially when divorce is involved."

"One more question," Sonja said. "How will they confirm that Kitty Currant is really Katherine Waite. Don't they have to have some DNA or something?"

"Yes, to positively identify her they would have to have solid evidence, most likely DNA. They do have several DNA samples here that the police collected at the time of the bombing. Someone would need to collect DNA from Kitty and then see if the two samples are a match. But we have to catch her first."

"Where do we go from here?" Sonja asked.

"It's a wait-and-see situation. But be extra vigilant in the days ahead. If Kitty shows up here, things could heat up," Tanya said. "She may try to contact you. If she's survived this long without being discovered, she's got formidable skills, and she's willing to use them."

"Right, I've got it. Thanks, Tanya. I appreciate the update," Sonja said.

"Stay in touch," Tanya said, and she hung up.

While Sonja digested the news from Fort Worth, Texas, Trygve rumbled down Losey Boulevard on the way to his job at the City Streets and Parks Department. His finger was throbbing with pain. He parked his pickup in the lot and walked into the superintendent's office. He intended to ask for light duty today since he was somewhat handicapped. He hated doing it. After all, he had a reputation as being a tough dude at work, and his status among his peers was well earned. Better to keep everyone guessing than to reveal his tender side.

Jeff Stokes, Trygve's boss, was the head of maintenance at the city streets department. As such, he was generally responsible for sending crews out to repair potholes, remove snow and ice, monitor traffic lights, and paint crosswalks, as well as manage the maintenance crews who repaired all the city vehicles and mechanical equipment.

"Ya wanna do what?" Jeff asked, cocking his head as he sat at his desk.

"I cut my finger in my shop last night, and it's still kinda sore. So, I thought I could go over to the south side and stencil those crosswalks down on 35 across from Eagle Bluff Elementary."

"How you gonna do that with a bum finger?" Stokes asked.

"I'll take the newbie with me and supervise him. He doesn't know how to do stencils, and I can teach him the ropes," Trygve explained. "You know, the finer points of stenciling blacktop," he added sarcastically.

Stokes walked to the door of his office and looked out into the main garage. "Newhouse! Come here!" He gestured impatiently to a young man leaning against the table where the coffee pot sat. Several workers were having a morning brew while waiting for their work orders for the day.

"Yeah, boss? What's up?" Newhouse asked, strolling up to Stokes. He was a skinny twenty-year-old kid with a ponytail protruding out the back of his Brewers baseball hat. He wore Carhartt coveralls, a worn blue-jean work shirt, and Red Wing work boots.

"You're goin' with Trygve today. He'll teach you how to paint pavement."

"Whatever you say, boss," he replied pleasantly.

Trygve came out of the office and waved at Newhouse over his shoulder as he walked to the corner of the garage where the sidewalk stencils and spray paint were stored. He ordered Newhouse to grab the stencils and safety cones while he picked up a couple of cans of white spray paint from the shelf. They loaded the supplies into a municipal pickup and drove south through city traffic to the roundabout on the south side, which connected U.S. Highway 14 to Highway 35 and bordered the Mississippi. Arriving in front of the school, they set up safety cones and directional traffic signs.

"When you're working with live traffic, don't count on the signs to keep you safe. You have to be constantly aware of your surroundings with one eye on your work, and one eye on the traffic flow," Trygve warned. Newhouse gave him a blank look.

"You mean the idiots can't read the signs?" Newhouse asked crossly.

"They might see them, and they might even read them," Trygve explained, "but that doesn't mean they won't drive through them. I saw one of our guys get hit by a car once because a driver was ordering his lunch from McDonald's on his phone, and he drove right over the cones and smacked into the guy who was raking blacktop into a pothole on the street. Broke his hip."

"Really?" Newhouse said.

"I'm not kidding," Trygve responded.

Trygve and Newhouse unloaded the equipment from the truck and were well into their task an hour later. They'd set up flashing safety lights, and the stencils were placed on the right lane of traffic. Trygve was about to hand the can of spray paint to Newhouse when he glanced over toward the roundabout and saw a beautiful baby blue vintage VW bug zip through the traffic heading toward Coon Valley on Highway 14.

Trygve shouted, "Here's the paint! I just saw something I

need to follow up on. I'll be back!" He shoved the cans into Newhouse's hands, turned and ran to the truck, jumped in, and wheeled into the traffic. Entering the roundabout from the south, he scanned the highway up ahead, looking for the VW bug. When a dash of blue disappeared around a corner, he stepped on the accelerator, following the tiny car for several miles until it turned into a farmstead between Coon Valley and Viroqua on Strangstalien Road. Trygve rolled into the driveway behind the vintage VW, creating a cloud of dust. He slammed the truck in park and stepped out onto the gravel.

"Have you been following me?" an older man asked as he climbed out of the Volkswagen. "Did I do something wrong?" he asked, noticing the City of La Crosse logo on the side of the truck. He was short and stocky with a bushy head of unkempt white hair tucked under a Funk's Seed Corn hat. Blue eyes and a tanned, wrinkled face gave him a weathered appearance. The man wore a worried expression.

Trygve held up his hands. "No, no, you're not in trouble, but I couldn't help noticing your VW bug. The color is rather unique. My wife's been looking for one, and when I saw yours go through the roundabout, I had to follow you."

The old man looked at Trygve with skepticism. "You followed me for ten miles to ask me about that car?" He gestured toward the little blue bug sitting comfortably under a big maple tree net to the driveway. Brilliant red leaves were falling gently on the roof. It was a beautifully preserved vintage Volkswagen.

"All I want to know right now is where you got the car," Trygve said.

"You wanna buy it?" the old man asked, confused.

"Not really," Trygve replied, but he could imagine Sonja happily shelling out the money to bring this reminder of her sister home to their farm in Barre Mills.

"The story behind this car is kinda weird," the old man began, leaning against the hood of the VW getting comfortable, but Trygve interrupted him.

"Sorry, I don't mean to be rude, but I'm on the clock, so would you object to me bringing my wife by this evening to see the car and tell your story. She wouldn't want to miss this."

"Well, I guess that would be alright," the old man said. "My name's Olson. Harvey Olson." He extended his hand.

Trygve held up his hand, exposing his bandaged finger, and said, "I'm Trygve Hovland. I'd shake, but I cut open my finger last night on my chop saw, and it's pretty sore. I work at the city streets department in La Crosse, but I live in Barre Mills. What time would be good for you?"

"Seven o'clock?" Harvey asked.

"Seven it is. I'll bring my wife then. Thanks, and I apologize. I didn't mean to scare you, but I gotta get back to work." Trygve climbed back into his truck, reversed, and waved to Harvey, who was still standing in his driveway with a very puzzled expression on his face. He hoped he wasn't getting himself into some kind of situation he couldn't handle. He guessed that at seven o'clock tonight, some of his questions might be answered if the guy actually showed up with his wife. *Was the guy some kind of radical collector of VWs?* He didn't think there was anything too unusual about the bug, but he wasn't an expert on Volkswagens by any means. He shrugged his shoulders and walked toward the house. *We'll wait and see,* he thought.

By the time Trygve returned to the work site in front of Bluffside Elementary, Ryan Newhouse had finished painting both lanes of the crosswalk. It looked sharp. Trygve parked his city truck off the pavement on the shoulder of the road and shut off the engine. Ryan had begun gathering the equipment into a pile alongside the road.

"Let me help you," Trygve said, feeling guilty for abandoning Ryan to his own devices. However, the greenhorn had done a nice job on the crosswalk. Trygve grabbed the traffic cones with his left hand and heaved them into the bed of the truck.

"Find what you were lookin' for?" Ryan asked.

"Don't know yet, but I think so," Trygve answered.

"You were gone for over an hour," Ryan reminded him. "What's the boss gonna say?" he asked as they climbed into the cab of the truck.

"I don't know. I guess he'll only know if you tell him."

Driving across town to the city streets facility, Trygve wondered at the serendipity of spotting what might be Katherine's missing VW. What role did the little bug play in the whole story of her disappearance? One thing he did know—Sonja was going to have a hard time believing it.

CHAPTER 13 • SONJA

Lean on Me

By noon, I was finishing my cleaning job at Helen Myhre's house on Ferry Street. Her little bungalow was time-consuming for a couple of reasons. First, she was lonely since her husband Fred died two months ago from heart failure, and I spent several moments listening to her reminisce about her husband Leland. Second, I spent a lot of extra time dusting all her memorabilia. Every square inch of available built-in shelving space in the living room, bedroom, and dining room was crammed with knick-knacks from their travels around the United States over the years. Dusting all of it ate up my time and prevented me from taking on new clients. However, I was extremely fond of Helen, and I didn't want to offend or hurt her in any way.

"I have a question for you, Helen," I said, hoping to start a discussion about decluttering.

"What's that, dear?"

"How attached are you to all of these souvenirs?" I asked. Helen looked up from reading the *La Crosse Sentinel*, and a muddled expression appeared on her wrinkled face.

"Why are you asking? I'm not sure I understand what you mean."

"I have a suggestion, just something for you to consider. How would you feel about boxing up some of these trinkets and placing them in the attic or basement for a while? It would certainly make cleaning your house easier for me, but I don't want to take away the things you enjoy looking at each day, things that remind you of your travels with Leland." I stopped what I was doing and sat in the recliner next to Helen. She suddenly looked sad and pathetic in her aloneness. I reached for her hand and held it tenderly in mine. The realization that Trygve and I were well into our middle-age years was not lost on me. The hands of time were ticking, and pretty soon scenes like this would be a reality for us, too.

Helen looked off into the distance, then refocused her attention on a shelf over the fireplace that was particularly crowded with South Dakota paraphernalia: salt-and-pepper shakers, small floral vases, toothpick holders, ashtrays, and other tourist keepsakes.

"Well, I guess I've never thought about it, but it is rather cluttered looking, isn't it?"

"Yes, it is, but I have a suggestion. You know, I've helped many people consolidate their collections, and most of the time, when it's all said and done, almost every one of them was happy to have less to take care of. So, my suggestion is this: Pick your favorite souvenir from each place you've visited over the years, and I'll pack the rest away for a while. You may decide you like the look of your shelves better, but if you don't, we can always put them out again."

"Let me think about it. When you come to clean next

time, I'll tell you what I want to do, okay?" Helen said, pursing her lips.

"Wonderful. We'll talk about it then."

I let go of her hand and chatted with Helen for a few more minutes, and then I walked to my car. Pulling out of Helen's driveway onto Ferry Street, I drove north a few blocks to Myrick Park, where I could eat my lunch and catch a view of the eagles who frequently flew above the marsh and perched in the trees along the banks. It was a beautiful fall day with a cloudless blue sky. As I sat at a picnic table near a hiking trail, I thought again about my sister. My life had been a string of disappointments when it came to finding out the truth about her story. I had run into so many dead ends I couldn't remember them all. The only thing I had left to cling to was hope—hope that someday I'd find out what really happened to her. Since my conversation with Chief Pedretti this morning, the hope I'd cradled in my heart all these years had finally paid in dividends. My dream of meeting Katherine again and talking to her might be possible. Of course, first she had to be found. While that seemed highly unlikely, I thought about the progress we'd made in the last few days, and I decided to dwell on the possibility that Katherine would be found. That thought alone buoyed my spirits. I was just packing up my lunch when my phone beeped.

"Sonja Hovland."

"So, what's this I hear about somebody reopening the investigation into Katherine's death?" snarled a caustic voice on the other end of the line. "Who was the genius who decided to do that? And don't tell me it was you, the bleeding heart of this family!"

There was no one who could stomp on my hopes and dreams like my sister, Darlene. She was the only one left in my small circle of immediate family, but I usually avoided her at all costs since every conversation between us became an assault on my worth and dignity as a human being. I have never been quite sure what Darlene's mental health diagnosis was. All I knew was she had a bitter, shriveled heart, and every time she called me, she tried my patience like nobody else I knew.

Trygve was very good at steering Darlene away from extended visits to our farm, making a valiant effort to protect me from her vicious attacks. He was very effective in keeping her at arm's length, although occasionally she succeeded in convincing us she could behave for a brief visit. She spent a weekend with us this past summer. We gritted our teeth through the ordeal, and when Darlene drove out of the driveway and headed back to Lake Elmo, Minnesota, Trygve and I breathed a sigh of relief and indulged in several glasses of wine as a reward for our patience and suffering, and then we made passionate love.

Now I was faced with telling her the latest news about our sister, Katherine.

"Dar, listen to me," I began. "I have something important to tell you."

"Yeah, I bet. Let's hear from the great amateur detective. By the way, have you had any more cases lately? I've been looking in the La Crosse paper for your name and your sidekick, the chief of police, but—"

"Darlene, listen to me, and don't say anything 'til I'm done!" I interrupted loudly. Amazingly, my sister became quiet, so I hurried on explaining to her about the shooting at the Innovative Fabrications factory in Fort Worth, how detectives thought Kitty Currant might be our sister, and how she was on the run, possibly heading north. "If all the news from Texas is true and Kitty Currant is our sister incognito—which I know is hard to believe—then she's still alive," I concluded softly.

I expected a rude outburst, which Darlene usually displayed when someone else knew more than she did. But nothing came. The silence at the other end of the phone had a chilling effect on me. Where was the combative, stubborn, rude sister I usually dealt with? I began to fidget. Had she had a heart attack over the shocking news and dropped dead on the kitchen floor?

"Dar? Are you still there?" I asked, disgusted by the desperate quality in my voice. "Did you hear what I said? Darlene?" For someone who cringed when my lioness sister roared, I sounded like a pathetic, whining kitten as I begged her to speak to me.

"Have you talked to Katherine's roommate?" she asked gruffly.

"What?"

"Her roommate? Have you talked to her?"

"I don't know who that is. How would I know that?" I asked.

"Her name is Sherry MacMann. She's in the phone book. Look her up, Sherlock," Darlene said rudely, and then the line went dead.

"Darlene? Darlene?" I couldn't believe my sister had capitulated so easily. This was not her normal battle strategy. How did she know who Katherine's roommate was? I walked to my car and slumped in the front seat, staring out the windshield of my Subaru as the traffic buzzed by on Losey Boulevard. *How is all of this going to be resolved?* I wondered. Then something struck me like a thunderbolt: Why didn't Darlene argue with me? Why didn't she vehemently deny that Katherine was alive? The fact that she knew who Katherine's roommate was left me wondering what else my sister Dar knew. Had she known all along that Katherine was in Texas and kept it hidden from me all these years?

I shook my head at that inconceivable idea and leaned over to start my car. Pulling out into traffic, I contemplated the extraordinary news I had received from Tanya Pedretti and the information I'd received from Darlene, but I didn't have time to obsess about it since I still had to travel to French Island to clean Dr. Fredrick Law's office. His bustling psychiatric practice is well-known throughout the Midwest. Lawyers appreciate his astute testimonies in court when they need an expert witness to explain the root causes of criminal and delinquent behavior. Members of the law enforcement community regularly consulted with him when they encountered aberrant behavior in the criminals they arrested.

Dr. Law's office was decorated in quiet tones of cinnamon, beige, and hunter green. Expensive oil paintings of quaint Italian scenes alive with community life hung on the walls, and the furniture was upholstered in rich, soft leathers and nubby tweeds. In one corner, games and cards were available to the patients who were waiting for an appointment with Dr. Law.

I entered the clinic through the back entrance and met Dr. Law coming out of one of the consulting rooms.

"Sonja, my dear," he said warmly, holding out his arms. "How are you, my friend?"

I walked into his arms for a bear hug. I could always count on Dr. Law to jumpstart my flagging confidence in mankind, especially on days when I had to deal with my impossible sister. After all, the guy saw crazy people every day, and he'd never lost his love for his fellow human beings. I greatly admired him for his stalwart position that mankind was basically good, even though I had plenty of proof that the opposite was true.

"I'm wondering if what I've heard about you recently is reliable," he said, looking deeply into my eyes. His dark brown eyes searched my face for possible clues. I squirmed uncomfortably under his scrutinizing gaze as I stepped away from our hug.

"Depends on what you've heard, Doc," I said, crossing my arms over my chest as I leaned against the wall. I recoiled with chagrin when I thought about Dr. Law analyzing my life.

"Your sister who died? Are you having issues accepting the truth of her demise?"

"How'd you know about that, Doc?" I asked.

"No, no, no," he said, shaking a finger at me. "You know I never reveal my sources. Professional confidentiality," he said, grinning widely. When I remained silent, he persisted, his expression turning serious again. "So, are you having feelings of denial and abandonment about your sister's death?"

"Not really, Doc, but what do I do about my other living sister, Darlene, who insists on demeaning me every time she talks with me? She's a nasty person, Doc, and I'm sure you've dealt with some real nutcases." Doc's bushy eyebrows crinkled together in an unpleasant frown at my use of the vernacular term "nutcase," and he ran his hand through his bushy, salt-and-pepper hair. "I've tried everything I can to change her, but nothing helps," I confessed.

"Aha! That is the problem! It's not her, it's you," he said, poking his finger at me.

"Me? Now listen, Doc, I'm not the one—"

Although Doc was one of the politest people I knew, he interrupted me quickly before I could get on my soapbox. "No, no, my dear. You misunderstand me," he continued, holding up both hands. "Of course, you are not the problem per se, but your reaction to your sister's behavior is. Is your sister rude, inconsiderate, overbearing, and foul-mouthed?"

I nodded my head in enthusiastic agreement. "Absolutely," I said. "That describes her to a T."

"It sounds like classic bullying behavior," Dr. Law continued. "You can't do anything about your sister, but you can control how you *react* to her. I can help you with that, you know."

"Hey, I appreciate the offer, Doc, but right now my life is on a skid into the ditch, and I just need to keep my hand on the plow, if you get my meaning. It'll all come out in the wash. Steady as she goes."

He frowned at my list of platitudes. "Do you honestly think that will work?" he asked, leaning against the wall and crossing his arms across his chest. Obviously, he'd heard those overused mantras before.

"It's the only thing I know how to do, Doc," I said. "You know the old saying: When life gets tough, the tough get tougher." Doc looked at me askance, his expression filled with doubt about my homespun, folksy philosophy.

"So, you think concentrating on your work and ignoring your problems will get you through your crisis?" he asked.

"Who says I'm in a crisis? Life happens to us all, Doc. There are good times and bad times. Besides, what other choices do I have?"

"We could talk about that—" he began, holding up his index finger, but I cut him off as politely as I could.

"No, Doc. I've got Trygve, and I've got my mules and chickens and Coco, and I've got my work. I'll muddle through somehow."

"Oh, believe me, I understand the value of work in keeping a healthy outlook on life. But even so, I am always open to a discussion about your past disappointments and your present difficulties." Doc Law smiled amiably and pushed himself away from the wall. He leaned toward me, wrapping his arm around my shoulders. "I am always available to listen. You know that, right?"

"I know that, Doc, and I appreciate the offer," I said, pointing to my cart of cleaning supplies, "but the dirt is calling my name, and I'm okay with that." I flashed a weak smile.

Doc shrugged his shoulders and walked down the hallway mumbling as he entered another consultation room. I got busy vacuuming, dusting, and wiping down all the counters, desks, and tabletops. In less than two hours, the office and consulting rooms were once again neat and clean. Although I felt no wiser than when I'd entered Doc's office, I was optimistic that Trygve and I would come up with a solution to the sticky problem of my missing sister. Was she really alive and heading back home? At this point,

I didn't know, but the lyrics of a Bee Gees song suddenly popped into my head: *How do you mend a broken heart?* If I could mend my broken heart, I'd be satisfied with the other cards I'd been dealt, including my vindictive, harsh sister Darlene.

Kitty Currant drove aimlessly without a specific destination, although she was making good time heading in a northerly direction. As the day wore on, her early start from the small motel in Kansas left her feeling drained and tired. Of course, it didn't help that she had no idea where she was headed, which compounded her feelings of insecurity.

She could not explain to anyone, much less herself, why she was inextricably drawn to Wisconsin. The seductive idea of home continued to pull her down the road like metal attracted to a magnet. She did, however, recognize the desire within herself to reconnect with her family, especially her two sisters. Her parents were gone; she'd watched their funeral services online from the Swedish Lutheran Church in Stickley. For most of her adult life, she'd avoided any contact with her biological family. She'd never searched for Darlene or Sonja online or tried to contact them in any way, so she had no idea what kind of family configurations they had. Were they married? Did they have children? It was a blank slate to Kitty—a mysterious unfinished page in a book that was still to be written. Maybe her curiosity about her family was the unconscious motivation that explained her trek across the midsection of the United States to the Midwest.

As Kitty drove northeast, the horizon began to lighten, and the sky turned grapefruit pink. Suddenly the sun roared over the skyline, flaming with the promise of a new day. Kitty grabbed her sunglasses from the visor overhead, found a radio station that played some soft jazz, and tapped her fingers in rhythm to the relaxing music as she drove down the road. By ten o'clock in the morning, she had made it to Leavenworth County, where she skirted the northern edge of Kansas City and entered Missouri. She turned off I-35 near the tiny town of Kearney and found a classic diner complete with black-and-white floor tiles and red leather booths. She indulged in some serious breakfast and several cups of coffee while she scrolled on her laptop looking for references to her disappearance from Fort Worth. Typically, events on Facebook, even sensational bits of news like the shooting at the IF factory in Fort Worth, only lasted twenty-four hours, and then they faded away. She saw no posts that called attention to the incident, for which she was thankful. It seemed the farther north she traveled, the less interest there was in her disappearance. So much for the attention span of a nation whose citizens were fixated on fleeting moments that titillated their senses.

Back on the road after filling her tank with gas, she continued to make her way across the northwest corner of Missouri and into central Iowa. The rolling hills morphed into flat, endless fields of corn that went on for miles, divided only by the crisscross of county roads and punctuated by clouds of yellow dust from combines rolling through the fields harvesting grain. Eventually, Kitty made her way east from Cedar Rapids, driving into Dubuque in the early evening. It had been a long, hard day, and she was tired.

She found an attractive B&B on a quiet backstreet in Dubuque. The room she rented on the second floor was in the rear of a fabulous Queen Anne monstrosity, complete with turrets and gingerbread fretwork. She climbed the steep stairs and, once in her room, indulged in a long soak in a deep clawfoot bathtub, then fell into bed sleeping soundly until early the next morning. Before she left the B&B, she had a lovely breakfast of quiche, toast, bacon, and scones with several cups of strong black coffee. She paid her bill, then sat in her old truck outside the B&B with a Wisconsin map unfolded across the steering wheel while she plotted a route, tracing it with her fingertip. Although her destination was unknown at this point, eventually she knew she had to stop somewhere. Analyzing several different routes, Kitty finally decided to follow the Mississippi River north.

The Great River Road followed the curves of the serpentine waterway and appealed to her affinity for small-town life. Was one of the villages and towns scattered along the shore of the big river a good place to end her journey, or should she continue to Stickley on Lake Superior, her old stomping grounds? The memory of the deep blue lake she'd come to know in her childhood had never left her. Despite being absent from the region for over thirty years, she could still feel the bracing wind in her hair and the brisk smell of the water in her nostrils invigorating all her senses.

In the end, she started her truck and headed north, connecting with the Great River Road. She slowed down and enjoyed the scenery, the bluffs, the thick forested hills, the wide river, and the sleepy little towns. Around noon, Lock and Dam No. 9 at Lynxville came into view. Kitty pulled off the main highway and watched several huge tows push their barges loaded with grain through the lock and dam as they headed downriver. The Mississippi was wide here, and the vistas were dotted with numerous islands all teeming with groups of canvasback ducks resting up for their journey south, where they would spend the winter.

Kitty parked in front of a small tavern called The Duck's Bill. The outside of the establishment had seen better days. The weathered gray siding and rickety awning that leaned at a precarious angle over the sidewalk gave the building a look of neglect and abandonment. A sign sporting a faded canvasbacked duck stuck out from the side of the building. The sign creaked gently in the cool breeze coming off the river. Despite its forlorn appearance, a neon sign in the window flashed the word *OPEN* every few seconds. Inside, the dark surroundings included a few round tables with wooden chairs, a long bar, and a pool table near the back entrance. The establishment had a limited menu, but its Friday night fish fry featuring river catfish and walleye was well-known throughout the area. Kitty sidled up to the bar, ordered a glass of wine, and drank slowly and thoughtfully.

"Travelin' through?" the bartender asked. He was a big guy with a beefy face, thick graying hair, solid, muscled arms, and large hands.

"Don't know yet. Give me some reasons why I should stay," Kitty said, smiling shyly.

"Friendly people. Beautiful scenery. Big river traffic. Great fishing," the bartender spouted. "How's that for reasons?"

"Huh, sounds pretty good. Any places for rent around here?"

"Now that's hard to come by. There are places you can buy, but there's not much for rent," the bartender informed her. "Around here, people either stay or leave, but my wife's got a friend who's a realtor up the road at De Soto. Let me give her a call." He picked up his phone from the counter, punched in a number, and walked toward the window overlooking the highway while he talked for a few minutes. He came back and stood in front of Kitty, the phone still in his hand.

"The wife says Marcy, her realtor friend, will meet you in Genoa at the Big River Inn about one this afternoon. She's got a few listings in the area, and she'll show you around," the bartender said. "How's that sound?"

Kitty nodded. "That sounds good. I'll meet her there. Thanks," she said. She left her wine glass on the bar and waved as she left the building. She drove leisurely, stopping ten minutes later at a hot dog stand down the road where she bought a Coney Island hot dog loaded with onions, hot peppers, pickles, and ketchup.

At one o'clock sharp, Kitty walked into the Big River Inn. A blonde with big hair stood up and approached her. She was a petite gal with a Bluff Country Realty name tag pinned on her leather jacket. "You must be the gal who's looking for rentals," she said holding out her hand. "I'm Marcy Lewellyn."

Kitty shook the realtor's hand and said, "Your friend at The Duck's Bill wasn't too optimistic there was anything to rent around here."

"Let's sit down, and I'll show you what's out there," Marcy said, pointing to a booth near a front window. For the next fifteen minutes, Marcy scrolled through various rental properties on her phone. Kitty wrote down the names of the properties that appealed to her on a napkin, and a half hour later, Marcy started up her Jeep Grand Cherokee and began driving through the coulees and valleys near Genoa. The last property they looked at was on Mundsack Road. The Bad Axe River, a Class I trout stream, meandered through the bottom of the wide valley, which was surrounded by steep hills and sandstone bluffs. It was a beautiful, peaceful place peppered here and there with a few dairy farms and several houses.

As soon as Kitty saw the little quaint cabin perched on a slight incline above the road, she was hooked. It had been neglected for about six months, according to Marcy, something about a divorce settlement that had gone haywire. But Kitty was sure this was the place for her. Although the front yard was full of overgrown vegetation, there were several large, majestic maples, oaks, and Scotch pines scattered next to the clearing where the cabin sat. The cabin itself was in good shape. It had a small, efficient kitchen, a roomy living room with a gas freestanding parlor stove on one wall, a standard bathroom, and a roomy bedroom. There was a small loft over the kitchen and bathroom that could be used for storage. Best of all, it had a good roof and was secluded and private.

"Whaddya think? Kinda rough, huh? No furniture," Marcy said. "Probably not interested?"

"It's perfect!" Kitty responded. "I can pick up some furniture. It's nothing that a little elbow grease wouldn't cure."

Marcy did a double take. "Okay, if you say so." She shook her head in surprise. The real estate business had taught her a lot about people and their personalities. She was still learning and was constantly surprised at what appealed to people. She supposed it had to do with their philosophy on life, or maybe it was more about what they were running toward or away from.

"How much is the rent?" Kitty asked.

"Seven hundred fifty bucks, electric and gas included."

"I'll take it," Kitty said enthusiastically.

"Okay. Let's head back to my office, and we'll sign the lease."

"Sounds good," Kitty said, grinning widely. *I've landed,* she thought. *I'm finally home.*

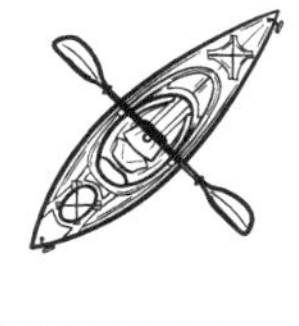

CHAPTER 14

I Got You, Babe

At five o'clock on Thursday afternoon, Sonja rolled into the driveway in Barre Mills and rumbled up to their small farmhouse. She was dying to tell Trygve the news about Katherine. When she parked her Subaru, Trygve was standing in the garage, his hands on his hips, staring into the rafters. Sonja got out of the car and walked up to him.

"Whatcha doin'?" she asked, looking up.

"Those good-for-nothin' barn swallows got in here somehow this fall and built a nest," he said, pointing upward to a clump of mud and sticks adhered to a rafter. "I'll have to knock it down and clean up the mess they made," Trygve explained.

"I suppose you will. What do you want for dinner?"

"Oh, don't make anything. I've got a little trip planned. We'll stop somewhere and get a bite to eat when we're done."

Sonja looked confused. "A trip? A trip to where? To do what?"

"I'll explain on the way. Half an hour? That's all the time it should take for me to knock down this nest and clean it up."

Sonja shrugged her shoulders. "Okay, I'll be ready." She walked into the house, suddenly feeling exhausted from all she had learned during the day. She wandered into the living room for a minute and sat down in the recliner cuddling Coco. She immediately fell asleep. A gentle tap on her shoulder half an hour later startled her awake.

"Are you ready?" Trygve asked gently.

Sonja jumped up from the chair, and they walked to the garage while she complained about the trip. "Where are we going?" she asked insistently.

"You'll see. It's a surprise," Trygve said grinning.

"I don't like surprises," she said grumpily.

"You'll like this one."

They meandered through the coulees and valleys and ridges of Barre Mills and La Crosse until they arrived in the little village of Coon Valley. "How much farther is this surprise?" Sonja asked impatiently, although it was a beautiful evening, and she was enjoying the colorful fall scenery.

"Not far now," Trygve said. He drove through Coon Valley on Highway 14 up a couple of steep hills and was headed toward Viroqua when suddenly he turned off on a country road, traveled past a small white clapboard country church, its steeple poking into the evening sky. He finally turned into a small farmyard which had several outbuildings and a mid-century ranch house. Checking his watch, he said, "We're a little early, but I don't think Harvey will mind. He'll come out when he's ready."

They sat in silence for several minutes until a screen door slammed and Harvey appeared in his stocking feet and waved them inside. Trygve and Sonja went into the house and sat at the kitchen table. Harvey's wife, Eleanor, welcomed them cordially and set a slice of jelly roll with a dollop of whipped cream in front of each one of them and poured coffee. Sonja couldn't remember a time when she'd had such a light, delicious dessert. The jelly roll reminded her of Stella Westley, her neighbor in Barre Mills, who made delectable desserts with plenty of eggs, cream, and butter. Though Sonja enjoyed the sweet treat immensely, her brain was counting up the calories in the jelly roll and whipped cream. She envisioned every calorie going straight to her hips.

"What kind of jam is in here?" Sonja asked.

"It's blackberry from my secret patch back in the woods," Eleanor said shyly. The foursome ate and drank coffee for a while until Harvey turned to Sonja and asked a question.

"Are you wondering why Trygve brought you here?" he asked, locking eyes with her.

"Well, as a matter of fact, I am," she said, giving Trygve a sour look. "My husband would only tell me it was a surprise."

"Let's go out to the shed, and I'll show you the surprise," Harvey suggested.

Everyone except Eleanor walked out to an old, abandoned tobacco shed about two hundred feet from the house. The shed was perched on top of a ridge above a steeply sloped hay field. Some beef cattle had bedded down for the night in a small grove of hardwoods toward the bottom of the slope. The view of the farmland from up here was beautiful. In the distance, Sonja could see several small farms, the barns and silos peeking out from the rolling hills, and stands of hardwood trees were scattered among the landscape. The fields were golden with ripe soybeans and corn. The double doors on the shed were held shut by a two-by-four, and Harvey took the piece of lumber out of its holder and swung the doors open. In the fading light, the little blue Volkswagen Beetle seemed to glow with a kind of otherworldly pride. Sonja covered her mouth with her hand and stared at the little car, speechless. Finally, she whispered, "Where did you find it?"

"I didn't," Harvey said. "It found me."

Sonja walked around the little blue car, admiring it, touching it, looking through the windows at the interior, wondering how it had arrived here of all places. It seemed impossible that she could finally touch something that had been such an integral part of her sister's life. "You'll have to explain this to me," Sonja said to Harvey. Then she turned to Trygve and asked him. "How did you find it, Tryg?"

"I was working on the south end of La Crosse this afternoon, and I saw Harvey drive it through the roundabout. I followed him home and promised to bring you back tonight to see it," Trygve explained. Her husband had several faults she could enumerate, but these were the moments when she remembered all the reasons she was so in love with him.

"So, you don't know how it got here either?" Sonja asked.

Trygve shook his head. "Nope," he said, "not yet, but I'm sure Harvey will tell us."

They both looked at Harvey. "You'll have to explain all of this to us," Sonja said again.

"Well now, that will take a while. Why don't we go back in the house and have a second slice of jelly roll and another cup of coffee while I tell you the story?"

"Sounds good to me," Trygve said.

They walked back to the house again and sat at the kitchen table while Eleanor bustled around the kitchen and served more jelly roll and coffee. Harvey began to explain. They bought their small farm of twenty acres and buildings two years ago when Harvey retired from his job as an engineer at a national company in La Crosse known for designing and building industrial heating and air conditioning units.

Harvey and Eleanor wanted a place where their city-dwelling grandkids could come and run and play and explore in the country, maybe have a horse to ride and raise a couple of heifers or pigs to show at the local county fair. The farm needed some tender loving care, and they spent several months commuting from their home in La Crosse repairing and painting the house, toolshed, and small barn. They hired several Amish to clear weeds, cut trees, and remove debris from the areas around the buildings. Harvey mowed the lawn, and Eleanor planted several beds of perennial flower gardens. They refinished the oak floors in the house and painted all the rooms. Finally, during the summer, they moved in and were able to relax and enjoy the farm as they'd imagined when they purchased it. Sonja related deeply to their story because that was exactly what they had done with their little farm in Barre Mills.

"The only building we hadn't explored was the tobacco shed," Harvey continued explaining. "I walked out there one day a couple of months ago, opened the doors to see what was inside since the owners had told us the shed was empty, and in the far corner was something covered with a tarp. I walked over and pulled off the tarp, and there it was—a vintage, baby blue VW bug. I don't know where it came from. I've been trying to track down the title since there wasn't one in the cubbyhole of the car. I was coming back from the DMV in La Crosse today, Trygve, when you spotted me going through the roundabout."

"How did it get here, do you think?" Sonja asked.

Harvey shook his head. "I really don't know, but why are you so interested in this little car? Are you a collector or something?"

Now it was Sonja's turn to explain. For the next fifteen minutes, she told Harvey and Eleanor the circumstances surrounding the death of her sister, Katherine, and her belief that her sister might still be alive. Although Harvey was politely listening to Sonja's account, he kept his eye on Trygve to see if he agreed with his wife's assessment of the situation.

"I always wondered what had happened to her Volkswagen since the police had never been able to track down its whereabouts," Sonja said. She sat back in her chair and crossed her arms over her chest. Eleanor clucked her tongue and slowly shook her head. "What a nightmare you've been through," she said sympathetically.

"What do you think, Tryg?" Sonja asked. "Do you think the VW is Katherine's?"

"It's Katherine's," Harvey said. "Her name is on the title."

Trygve leaned over the table and clasped his hands together looking thoughtful.

"What about ownership?" Sonja asked.

Trygve glanced at Harvey."Since you found it on your property and by reason of property laws, you are now its rightful owner. But the car is in the vicinity of her disappearance. If Katherine hid it here and covered it up with a tarp, she did a good job. It's been missing for over thirty years, and nobody noticed it. I'm surprised it still runs."

"Runs good. I just added a little gas and oil, and it started right up," Harvey said.

"One other thing," Trygve said, holding up his pointer finger midair. "The previous owners who lived here at the time of Katherine's disappearance might have had a connection with her somehow. Do you know who that might be?"

Harvey shook his head. "The place changed hands several times before we bought it, so I'm not sure who owned this place thirty years ago, but you could check at the Vernon County courthouse. They would have a record of ownership and transfer of property titles."

They chatted for several minutes. Finally, Trygve and Sonja got up, thanking their hosts for the information and coffee. Walking to the truck in the growing darkness, Sonja thought about the news she'd received this morning from Tanya Pedretti and the phone call from her sister, Darlene.

"Tryg, I have some things to tell you," Sonja said.

"I have something to tell you, too," Trygve replied as he started the pickup. "I'll go first."

"Okay, go for it. I'm listening," Sonja said buckling her seatbelt.

"I got fired today," he said quietly. He stared out the front windshield of the truck.

Sonja thought she had misunderstood. "What? Did you say you got fired?" When Trygve nodded and turned to look at Sonja, the surprise and shock reflected on her face stopped him in his tracks. He wished he could erase her expression; he hated disappointing his wife.

"I'm sorry, but following Harvey with my municipal vehicle is against the rules at the city streets department. Municipal vehicles are not to be used by employees of the city for their own personal use. I knew that, but I took a chance, and somehow my boss found out, called me in at the end of the day, and 'terminated my employment,' to quote his exact words."

There were a hundred questions on the tip of Sonja's tongue, but in the end, none of them would change the fact that Trygve was now unemployed. "What are we gonna do?" Sonja asked, feeling the panic gathering in her chest.

"They're hiring at the same company that Harvey worked at—Meyers Corporation in La Crosse. I stopped by their office on the way home and got an application. I'll fill it out tomorrow and see what happens. Don't worry, honey. I'll find something to do. If nothing else works out, I can keep making my chairs. I've got fifteen orders to fill before Christmas, so that will bring in some cash."

"Well, as shocking as your news is, I think my news is going to blow your socks off," Sonja said. "Are you ready?" As they drove toward La Crosse, Sonja told Trygve about the shooting at the IF plant in Fort Worth and the possibility that Kitty Currant was, in fact, Sonja's long-lost sister, Katherine Waite.

"What are the chances? I can't believe this!" Trygve replied. "Does Tanya think Kitty's headed this way?"

"I don't think she really bought into that idea, but two detectives from Fort Worth think that's what Kitty is doing, traveling north to Wisconsin. Nobody has seen her since Monday when she left the plant after the shooting," Sonja said. "But there's more."

"I don't know if I can handle any more," Trygve groaned.

"Darlene called—"

Trygve cursed. "And she was her wonderful, charming self, full of happiness and joy?" he snarled, his face dark with anger as he gripped the steering wheel.

"Now, now. Let's not be negative," Sonja chided. "I got the distinct impression she knows something about Katherine that we don't."

"Oh, really? Like what?"

"I can't put my finger on it except that when I told her about the shooting and the possibility that Katherine was still alive, the line went silent," Sonja said. "She was speechless."

"That's impossible! Darlene is never speechless! You mean she had nothing to say? No well-timed cuss words?" Trygve spouted. "No mightier than thou attitude? Why doesn't that ever happen when I talk to her?"

"She can't resist your charms, honey. She saves her most colorful language and worst behavior for you, but I couldn't believe it either. And get this. She knew Katherine's college roommate still lives in La Crosse. It's almost like she had talked to her recently, and she knew the news about Katherine already. Isn't that weird?" Sonja asked.

"Not really. Darlene likes to pretend she's smarter than everybody else, but it wouldn't surprise me if she knows where Katherine is. Maybe she's been in contact with her.

I'll bet she's up to her neck in—" Tryg's voice had gotten louder until he was almost shouting.

"Whoa! Whoa, Tryg," Sonja said, noticing the vein sticking out on his neck. "You're getting carried away with the emotion of the moment. The only time you get to do that with me is when we're having sex," Sonja said, smiling. She laid her hand on Trygve's thigh. "Take it easy, big guy. Somehow, I will get the truth out of Darlene, but in the meantime, you and I have some unfinished business."

Trygve let out a huge gush of air. "You mean the sex or the business of finding your sister?" Trygve asked.

"Both," Sonja said.

CHAPTER 15

It's a Jungle Out There

Fort Worth detectives Jason Dreves and Ken Stanton stood in front of the storage shed and stared into the empty yawning space that had once held Kitty Currant's old pickup truck. The storage shed was located on Willow Way in a northside Fort Worth neighborhood. Someone noticed a 2020 Honda Civic parked near the shed for several days, and they called the Fort Worth Police Department. Chief Allbaugh had been waiting for an opportunity to send Jason and Ken on a wild goose chase. *This is too good to pass up,* he thought. *Maybe these two guys will learn the real meaning of dead ends and beating the pavement when I send them on this assignment.*

The two detectives walked into the empty lot next to the storage shed, kicking the grass, and found the keys for the Honda that was parked on the street. They opened the car. Inside they found the registration papers, which identified Kitty Currant as the owner of the vehicle. Jason turned to his partner. "Whaddya think? Should we call the chief?"

"Not yet. Let's walk through the neighborhood and see if

anybody knows what was in the storage unit."

They crossed the street and began knocking on doors. One lady told them a woman had arrived at the shed mid-afternoon on Monday in the Honda Civic. "I was busy with a load of laundry, and when I looked out the window again, the door of the storage shed was open, and the Honda was still parked under the tree. I didn't think anything was weird about that, but then several days went by, and the Honda was still parked on the street, and I began to wonder why it was still there. That's when I called the police department."

Another older gentleman three doors down knew the owner of the storage facility and gave Jason and Ken his name and phone number. They called him, identified themselves as police officers, and asked about the renter for space #14. There were some shuffling noises on the other end of the line while the man went to his desk and looked up the information about the renter.

"From my records, it looks like the renter's name is Kitty Currant. She's rented that space since 2007, when I first built the storage facility. Always on time with her payment. Never caused any trouble," the man said.

"You wouldn't happen to know what she stored in the space, would you?" Jason asked. "Because it's empty now."

"Oh, I've talked to her several times over the years. Real nice gal. She had an old pickup in there, a 1978 Ford F-150 that she said belonged to her grandpa. He was pretty nostalgic, and she was hanging onto the truck for him."

"Anything else in the storage unit that you noticed?" Jason asked.

"Nope, I never really looked inside the unit. I just stood outside when we talked. She was always so respectful and nice."

"Do you remember the color of the pickup?" Jason asked.

"Umm . . . as I recall, it was a dark forest green. I have the license plate number somewhere. Just a minute . . ." Jason could hear the rustle of paper. "Yeah, here it is. Wisconsin plates AST-6720. Does that help you?"

"Yes, thank you so much." Jason disconnected, then walked with Ken back to the storage unit. "I'm glad we can tell the chief that we actually found something that might move this case forward."

"We'll see about that. Right now, you and I are at the bottom of the heap. If he considers this progress, I'll be surprised," Ken said sourly.

"I'll call that Pedretti cop in La Crosse and give her this information. We can put out an APB on the truck. At least they'll have something to look for on their end in Wisconsin," Jason said, "if that's where she's headed."

SONJA

One thing you should understand about my marriage to Trygve is that we differ in a lot of ways that significantly impact our relationship. My husband is loyal to a fault, quick to forgive, thoughtful, but reticent to share his opinions with people he doesn't know. He has low regard for those who pepper their conversations with profanity; he rarely swears unless he is highly provoked. He is a great provider, as proven by his years of employment at the City Streets and Parks Department. His circle of friends is small but very loyal.

I, on the other hand, have many, many friends scattered

throughout the La Crosse area. I develop friendships easily and tend to keep them for a long time. I'm honest to a fault, but I frequently lose patience with people who disagree with me or challenge me. I try not to hold grudges, and I'm still learning to forgive. All I can say is that Trygve and I bring different things to the table, and I believe our differences are what make our marriage so successful. Whether it helps us in our detective work, only time will tell. The jury's out on that one.

We'd gotten home late the previous night after stopping in La Crosse for a pizza. On Friday morning we discussed our strategy for the day. Several problems had reared their ugly heads all at once, and unless we capitalized on our strengths, I feared we would never get to first base and find my sister, but Trygve's current unemployment dilemma had now moved to the top of the list. I still do not understand how you can be fired for driving a work vehicle out into the countryside to follow someone who might hold the key to a thirty-five-year-old mystery. The narrow-mindedness of some people is appalling, and I told Trygve that in no uncertain terms.

"Listen, babe," Trygve tried to explain to me. "My termination from my job makes perfect sense. I was wrong to assume I could use a city vehicle to carry out a personal errand. Think about it, honey. What if everyone did that? There'd be no end to the abuse and misuse of public funds and assets. It'd be a nightmare. Jeff had every right to fire me."

Leave it to my husband to be open-minded enough to see the viewpoint of the person on the other side of the fence. Me? Not so much. I stayed silent, trying to comprehend how our lives were going to change with Trygve's unemployment. I envisioned us standing in a soup line with our empty bowls and empty eyes, longing for a delicious square meal of meatloaf, mashed potatoes, green beans, and chocolate cake, only to get a thin broth with a few carrots floating in it.

"Honey? Did you hear what I said?" Tryg asked, taking a sip of coffee, enclosing my small hand in his large one.

"Have you ever stood in a soup line?" I asked him.

"What?" His expression reflected his total confusion.

"A soup line. You know, like the ones during the Great Depression?"

"No. What's that got to do with anything?" He let out a frustrated sigh. "Have you lost your mind? Honey, you need to get a grip."

I switched tactics. "Okay, okay, never mind. Ignore that comment. We don't have time to talk about it anyway. So, you're going to Meyers today to apply for a job, right?"

"Yep, it's the first thing on my to-do list. I've got my application all filled out. What about Katherine's roommate? You're going to look her up, correct?" Trygve asked.

"Yes, I already have her address. She's listed in the phone book." I pushed Sherry MacMann's street and house number across the table to Trygve. He glanced at it and made a wry face. "Oh, she lives by the golf course at the bottom of Grandad Bluff," he said nonchalantly.

"I was wondering where that was. You better check on me to make sure I'm still alive at noon," I said.

"Don't be dramatic. It doesn't help our situation," Trygve said wisely. "Besides, she probably doesn't know anything about your sister's whereabouts, but she might know some other piece of information that would be helpful. Maybe she knows how the VW got out by Viroqua. You could ask her that. But you'd better be ready to pick her up off the floor when you tell her Katherine could still be alive."

"Well, now look who's being dramatic," I muttered under my breath.

"Just trying to keep things realistic, sweetheart," he said, finishing his piece of jelly toast. He brushed his hands together to get rid of the crumbs. "When I finish the job application stuff, I'll call the courthouse in Viroqua and hunt down the history of the previous owners of Harvey and Eleanor's land. Maybe something will come from that, although I can't imagine what it would be."

"Worth a try," I said softly.

We cleaned up our breakfast dishes and deposited them in the dishwasher. At the last minute, we decided to meet at our favorite sub shop downtown on 14th Street near the university at noon sharp. From there, we'd reevaluate our progress and make another plan to maximize our time and energy.

Trygve headed to Meyers Corporation on Losey Boulevard and went into the main office to turn in his job application. While there, he interviewed for a position on the shipping line, and when he walked out at ten-thirty, he'd been hired; he would report to work on Monday. From there he drove to Apple Blossom Lane to see Art Ravenwald. Art had become a close friend and mentor to Trygve in his pursuit of creating unique twig chairs. His sense of balance and proportion was finely tuned from his years of making beautiful mobiles, and he had given Trygve several helpful suggestions concerning his chair construction and design. As a result, a chair that once seemed destined for the scrap heap was salvaged into a thing of beauty, a unique creation that appealed to those with a whimsical sense of style.

Trygve parked his pickup along the curb and walked up the driveway. Art's garage door was open, so Trygve walked through the garage and casually entered the kitchen.

"Yoo-hoo!" Trygve yelled. "Are you home, Art?"

"I'm in my studio. Come on in," Art yelled back.

Trygve walked into the studio and was immediately greeted by Jocko, Art's colorful pet parrot.

"Who's here? Who's here?" the parrot cackled dramatically from his large cage by the window where the sunlight poured into the room. He fluffed his gray feathers, sending a cloud of dust into the air. Trygve walked over to the cage and produced a banana from his pocket, which he peeled and slipped through the wires of the cage. Jocko trilled in delight and began pecking at the fruit, gobbling chunks of banana.

"I see you've resorted to bribes," Art said smiling. "You're a fast learner, but I'm not sure it will change Jocko's behavior."

"How are you?" Trygve asked, eyeing up his friend. Art loved the sincerity in Trygve's voice and the concern for his well-being. Just seeing Trygve or Sonja lifted his spirits almost as much as creating his artwork. He was getting along in years now, fast approaching eighty. He'd recently had a fall, but fortunately hadn't been seriously injured, just a couple of bumps and bruises. He has lived alone since his wife, Marion, passed away two years ago. Trygve faithfully checked on him when he was in the area.

"You asked how I am? Well, I'm just as cantankerous as always, I guess," Art said gruffly, but Trygve detected a note of gratitude in his voice. "When you talk to a parrot all day long, you get to wondering about your mental health sometimes, so human conversation is a gift."

"Mental, mental," Jocko chirped from his cage.

Art rolled his eyes at Jocko's rude interruption, then locked eyes with Trygve and smiled warmly. "What have you been up to? Got a problem with a chair?" Art asked.

"Yes, but I've got several other problems bubbling on the back burner, too," Trygve began. He pulled up a stool from Art's work area, plopped down, and began explaining his dilemma: how he lost his job at the city streets department, was hired this morning for a new job at Meyers over on Losey, and Sonja's most recent fixation with her long-lost, supposedly dead, but maybe not dead sister. Art listened respectfully, his expressions changing as the narrative about Trygve's problems unfolded.

"Wow! You do have a plateful," Art finally commented when Trygve was done talking. "That little wife of yours is a crackerjack; there's no doubt about that," he laughed. "She can get herself in more jams than anybody I know!"

Just when Trygve thought Jocko was done with boisterous comments, he taunted the two men, screeching, "Crackerjacks here!" Art walked over to Jocko's corner and spread a large tablecloth over his cage, which had a calming effect on the big bird.

"Just ignore him," Art advised with a swipe of his hand. "He gets pretty wound up when company comes." Art returned to his studio office chair and refocused his attention on Trygve. "When Sonja gets an idea in her head, there's no stopping her, is there?" He smiled, but then his expression turned serious. "I remember that whole bombing incident like it was yesterday, although I had no idea the drowned girl was Sonja's sister. Does she really believe her sister is still alive? That seems too good to be true after all these years."

"Almost everybody who knows anything about the bombing and drowning has been telling her that over the years, but it doesn't seem to faze her. This latest news from Fort Worth has her in a tailspin. If Katherine is alive, she must have some finely honed skills to be able to hide in plain sight for over thirty years. If I ever get to meet her, it'll be an experience I'll never forget, I'm sure," Trygve said glumly. His shoulders slumped, and he let out a groan. "I just don't know how Sonja's going to handle the situation if Katherine really is dead. That might be too much for her."

"People are very resilient," Art said. "If Sonja believes a narrative other than the one that's been told to her all these years, then the denial over her sister's death comes from deep within her—and keeps her hopes alive. If Katherine is dead and Sonja's hopes are destroyed, then you can start worrying."

Trygve nodded in agreement at the wise words of his friend. "In the meantime, we're running all over the country checking out preposterous leads," he said. "The other night we ended up near Viroqua looking for a vintage Volkswagen. It seemed like a waste of time, but believe it or not, we found the VW bug. Of course, I lost my job over it, but maybe the car will lead to something we can actually use to determine whether Katherine is still alive, although I doubt it. I guess that's the price you pay when you buy into conspiracy theories."

"You're a good man, Trygve," Art said quietly. "You're doing the right thing by supporting Sonja. That's all you can do right now. Be there through the good and the bad."

"Well, believe me when I say that sometimes I question my own sanity," Trygve said. He pulled out his phone. "But the real reason I stopped was to show you this chair I designed." He scrolled through his photos and stopped, tapping a particular photo. "Check this out and tell me what you think."

For the next half hour, Art studied the whimsical chair Trygve was constructing. They talked about its basic composition elements, the crossed twig forks in the back of the chair, whether he should use smooth, peeled wood or leave the bark on the twigs, or add other elements such as a fishing rod or a garden hoe to create interest. The lively discussion and the wisdom of Art's suggestions invigorated Trygve's enthusiasm for the project, and he left Art's home feeling fortunate to have such a creative friend who understood his artistic ideas.

Trygve walked to the curb and was just climbing into his pickup when his cell beeped.

"Tryg, did you forget our lunch date?" Sonja asked impatiently.

"Nope. I was at Art's, and the time got away from me. I had a couple of chair questions for him. I was just about to leave. I'm on my way," Trygve said. Ten minutes later he pulled into the parking lot at Sandwich Heaven near the university. Walking into the sub shop, he went to the counter and ordered his sandwich. Sonja was already devouring her lunch in a booth by the window that faced the street.

"Hey, honey," Trygve said as he sat down and opened his sandwich. "You're looking at the newest member of the shipping department at Meyers."

Sonja bounced up and down in her seat and clapped her hands together. "Oh, Tryg. I never doubted that you'd get a job."

Trygve frowned. "Yeah, you did. Remember, you asked me whether I'd ever stood in a soup line?" He lifted his eyebrows and smiled subtly, then took a bite of his sandwich.

Sonja swiped her hand through the air. "Oh, forget that. You know me. I always overreact to bad news."

"That's true, you do. So, what did you find out from Sherry MacMann?"

Sonja shrugged and remained silent, which made Trygve wonder if her nonchalance was just a cover-up for indecision and doubt.

"I haven't talked to her yet." She slid down in the booth waiting for the tirade she was sure would come.

Trygve stared at her. "What? You haven't talked to her? Why not? You aren't chickening out, are you?" he asked, his eyes widening with surprise. "Honey, I put myself out there chasing the VW and lost my job over it. The least you can do is go see this gal. She might be able to give you a little peace of mind about your sister." He waited while Sonja thought about what he'd said. He knew her well enough to know this was not the moment to pressure her; she had to make her own decision.

They ate in silence for several moments before Sonja reached for his hand across the table and squeezed it. "Tryg, you have no idea how much I appreciate all you've done."

Trygve waited for the big BUT that he was sure was on the tip of Sonja's tongue. However, she surprised him again.

She began to explain. "I haven't talked to Sherry yet because frankly, I don't know what the heck I even want to ask her. I mean, really, Tryg, can you imagine some random woman appearing at your door and asking questions about your college roommate from thirty-five years ago? Who does stuff like that?"

"You do," Trygve said bluntly. "I've seen you ask people questions that I wouldn't think of asking. Remember how you confronted Beck Watson in the basement of that house when he tied you up and threw you in a corner like a rag doll? Come on, honey! Watson was an absolute whacko who could have shot you and left you dead. Talking to Sherry will be a walk in the park compared to that, don't you think?"

Sonja chewed thoughtfully on a mouthful of sandwich. "Nothing about this whole thing has been a walk in the park, Tryg, but since you're still technically unemployed, would you consider going with me?"

Trygve leaned forward across the table, his brown eyes flashing with impatience. "Am I missing something here? What's wrong with you? You've got this great lead, and you're waffling. What good am I going to do? Besides, I've got my own assignment of trying to find out who owned the farm where Katherine hid the VW."

"That's true," Sonja replied, looking despondent. "I guess I'm feeling a little burned out. Everything we've found out about my sister makes me second-guess myself." Sonja paused and Trygve stayed silent. "I thought I knew her, but she just isn't the person I thought she was. She seemed to have so many secrets. Why is that? Was she always that way, and I just didn't notice it because I was ten years younger? Even Darlene seems to know more about Katherine than I ever did."

"Leave Darlene out of this. Don't make this into a competition with your sister."

Sonja looked peeved. "Oh, for Pete's sake, don't be ridiculous, Tryg. Just remember, though, that there is a vintage VW at stake."

"Whatever," Trygve mumbled with disgust. He gathered up their sandwich papers and cups and walked to the wastebasket to deposit them. When he slid into the booth again, he leaned back and watched his wife for a moment. *A more stubborn, wonderful woman does not exist anywhere on this earth,* he thought, *but dealing with her sometimes is a complete pain in the ass.*

He leaned forward and placed his elbows on the table. His penetrating stare got Sonja's full attention. "At the beginning of this whole affair," Trygve began lecturing softly, "you told me you were doing this because you wanted closure and you wanted to know the truth. If Katherine's roommate is still alive, you need to talk to her. She might know something that will shed some light on this whole mess, something that will help you move on and celebrate your sister rather than wallowing in constant regret and sadness."

Trygve's remarks agitated Sonja. Her face had turned pink, and her features were scrunched up in exasperation. Trygve thought she was on the verge of tears. "Okay, okay, don't badger me, Tryg," she said, holding her hands in front of her. She briefly squeezed her eyes shut, then opened them again and said, "I'll go and meet her, but it'll probably be a complete waste of time."

"Don't be a Debbie Downer. You don't know what will happen until you've actually talked with her," Trygve said, feeling relieved that he was off the hook.

"Well, thank you for all the support," Sonja rasped angrily as she stood up and threw her purse over her shoulder.

"My pleasure, honey," Trygve said sweetly. He watched Sonja stomp through the shop and across the parking lot to her Subaru. *The price we pay for love*, he thought.

CHAPTER 16

Big Girls Don't Cry

Sonja fidgeted nervously as she stood on the porch of Sherry MacMann's impressive residence. The imposing facade of the house on Pine Street didn't reassure her or calm the panic she felt rising in her chest. She thought back to Trygve's warning: Don't be a Debbie Downer. She supposed it was good advice. During her intense search for the truth about her oldest sister over the past week, she had been proven right—her sister was alive somewhere. Her death by drowning had been staged, and now Sonja was overwhelmed with the hope of finding her. But she also had to face the stark reality that her oldest sister seemed to have a talent for hiding. In addition, the police in Texas had not officially confirmed Katherine's identity, and the only reason she had been discovered was the freak shooting at her place of employment and her subsequent disappearance from White Settlement.

The red brick home of Sherry MacMann was large and imposing. Set against the backdrop of Grandad Bluff, which soared six hundred feet in the air, the house was majestic by Midwest standards. Black shutters embellished the oblong windows along the front of the house, and four white columns supported a porch with an ornate black wrought iron railing that ran along its edges. The two columns closest to the door were decorated with beautiful arrangements of sunflowers, mums, pumpkins, and various types of squash and gourds.

Sonja leaned over and pressed the doorbell. From inside, she heard the bell's soft chime. While she waited at the door, she thought about the information her sister Darlene had shared with her. Anytime Darlene volunteered information, the alarm bells in Sonja's mind began clanging. Had Darlene manipulated her into seeking out Sherry? How long had Darlene known Sherry, and more importantly, had she kept Sonja in the dark all these years out of meanness and selfishness? Sonja had a bad feeling about this, but she guessed she'd soon find out the real reasons behind Darlene's revelation. As she stood on the porch, her nervousness increased until she felt like turning around and running back to her Subaru.

However, before she could escape to her car, the solid oak door suddenly opened. Sonja quickly recovered her sense of decorum and flashed a friendly smile. The woman who answered stood impassively with her hand on the door handle as if she would slam it shut in Sonja's face. She was tall and lithe with medium-length gray hair, dark brown eyes, and a solemn manner. A pair of reading glasses hung from her neck, and she had tucked a pencil behind her ear. She wore a pair of dark brown corduroy slacks and a burnt orange sweater. The woman evaluated Sonja's presence at the door of her house with one sweeping downward glance, which reminded Sonja of Cruella, the wicked witch in the Disney movie *101 Dalmatians.* The woman displayed a restless, impatient energy. Underneath her calm exterior, Sonja sensed a cold, haughty spirit. "Yes? Who are you?" she said, tipping her nose slightly upward.

Sonja reminded herself to remain still and not fidget, to stand tall and be confident. "Hello. My name is Sonja Hovland. I'm looking for Sherry MacMann."

"I'm Sherry," the woman replied. "What do you want?" Her voice was deep and sonorous, but her attitude was tinged with annoyance. She wasn't used to being interrupted.

Well, la-de-da to you, too, Sonja thought. "I wonder if I could have a few minutes of your time to talk to you about my sister, Katherine Waite. I believe you were her roommate when you attended UW–L back in the nineties." Sonja watched the woman's face carefully. Her simple statement produced a gamut of emotions that crossed Sherry's face in a flash—surprise, sorrow, disappointment, and then anger.

"You're Katherine's sister?" Sherry replied, pointing her index finger at Sonja. Sonja felt herself shrink inside at the gesture, but she straightened her shoulders and found her voice.

"Yes, I am."

"What are you doing here? She's been dead for over thirty years. I can't imagine there's anything I could tell you now that would make a difference."

"Well, you haven't heard what *I* have to say, have you?" Sonja began, her cheeks flushing with irritation. "And believe me, it will be something you'll never forget."

"I doubt it," Sherry said pompously, "but . . . come in anyway." She stood aside as Sonja stepped into the foyer.

"Why don't we go into the kitchen?" she suggested, pointing down the long hallway. "I just made a pot of coffee."

"That sounds wonderful," Sonja said, although she doubted there was anything about this woman that could be wonderful. As she followed Sherry to the kitchen, Sonja walked past a large library on the right, complete with a massive oak desk that must have also served as an office, and on the left was a beautiful living room filled with high-quality furnishings, a large collection of books, and expensive paintings. They arrived in a spacious, comfortable, well-used kitchen. The dishwasher was quietly humming, and a freshly baked coffee cake sat on the kitchen island filling the room with a lovely cinnamon scent.

"Have a seat by the window while I get a few cups. Do you take cream or sugar?" Sherry asked, reaching into the cupboard for coffee cups.

"No, just black, please."

Sherry poured two cups of coffee and carried them to the small table by a window that overlooked a manicured backyard. "It's a nice view here," she said, setting the cups on the table. Sonja sipped her coffee, but things suddenly seemed awkward. *Why did I agree to do this?* Sonja wondered.

Sherry looked at her and said, "You had something to tell me? So let's hear this earth-shattering news you have about Katherine." Her statement bristled with hostility.

"There's a possibility that my sister is still alive," Sonja blurted.

Sherry continued to stare at Sonja as if she'd lost her mind. The quiet of the kitchen made the silence that followed even more uncomfortable. Somehow, this was not what Sonja anticipated when she had agreed to interview

Katherine's former roommate. The austere woman sitting across from her seemed to be immune to surprising news of any kind. Sonja imagined running into Sherry's kitchen screaming horrible news that someone had been stabbed to death in her front yard, and Sherry would turn to her and say with cool aloofness, "What proof do you have that this is true?"

Sherry dipped her head slightly at Sonja's outburst. Finally, after several moments she spoke. "It seems highly unlikely that she's alive, don't you think?" she said as if she were talking to a child. "She drowned in a kayaking accident after the bombing. Those are the facts according to the police." She paused and continued to stare at Sonja as if she were unhinged. "What's so hard to believe about that?"

"If I could explain what's happened recently, you might change your mind about what you've been told," Sonja said.

"Have at it," Sherry said, with a nonchalant wave of her hand. "I'm always up for a good argument." She leaned back, crossed her arms over her chest, and focused her full attention on Sonja. The scrutiny of her hard eyes made Sonja very uncomfortable, but she steeled herself and began her explanation.

For the next fifteen minutes, Sonja reviewed the latest developments in her search for the truth about her sister, beginning with her mysterious death and missing body. Then Sonja mentioned the vintage VW bug that had disappeared on the day of her death but had now been found near Viroqua. Finally, she outlined the shooting event at the Innovative Fabrications plant in Fort Worth, where Kitty had disarmed the assailant who'd shot a coworker to death and then gone missing after the incident. Two Fort Worth detectives had examined Kitty's personal records, Sonja explained, and tentatively identified her as the deceased Katherine Waite from La Crosse, Wisconsin, who'd been presumed dead for thirty-five years.

"How do they plan to confirm her identity?" Sherry asked.

"DNA, I guess," Sonja answered. "Of course, they have to find her first."

"So you think these are compelling reasons to believe she might still be alive. Is that what you're saying?" asked Sherry.

"Well, don't you think these discoveries prove she's still alive? And doesn't all of this beg the question of a screw-up by the police in the first place?" asked Sonja.

"The police screwed up? The company where she worked in Fort Worth confirms she's Kitty Currant, but the police believe her personal records have been falsified? You've located her missing VW bug? So what? What does all of that prove? You have no concrete physical evidence to support your arguments. It's all hearsay and gossip and conspiracy theories. If she's still alive, then where is she?"

Sonja blinked rapidly. "Well, right now, we don't know where she is, but we think my sister Katherine—"

"Katy," Sherry corrected.

Sonja frowned, confused by the name. "Katy? Who's Katy?"

"That's what Collin called your sister. He called her Katy," Sherry stated, lifting her eyebrows slightly.

"Collin? You mean Collin Ainsworth, the bomber?"

"Yes, Collin, the bomber, always called your sister Katy. He was in love with her, you know."

Sonja sat frozen in her chair. Her coffee had grown cold. Katy? Katy in love? Katy in love with the bomber? Sonja felt as if her mind would burst from all the new information she was learning about her beloved sister. She was beginning to realize that she really didn't know Katherine at all, and she felt a growing dread about meeting her in the flesh. This growing ambivalence led her to reconsider whether she should continue her investigation. She was beginning to grasp the reality that Katherine might not be the person she thought she knew.

"Do you know Collin?" Sonja finally asked after several moments of silence.

"Not personally," Sherry said. "But I know he spent about five years in prison near Green Bay and that he was released about twenty-five years ago when his sentence was commuted. Since then, I don't know where he went or what he's doing."

"How do you know about his sentence?" Sonja asked.

"My father was the attorney who prosecuted the case that sent him to jail."

Suddenly, Sonja had a light-bulb moment. "Of course. MacMann, Hollingsworth and Smith, the law firm downtown," she said in a hushed tone.

"Yes, my father, Ralph, was a very competent prosecutor. That was the most famous case he worked on in his career."

"And what do you do?" Sonja asked, although she already knew the answer.

"I'm a lawyer. I took over my father's practice when he passed away suddenly from a heart attack five years ago, but I've worked at the firm for several years."

"Do you know my sister, Darlene Waite?"

The question must have surprised Sherry because she paused before she answered. "In passing," she said cooly. "All of this happened a long, long time ago. I don't see the purpose of digging it all up again. It's ancient history now."

But Sonja knew she was lying about knowing Darlene. Dar loved to keep secrets and use them to lord it over other people. She was a classic manipulator and bully. Sonja suddenly had a stark moment of clarity. She could imagine this cold fish of a woman getting along famously with her irascible sister over the years since the bombing, the two of them plotting, planning, and devising ways to keep the other dumb little sister in the dark, to keep her from finding out the truth. Suddenly Sonja was furious. She'd been insulted, dragged over the coals, misunderstood, ridiculed, and abused. She stood up suddenly, spilling her coffee onto the table.

"I'll let myself out," she rasped. "Thanks for the coffee."

As Sonja stomped toward her car, she could feel tears wetting her flushed cheeks. She climbed into her Subaru, slammed the door until it rattled on its hinges, and squealed out onto the street, leaving two heavy black marks on the pavement. Someone honked their horn at her and flipped her off. Screeching to a stop on Losey Boulevard, she pounded the steering wheel of her car and sobbed uncontrollably. "I've been so stupid!" she exclaimed. "I've been so, so stupid."

As Sonja sped away from the curb, Sherry McCann watched her from the living room window in the front of the house. *What an odd woman,* she thought. *So bold, but very stupid and naïve.* But secretly she worried about what Dar had told her sister Sonja. *Dar never could keep her mouth shut.* Sherry had seen the police reports about the drowning death of Katherine Waite, and there was no doubt in her mind that Katherine was still alive—somewhere. She'd always assumed Katherine had left the country and was living abroad. Now it seemed that she might be closer than anyone realized.

Sherry picked up her cell from the counter in the kitchen and dialed Dar, who answered on the third ring.

"Dar, we need to talk," she said quietly.

PART 2

"TO LIVE IN THE PAST IS TO DIE IN THE PRESENT."

Bill Belichick

CHAPTER 17 • SONJA

The Weather Outside Is Frightful

DECEMBER

By mid-December, the La Crosse area had had several significant snowfalls, which blanketed the land surrounding our farm in white. Everywhere I looked, the fields of corn stubble were disappearing under newly fallen layers of brilliant, clean snow. The evergreen branches were laced with frost, and the deciduous trees cast black shadows on the snowy tableau outside my window. I had gotten Trygve to set up multiple birdfeeders near our house so I could watch the winter birds' movements and enthusiastic pecking of the seeds I fed them every day.

I was at a low point in my life. Trygve was understanding, loving, and kind as he always had been in any crisis, but the disappointments that had plagued me in my search for my sister had struck me low as surely as an axe fells a tree. My friend, Police Chief Tanya Pedretti, had reached out and taken me to lunch several times in an attempt to console me, trying to minimize the damage I'd experienced. I vaguely recalled Tanya's statement several months ago when I insisted on reopening my sister's case: "Prepare yourself for disappointment." Truer words had never been spoken.

Together, Tanya and I rehashed every aspect of the investigation of my sister's death. We examined the police records concerning the case and reviewed the information Tanya had received from the two detectives at the Fort Worth Police Department who stepped forward to share their findings with her. Trygve had investigated the ownership of the farm in 1990, where the Volkswagon beetle has been stored, but it did little to solve the mystery of how the car had gotten there and stayed hidden all those years since Katherine's escape. However, there was one bright note of encouragement. We now knew that Kitty Currant was indeed my sister Katherine Waite. DNA samples extracted from items at her work station in Texas were a positive match to the DNA that police had gathered from her apartment the day after the bombing, but all of it seemed to fly in the face of common sense. Kitty appeared to be as elusive as the fog that hung over the river on cold winter mornings. Her identity had been firmly established, but no one had spotted her or knew where she had gone since the day of the shooting at Innovative Fabrications. Apparently, she was a master of disguise and intrigue—a ghost of the past who refused to come into the light of the present.

It was Thursday, December 18. I met Tanya at the Freighthouse in downtown La Crosse for Christmas lunch. She greeted me with a hug and led me to one of the more private areas of the restaurant where we could talk without being overheard. Outside the window, the river was silent and white, frozen in stillness. We sat down in a cozy booth and ordered two glasses of Moscato wine and the lunch special, shrimp pasta salad with crusty French baguettes, followed by a plate of Christmas goodies. While we waited for our food and sipped our drinks, Tanya chattered happily about her family Christmas plans. Her identical twin boys, Scott and Skipper, were home from the university in Madison, and she was pleasantly surprised that they seemed to be enjoying the company of their family.

"Go figure, Sonja. When Scottie and Skipper were seniors in high school, they treated us like we had the plague; they couldn't get away from us fast enough. Now, they've come home with a brand-new attitude. We even broke out the Monopoly game the other night. We haven't done that for years," Tanya finished with a grin. Despite her attempt to spread some holiday cheer, my sad countenance put a damper on everything.

I smiled weakly at her effervescent mood and chewed on my baguette. I'd lost my appetite in the last few weeks, and I'd even dropped a few pounds. Nothing tasted good to me, even though Tryg had cooked some delicious meals, trying to entice me to eat. I appreciated his efforts, but I just wasn't interested in food. I stumbled through my cleaning jobs, barely remembering where I'd been or what I'd done. I wasn't sleeping well either. My nights were a never-ending movie screen of moments I'd never recover: shopping with Katherine, cooking together in the kitchen, kayaking, swimming, and skiing on Lake Superior and the Mississippi, showing her my farm animals, and introducing her to Trygve. Unless I could locate her, none of it would ever happen. I had never felt so alone. To put it bluntly, I was a wreck, and I knew it.

"It sounds like your kids are finally appreciating all the effort you put into giving them a loving home," I said, trying to take an interest in our conversation.

"Well, what goes around comes around, I guess," Tanya said. She paused.

I could see her weighing whether she should go on with this mindless chatter or get to the heart of the matter. Striking a balance in consoling other people in their troubles is always a hard thing to do, isn't it? In my experience, people often are so focused on avoiding tough topics that they say nothing at all, ignoring the elephant in the room, so to speak. I knew Tanya wasn't about to spout off some classic one-liner like, "I'm thinking of you and praying for you." *How many people who said that really prayed?* I thought bitterly. That was probably the most overused and abused statement people repeated to those who were going through a difficult time. But I could see the moment had come. My friend had a distinct look in her eye, and I knew she was about to give me some down-home nitty-gritty advice. I could almost read her thoughts. *Enough of this sour attitude, Sonja. Something's gotta give.* For just a moment, Tanya stepped out of her comfort zone and into my world.

"Sonja, I'm worried about you," Tanya started softly but firmly.

I stared at her, then shifted my gaze to the twinkling Christmas tree in the corner of the restaurant with its sparkling lights and shiny ornaments. Outside, the streets were busy with shoppers carrying packages, the traffic rushing by in its usual hubbub and noise.

"You've lost weight, and I can see you're devastated

about your sister. How can I help you?" My friend reached across the table and clasped my hand. Her tender concern and the warmth of her touch loosened something within me that had been festering for a long time.

"I wish I knew what you could do to help," I began. I choked back a sob, and tears flooded my eyes. All the anguish I'd experienced the last few months came boiling out of me. "You tried to tell me I'd be disappointed, but of course, I wouldn't listen. I just had to try and find out about my sister. Boy, was I stupid! The stuff I believed about her was not even close to the truth. Sometimes I think I would have been better off if I'd stuck my head down a rat hole! Why didn't I listen to you and take your advice?" I spouted loudly. "What did I accomplish for all my efforts? Nothing! Absolutely nothing!" I slammed the table with my fist, my fury and frustration spilling over in a loud outburst.

Thank God for Tanya. Just try to rock her boat! She wasn't embarrassed by the stares from the other people near our booth, and believe me, they were looking at me like I was some kind of lunatic. Tanya has seen a lot of crises in her police work, and outbursts of strong emotion were nothing new to her. You wanna talk about shockability? Tanya has seen things I couldn't even imagine: victims of murder, drug overdoses, teen suicide, car accidents that had snuffed out a parent's life and left their kids traumatized, shattered rape victims. The list went on and on. If I was ever thankful for my friend, then this was the moment when my cup overflowed. She cared. She listened. She accepted me in my confusion, anger, and sorrow.

Tanya squeezed my hand again and motioned to the waiter, who hurried to our table. "We'll have two brandies on the rocks," she ordered sternly. The waiter nodded his head and scooted away. "Have you thought about anger management?" she asked me seriously, but I noticed a sly smile teasing the corners of her mouth.

"You offering your expertise?" I asked.

"What do you think we're doin' right now, girl?" she asked. "This ain't no slouch you're talkin' to. When it's all said and done, you're gonna have one big-ass bill."

"Hundreds of dollars?" I said, a smile creasing my cheeks.

"Thousands," she bantered back. We began to laugh. We nibbled cookies from the Christmas platter and drank our brandies. Over coffee, my mood turned a corner. We reviewed some of the discoveries we'd made about Katherine. Tanya cautiously expressed the hope that one day Katherine might be found and our relationship could be restored. I vowed to recall the good things about my sister before she'd participated in an infamous crime and staged her own demise.

"Do I have your word that this investigation you've been conducting has finally come to an end?" Tanya asked after several minutes of discussion.

I moved my finger back and forth like a metronome. "Not totally," I said carefully. "I'm giving myself permission to keep the door open, but . . . with realistic expectations."

"What does that mean?" she asked. "Sounds like psychobabble to me." She had every right to be suspicious of my motives. I'd put her and Trygve through the wringer in the last few months.

I began to explain. "Well, the guy who ended up with Katherine's VW bug has offered to sell it to me. It's something that will remind me of the happy times I had with my sister. Every time I drive it, I'll remember the joy I felt being with Katherine when she took me for a ride along Lake Superior."

"That's a step in the right direction, a positive memory," Tanya commented. "That's good. What else?"

"You're a tough taskmaster, you know that?" I said impatiently, my eyes flashing with irritation.

"Only because you need it," she replied calmly. "What else?" She wasn't letting up, and I knew she'd hold me to the promises I was making, forcing me to be realistic in my expectations.

"Okay, okay," I said, making a wry face. "I'm going to talk to two people, and then I'm done." I held up my index finger, "First, I'm going to look up Mrs. McClintock. I know she lives in Trempealeau."

"Are you sure you want to do that?" Tanya asked.

"Yes, I do. I know Katherine hurt a lot of people through her actions, and I want to be sure Mrs. McClintock knows how very sorry I am for the death of her husband and all the grief my sister caused. It'll be hard, but it's something I feel I must do."

"Okay, I understand, but it won't be easy. And just remember, some wrongs you can never make right." Tanya's brown eyes blazed until Sonja had to look away.

I'm sure she knows what she's talkin' about, I thought. I nodded my head in silent agreement. Throughout this conversation, I was dealing with Tanya Pedretti, the cop. Despite the friendship we shared and the fondness we had for each other, her questions were tough, and her expectations were high. She didn't spare my feelings, but I also realized it was coming from a place of love and concern.

"You mentioned two people. Who's the other one?" Tanya demanded.

"Retired Detective Rolly Gulbrandsen. He lives in an assisted living facility in Middleton down by Madison," I explained.

"Never met the guy. Why do you want to talk to him?" Tanya asked. Her demeanor was unrelenting and challenged my assumptions that what I was planning to do would be easy. For once, I listened and agreed. Everything about the goals I'd set for myself was going to be difficult and laden with guilt and emotions I would rather have buried somewhere on the back forty of our farm.

I took a deep breath before I answered, thinking through my response. "I want to hear from someone who actually investigated the crime and was assigned to the case. I want to ask a few questions that only someone who was closely involved would have answers to. And don't ask me what they are, 'cause I'm not going to tell you," I said adamantly, my temper flaring.

Tanya nodded in agreement. "I can live with that. One other thing before we go."

"Yeah, what's that?"

"I made an appointment for you with Doctor Tom at his south side clinic on Mormon Coulee Road," Tanya said.

"What?" I was instantly angry. "What gives you the right?"

Tanya leaned forward, her eyes flashing, challenging me to argue with her in public. By the look on her face, I knew I'd come out the loser. "Being your friend gives me the right to do things for you that you probably wouldn't do for yourself. Besides, Trygve called me, and he's worried sick about you. Sonja, you're his entire world, and you owe it to him to get checked out. Tomorrow at ten in the morning. Doctor Tom. Be there."

Tanya slid out of the booth, grabbed the check, gave me a peck on the cheek, and disappeared before I had time to launch an argument. I sat in the booth for a while after Tanya left, thinking about what it meant to have a friend who wasn't afraid to be honest. Coupled with love, humor, and concern, was there any greater gift?

CHAPTER 18

If I Could Put Time in a Bottle . . .

It took Collin Ainsworth several weeks of intense searching using various sources on the internet to understand what Kitty had been doing since the bombing at the university in 1990. Innovative Fabrications in Fort Worth had been her place of employment for over thirty years. In a phone call to the factory, Collin hooked up with a supervisor, and during a brief conversation, he learned about her value as a team department leader at the plant. They missed her input every day, the supervisor said, and he hoped she would return soon because she was desperately needed at work. Collin wasn't surprised. When he'd met Kitty at the university, she'd been a stand-out from the beginning—smart as a whip with a solid, Midwest work ethic coupled with dogged determination. It didn't take a rocket scientist to figure out she was going places.

In another phone call to the Fort Worth Police Department, he pretended to have information about Kitty's disappearance. He was connected to a detective assigned to her case. Ken Stanton was guarded and distant, hesitant to share specific information with a stranger over the phone.

"Who did you say you were?" Stanton asked gruffly. "How do you know Kitty?"

"I'm a friend from years back. I returned to the La Crosse area after a long absence, and I was interested in hooking up with her again. We were good friends in college. I heard about the shooting at the factory from another college acquaintance," Collin explained.

"You haven't kept in touch over the years?"

"No, my work took me to other places, I married and divorced, and we lost track of each other. Can you give me some information?"

"We probably know about as much as you do. She lived in White Settlement for over thirty years, but she had very few friends she was close to. She seemed to be something of a loner," Stanton explained. That was as much information as he was willing to give to a stranger.

"Can you give me the contact information of a few of her friends?" Collin asked. "I can take it from there."

Reluctantly, Stanton bent his own rules. "There's a gal she worked with named Gwen Delaruso, who seemed to be a friend of hers. She has a Fort Worth number. You can call information to get it."

Following that conversation, Collin called Gwen's number, but the call went unanswered, so he left a message.

When Gwen listened to the message, she scoffed at the gist of the content. Someone from college was looking for Kitty? She doubted it. Ever since her friend's disappearance after the shooting, Gwen had been fighting off curiosity seekers who saw a reference to the shooting on TV or others who had scoured the internet searching Facebook,

Instagram, Twitter, and Snapchat for information about the woman who'd disarmed a shooter and suddenly, mysteriously disappeared from White Settlement. The rumors and speculations had elevated Kitty into something of a celebrity and folk hero in the Fort Worth area, although Gwen was sure Kitty would have been horrified by the attention. Gwen had reluctantly consented to an interview by a reporter from a local Fort Worth television station after the shooting incident at the plant in the hope that it might be helpful in locating her, but it had turned into a fiasco. Every Tom, Dick, and Harry in her neighborhood came out of the woodwork trying to get information about Kitty, so when Collin called and left a message, Gwen was in no mood to deal with another person pestering her for the inside track on Kitty's whereabouts—as if she knew where she had gone. However, she returned his call because she was curious about his connection to her from college. Kitty had never talked about anyone from college, but maybe this person could shed some light on where she might have gone.

"What did you want to know about Kitty?" Gwen Delaruso asked. She squirmed uncomfortably, feeling guilty about her participation in something that felt like nothing more than a gossip session. She was doing exactly what she deplored in all the people who'd called her about Kitty—trying to find a salacious tidbit that would lead to her location. But Gwen was beginning to realize that Kitty had kept her secrets well. Despite knowing her for over thirty years, she realized she really didn't know her at all.

"We were good friends in college," Collin explained, "and then I lost track of her when I transferred to another university. I'm divorced now, and I'd like to see her again." *Nothing but a pack of lies*, he thought as he spun his story.

"She never talked about her family or anybody else for that matter," Gwen said. "After the shooting that day, she said she was going home to lie down, but later, when I went to check on her, she was gone, and I haven't seen her since."

"Do you think she's headed to Wisconsin?" Collin asked.

"It's possible, I guess. I recently found out she has a sister in La Crosse, so maybe she's decided to reconnect with her family. I don't know. Kitty was always a mystery."

"What kind of vehicle was she driving?"

"Why do you want to know that?" Gwen asked sharply.

"It might help me locate her," Collin said, although he was irritated by Gwen's distrust and vague answers.

"The police put out an APB on her truck, a dark green Ford F-150 pickup, 1979 model."

"Okay," Collin said, jotting the description on a piece of paper. "That might be useful somewhere along the line. Thanks for the information." He clicked off and stared into space. Trying to locate an old Ford pickup in southern Wisconsin seemed like searching for a needle in a haystack. He could think of at least ten farmsteads between his house and Viroqua that had several old, dead vehicles languishing in and around their places. However, Collin hit a lucky streak when a few nights later someone on Facebook posted a photo of a dark 1979 Ford truck with Wisconsin license plates parked at a bar in Lynxville with the comment, "Could this be the vehicle of the missing woman from Fort Worth?" Collin sent a private message to the person, then waited impatiently for an answer. Several hours later, he received a response: "Bartender says woman showed up this fall driving an older Ford F-150. Renting a place somewhere near Romance. What's your interest?"

Collin refused to take the bait. The location of the rental property was not specific enough to be helpful, which left him in a quandary, but studying a local map of the area on his phone, he deduced there were about a half dozen roads connected to the little place called Romance. For several weeks he cruised the roads throughout the Bad Axe Valley searching for Kitty's vehicle. It seemed like a pointless mission, but he couldn't let it go. Finally, about six weeks later, while he was driving on Mundsack Road, he spotted an older dark green pickup parked next to a tiny cabin. He stopped on the road below the cabin and watched for any signs of life, but the cabin remained quiet. He drove away after an hour convinced that Katy was somewhere nearby, and decided to return later.

On December 19, Collin hopped in his pickup and drove back to the hunting cabin. He felt a deep sense of purpose he hadn't had in a long time. Instead of driving aimlessly through the countryside looking for a random pickup parked in someone's yard, he stared straight ahead, his destination clear in his mind. When he thought about the mission he was on, his heart thumped wildly in his chest. He was nervous, and anyone who knew what he was about to do wouldn't blame him.

He drove west on Highway 27/82 from his cabin on Roller Coaster Lane near Mount Sterling until he dropped down from the bluff into the village of De Soto on the Mississippi River. The scenery in his windshield displayed a panorama he never got tired of—steep wooded bluffs, small bubbling creeks, and the wide wild river dotted with small towns along its shore, eagles soaring in the air above him, deer browsing in the valleys and fields, all of it swaddled in a deep layer of white, peaceful snow.

Turning left on Mundsack Road, Collin drove along the winding route until Katy's rental cabin came into view. He drove past the cabin, noticing the smoke from the chimney rising in the still air and the old pickup parked near the house. Someone was home. Driving down the road, he found a place to park his truck on what looked like some kind of logging trail that headed deep into the thick woods. He walked down the gravel road and climbed the hillside behind the cabin, where he sat under a huge evergreen tree with branches that swooped near the ground. It was crisp, and the snow was deep, but he had dressed for the cold. He waited beneath the pine boughs and watched the cabin with a set of binoculars he had brought along. Finally, after his patience had worn thin and his toes and fingers were stiff from the chilly temperatures, Katy came out of the back door of the cabin, threw a bag of garbage into a can sitting against the cabin wall, and went back into the house. Collin could barely contain his excitement. He had actually tracked her down! He almost yelled out her name. His thoughts of their romance on campus had returned as he sat under the huge evergreen. Swallowing hard, he had to remind himself this was no picnic he was on. He had found a fugitive from the law with an active warrant for her arrest who had successfully built a life for herself several states away by creating an alternate persona. He knew nothing about her motives. What was she doing in Wisconsin? Would she resent him for convincing her to drive the getaway truck after the bombing so many years ago, forcing her to run for her life? Had she contacted her sisters, or was she still alone and undiscovered, hiding in this quiet valley?

He had doubts about many things. He had changed, and he was sure Katy had changed, too, but he was hopeful he would have the opportunity to talk with her. Whether they could revive their feelings for each other was unknown. As Collin sat under the tree, his mind was crowded with feelings, facts, and emotions all jumbled together in a confusing knot.

Fifteen minutes later, Katy came out of the cabin, climbed into her rickety truck, and disappeared down the road. Collin stood up, stretched his cramped muscles, and climbed back down the steep hill to the road below. He was unsure what to do. Should he go into the cabin and wait for her to return? Should he leave without making contact or write a note and tuck it in the door? That seemed like a childish thing to do. *This isn't junior high where you write notes to somebody you have a crush on*, he thought, disgusted at his immature solution to a sticky problem. He walked back to his truck on the logging trail and took a nap. When he woke up, he felt braver and surer of himself. After much consideration, he drove his pickup to the cabin and parked along the road below the house. Katy had returned. He climbed the steep driveway, walked up to the door of the cabin, and knocked. A few moments later, the door flew open.

"Hello, Katy," Collin said softly. She looked much as he remembered her, just an older version of herself—softly curled hair, intelligent, hazel eyes, petite nose, compact body, little hands. She was dressed in a well-worn pair of tight blue jeans and a comfortable plaid flannel shirt.

"Oh, my God. What are you doing here, Collin?" Katy asked, laying her hand over her heart. Her eyes were huge, and he could see panic in the shadows of her face.

"I came to see you," he said. "Don't be scared. I won't hurt you."

Katy stood in front of him, staring in disbelief. Several awkward moments passed.

"This is where you invite me in for a cup of coffee . . . or a drink . . . or something," Collin finally said.

Kitty shifted nervously on her feet and looked beyond Collin out to the yard.

"Don't worry. I'm alone," Collin reassured her.

"I'm sorry. I didn't mean to distrust you. It's just . . . It's just that I never expected to see you again," Katy stammered. Later she remembered this exact moment in her mind when Collin, her former lover, stood on her doorstep, and she thought, *You should never invite a convicted felon into your living room. Especially one with dark brown eyes and curly hair and a winsome smile.* But she did anyway, and in the end, she wasn't sorry at all.

CHAPTER 19

It's a Hard-Knock Life

Sonja sat on the edge of the examination table in Dr. Tom Nielson's office on Mormon Coulee Road on Friday morning. Dr. Tom was as irascible as ever, asking blunt questions and responding to Sonja's answers with grunts of dissatisfaction. His thick, wiry red hair stuck out in every direction. He wore a pair of weathered blue jeans and a Western shirt underneath a leather vest, which hung loosely on his lanky frame. A red bandanna tied around his neck moved up and down with his protruding Adam's apple whenever he swallowed. He was opinionated, grumpy, and probably would have liked a whiskey sour on the rocks if he hadn't been so busy giving Sonja a thorough physical exam.

"You been eatin'?" he asked, leaning against the wall with his arms crossed over his chest. "You've lost a couple of pounds."

Sonja sighed loudly. "Well, of course I've been eating. You know that Trygve is a great cook. You've had his food, remember?"

"He can make it, but it doesn't mean you have to eat it, does it?" Dr. Tom responded rudely, his wooly eyebrows scrunched together like a Brillo pad.

"Point taken. If you want the truth, my appetite has fallen off a little bit lately," Sonja said sheepishly.

"How about your bowels?"

Sonja's forehead creased in a frown. "What about them?"

"They workin' okay?"

Sonja stared at Dr. Tom and made a face. "Yes, I'm having regular bowel movements, if you must know."

"I do need to know; I'm your doctor. Your blood work shows you're a little anemic. I'll give you an iron supplement. Take it with food. Otherwise you might get a little queasy from it."

"Got it, Doc. Can I go now?" Sonja asked, ready to jump down from the table.

"No. There must be something else bothering you," Dr. Tom said. "I've checked all the boxes I need to in a regular exam, but you're not telling me everything." He plunked himself in a rolling office chair and propped his well-worn cowboy boots up on the small desk attached to the wall while he continued to spout his observations. "Your blood pressure is a little high, and I can tell there's something else on your mind. You're nervous and jittery. That's not like you. So, what's going on? Come out with it. I can't help you unless you're upfront with me about your problems. What's worrying you?"

Sonja shook her head and let out a loud sigh of frustration. "Why does everyone have to stick their nose in my business?"

Dr. Tom slammed his feet on the floor and barked a response. "Because they care about you, Sonja, that's why. Does this have something to do with your sister?" he asked. Sonja looked at him with a startled expression.

"Which one?" Sonja asked brusquely. "They're both nightmares from hell but in different ways."

"I'm talkin' about your sister who drowned over in Pettibone way back when, how she was never found, and now someone thinks she's still alive and has been hiding out in Texas." The dubious look in his eyes left an impression Sonja wouldn't easily forget, and she wisely decided not to challenge him. "Doesn't seem likely to me," he continued. "Common sense tells you it probably isn't true, but I can see where something like that would tend to keep you awake at night."

Sonja stared at him, amazed at his perceptive analysis of her situation. Despite his outspoken opinions, she loved him for his honesty and his concern for her well-being.

"Well, what have you got to say for yourself?" Dr. Tom rasped. "Does this have something to do with your missing sister or not?"

"When it comes right down to it, I never accepted that her death was real," Sonja began to explain. "I've had questions nobody has been able to answer, and I've been looking for answers my whole life. Now I'm right on the doorstep of finding her, but she keeps running away." Sonja's eyes filled with tears, and she angrily swiped her hand across her cheeks. "I'm sick and tired of chasing her, if you want to know the truth."

Dr. Tom remained silent for several moments, studying

Sonja while she cried softly. A few moments later, in a gentler voice, he asked, "Sonja, the question you have to answer is this: Are you happy chasing your dream?"

"You mean my dream of finding my sister alive?"

"Exactly."

"Well, after I made the decision a couple of months ago to get to the bottom of this whole mess, I've been pretty miserable," Sonja admitted. Dr. Tom handed her a tissue, and she blew her nose loudly. "I've been turning over rocks for a long time, and I'm so tired of it. Tryg has tried to help me, but I haven't been very cooperative . . . or appreciative."

Dr. Tom waited a moment, then he said, "It seems to me that chasing your sister is like chasing a butterfly; the more you chase her, the more she eludes you. Maybe if you stop trying, your sister will come and sit down next to you just like the butterfly does when it's not being chased." Dr. Tom cocked his head and waited. "It's worth considering, don't you think?"

Sonja had never thought of Dr. Tom as an empathetic personality, but at that moment, she knew he understood the angst and frustration she'd experienced over the years in her search for the truth about her sister. But he was also wise enough to see what it was doing to her.

"I'll have to think about that," Sonja remarked thoughtfully. "Should I give up my search? Is that what you're suggesting?"

"No one can make that decision except you, but I can tell you that your obsession is taking a toll on your health, and you're the only one who can change that. You might want to consider some other options," Dr. Tom concluded. He stood up and walked to the door, but before he could leave,

Sonja jumped down from the table and hugged him tightly.

"What's that for?" Dr. Tom snapped belligerently.

"That's for telling me what I didn't want to hear," Sonja said, tears glistening in her eyes. "Thank you, my friend."

Meanwhile, Tanya Pedretti was responding to a fire within the city at an apartment complex. She grabbed the looped handle in the ceiling of the squad car as Lt. Chad Hepple raced through the streets near the university, lights flashing and siren wailing. Weaving in and out of traffic, they arrived at the Ferry Street apartment building, which was engulfed in flames. Lt. Hatchet Brousard blew out a sigh of relief in the back seat when the cruiser skidded to a halt next to the curb.

It was Friday, about mid-morning. Tanya had been having a pow-wow in her office with Chad and Hatchet about the disappearance of Kitty Currant, aka Katherine Waite. When the fire alarm came through to the law enforcement center, Tanya jumped into action, commandeering Chad and Brousard in the process. As soon as Lt. Hepple ground to a halt at the scene of the fire, Tanya jumped out and ran up to Scott Chandler, the fire chief, who was standing on the sidewalk barking orders to his crew.

"We'll need another pumper!" he yelled into his phone. He stumbled briefly as crewmen pulled more hose toward the raging fire. "Get on the roof!" he yelled to his men, pointing to the smoking shingles. "The roof! It's about to go up in flames. Knock it down!" he yelled loudly. A truck equipped with an extendable ladder backed over the curb and up on the lawn. Chief Chandler turned, noticing Tanya for the first time. Despite the chaotic mayhem all around, Tanya was confident the fire crew had the situation under control.

"What do we know, Scott?" Tanya asked. "Are there people inside?"

"Don't know yet, but as soon as we can knock the fire down, I'll send my men inside, and they'll sweep the building."

"Looks like you've got it under control," Tanya responded, covering her mouth with her arm as a gush of sooty black smoke blown by the wind threatened to overwhelm them.

"Yep, we're doin' our best, but it's going to take a while to get this tamped down. I'll keep you in the loop," Chandler promised.

Tanya, Chad, and Hatchet retreated briefly and stood next to the squad car parked along the street. A small crowd of bystanders talked quietly as they watched a familiar building in their neighborhood crackle and roar with flames, the heat radiating outward toward the street. Suddenly, part of the roof collapsed in a loud whoosh, the heat and flames scorching the nearby trees.

Tanya turned and said, "There's not much we can do here. Let's go back to the office."

The trio trudged to the police cruiser and returned to the law enforcement facility on Ranger Street. They took the elevator to the second floor, entered Tanya's office at the end of the building with the view of the bluffs and river, and continued the discussion they had been engaged in before they were called out to the fire, namely, Kitty Currant, the missing fugitive from Texas.

"Do you think Kitty's back in the area?" Tanya asked.

Just this morning she had gotten a call from the Fort Worth police wondering if anyone had spotted the woman in Wisconsin. "The Fort Worth people are anxious to talk to her."

"I can understand why," Hatchet responded. "She lived right under their noses for over thirty years, and they never caught on. That's gotta be a little embarrassing for them." He cocked his head at an angle and frowned. "Tell me again why we're spending all this time on someone nobody can find? This Kitty is obviously an expert at keeping a low profile. She's probably in Canada by now."

Tanya shook her head in frustration. "Maybe, but I have a hunch about this. Something tells me she's around here somewhere."

"A hunch? Based on what?" Hatchet asked.

Tanya shrugged. "Just intuition, I guess. You know I put surveillance on Collin Ainsworth." The two officers nodded. "We'll see if anything comes of that. But the question we should be asking ourselves is: What would motivate Kitty to return to Wisconsin? What's here that would draw her back? What would make her risk returning to her old stomping grounds?"

"I'm sure you have an answer to your own question," Hatchet said. "Or is this part of your hunch?"

"People are motivated sometimes by feelings they don't always understand," Tanya began. "I did a search of the official records concerning Collin Ainsworth. Rumor has it that Katherine and Collin were lovers at the time of the bombing. I was surprised to learn he's been living in the Mount Sterling area for the past ten years or so, working odd jobs, hanging out. I talked to his employer at the orchard where he works. He vouches for Collin, saying he's a hard worker, dependable, but extremely shy. He doesn't have many friends, but he seems to have rebuilt his life after his stint in prison. So, I wondered if Katherine would be drawn back here because of him. Have they been in communication over the years? The other factor, of course, is her sister, Sonja Hovland. Maybe she wants to reconnect with Sonja again, or is there something else we don't know about that could be a factor in her returning to the area?"

"All of those things you mentioned are a hard sell," Chad said. "Coming back here for any reason would be pretty risky. There's still an active warrant out for her arrest. Her participation in the bombing in 1990 is not going to go away despite the years that have passed. If she shows up, we'll have to arrest her, she'll have a trial, and then . . ." His voice faded away as he considered the ramifications, but Hatchet picked up the storyline.

"Then she'll be spending time in jail," he finished.

"Probably, but only if she's convicted," Tanya reminded the two men. "Remember, she's still entitled to a trial. And even if she's found guilty, the judge has a lot of prerogatives in the sentencing of her case."

"Really? Like what?" Chad asked skeptically.

Tanya leaned back in her chair as she talked. "Well, first of all, the judge must take into consideration the sentencing guidelines for this type of crime. Secondly, he has to consider victim impact statements. In this case, that would include testimony from James McClintock's family, his wife and children. But then the judge has some lateral freedom to consider other factors like Katherine's life over the last thirty-five years: her successful employment at Innovative

Fabrications, the fact that she has never committed another crime, not even a traffic violation. He'd have to determine whether she has any remorse for her participation in the bombing; things like that. So the judge must weigh the conflicting factors and deal out a sentence that is fair for everyone."

"I'm glad that's not my job," Hatchet said somberly.

"You and me both," Chad chimed in.

"Well, none of that will happen until someone finds her," Tanya said bluntly.

"Any news on that front?" Chad asked.

"Not that I'm aware of," Tanya said, "but I've got a few ideas I'm tossing around. I'm hoping the gal I assigned to watch Collin will come up with something. The guys in Fort Worth said there have been a few wild reports that someone spotted her in Iowa and Kansas, but witnesses are not coming forward and can't be found. It must be rumors, I guess, or wishful thinking, the internet run amuck, a Facebook frenzy—whatever. Take your pick," Tanya said, waving her hand. "Everybody today loves a conspiracy theory, so until we get a call from a reliable source, Katherine has disappeared—again."

CHAPTER 20 • SONJA

News From Nowhere

When my appointment with Dr. Tom ended, I headed out the door with renewed purpose. The night before, I looked up Joy McClintock's address in Trempealeau and decided there was no time like the present to express my sincere apologies concerning the death of her husband, James, during the bombing in 1990. Although I knew the task would require a heavy dose of true humility, I worried that my apology would be viewed only as a way of cleansing my family's name and reputation when what I really wanted was to be forgiven so I could get on with my life and experience freedom from the heavy burden of guilt I had carried over the years. As Kermit the Frog used to say, "It ain't easy bein' green." I had found the beloved amphibian's quip applicable in my own life. "It ain't easy being a sister to a notorious criminal." This cloud of uncertainty hanging over my life had rained on my parade long enough. I was ready for absolution.

Traveling along Highway 53 through Onalaska and Holmen on my way to the river city of Trempealeau, it began to snow—a heavy, wet affair that immediately made the highway slick and treacherous. I was distracted by my mission, preoccupied as I composed my speech of remorse I'd planned for Joy McClintock. In my absentminded state, I continued traveling down the road failing to decrease my speed until another driver pulled out suddenly several hundred feet in front of me. I hit the brakes, but when you're driving too fast for conditions, things don't always go as planned. I went into a skid and rear-ended the other driver, sending him into the ditch. I, on the other hand, did several donuts on the slick road and ended up in the other lane of traffic, where I was rear-ended by another driver who couldn't stop in time either. During the crash, the airbags went off with a loud bang, but they didn't protect my head, which slammed into the driver's side window, rendering me unconscious.

Several minutes later, someone knocked on my window. In a painful fog, I powered my window down while the man forced my door open.

"Ma'am, you've been in a crash. Are you hurt? How are you feeling?" a policeman asked, hovering over me.

I realized then I must have been knocked unconscious and been out of commission for several minutes. How did I end up in the ditch? I noticed the crumpled hood of my Subaru and groaned. It would take a small fortune to fix my hood and trunk. Obviously, I was having a moment of major confusion and amnesia. My dazed expression told the policeman that my injuries were probably more serious than he realized.

"Don't worry," the cop continued. "We'll get you out of your vehicle and into the ambulance as soon as it gets here.

They'll take you to the hospital so you can get checked out."

"Trygve, my husband," I whispered, noticing a distinct throbbing pain on the left side of my head. "Someone needs to call him." I mumbled the phone number to the cop, then drifted in and out of consciousness as the EMT crew got me on a stretcher and loaded me into the quiet safety of the ambulance. I was dizzy, disoriented, and had an awful headache. I threw up. I felt a surge of gratitude for the medical attention, closed my eyes, and drifted in a fog of pain and disorientation.

The next thing I remember after the ride to the hospital was a big, warm hand encapsulating mine. My eyes fluttered open, and Trygve leaned down and gave me a tender kiss.

"How you doin', baby?" he asked quietly next to my ear.

"I'm here, ain't I?" I said with a surly attitude. "I have a terrific headache if you wanna know the truth, and I feel like I might puke again." When I thought about how much worse everything could have turned out, and I saw the concern on my husband's face, I softened my response. "I'm okay, I guess, but what are the doctors saying? What actually happened? I don't really remember."

"You went into a skid and rear-ended another driver, and then you did some donuts, and you were hit from behind by another car. You probably have a major concussion, so they're going to get a CT scan to make sure you don't have a brain bleed. You've got a bruised shoulder and a couple of purple bruises on your legs and back, but all in all, I'd say you're going to live," Trygve informed me. Tears filled his eyes, and he touched my hair tenderly and patted my arm. When I looked into his big brown eyes, my heart swelled with love, and I began to cry.

"I'm sorry, Tryg. I suppose my car is totaled, huh?"

"You can replace cars, but you can't replace people," he said soberly. "Now, just rest and go back to sleep. I'll be right here when you wake up."

While Sonja slept and the doctors read the reports and tests to determine a protocol of treatment, Trygve stepped into a lounge next to the ER and called Tanya Pedretti.

"Tanya, it's Trygve. I'm at Mayo. Sonja was in a three-car accident up on 53 north of Holmen."

"Oh no! I saw the report come over the scanner. Is she alright?"

"She's concussed and has a few bumps and bruises, but I think she'll be fine."

"Thank goodness," Tanya replied. She went on in a rush. "Hey, I'm glad you called. A couple of weeks ago I put one of my officers on Collin Ainsworth. He's been under surveillance to see if he might lead us to Katy, and we lucked out. I just got a call. Apparently, the two of them have been in communication. Our officer followed him and found Katy holed up in a little cabin down by Genoa. We're going down right now to arrest her. Tell Sonja when you think she's ready to hear it. I gotta run! My team is waiting for me." And the line went dead.

Trygve stared at his phone as if it might tell him what to do next. He shook his head and decided he would wait to tell Sonja about her sister until she was in police custody. Telling Sonja anything prior to that seemed like cruel and unusual punishment, especially in light of the accident.

Trygve leaned back in his chair and rested his head against the wall. *When was all of this cloak-and-dagger drama going to end?* he thought. *Or was it just beginning? Why couldn't his wife leave the past behind?* He didn't have any answers, but trying to protect Sonja from her own instincts was a full-time job, one he was only beginning to comprehend.

The little cabin on Mundsack Road sat smugly on the crest of a small hill overlooking the Bad Axe Valley, smoke curling softly from the stovepipe chimney, snow covering the hills and bluffs in a layer of white, which softened the sharp edges of the jutting rocks and trees. The whole scene looked like a Currier and Ives print. Tanya Pedretti, Lt. Chad Hepple, and Hatchet Brousard sat in a standard department hatchback cruiser on the side of the quiet country road about one hundred feet away from the cabin and watched for any sign of Katherine Waite.

Tanya was in a rare philosophical mood. As she sat in the cruiser, her thoughts rambled. She wondered how Katherine had arrived in such a seemingly isolated, quiet valley. Was she trying to run away from the history she had created in her initial crime spree, or was she returning to Wisconsin because of a psychological hunger for home and family connections? Since national television and internet outlets had thrust her into the spotlight, this idyllic setting tucked away from the glare of the world offered an escape that would be hard to resist.

By contrast, Chief Pedretti's life in the city was so busy it sometimes made her head spin, but she knew that real peace had nothing to do with your location. You could run and try to hide from the realities of life as Katherine Waite had done, but sooner or later, the real world came knocking on your door, as the infamous fugitive was about to find out. Tanya couldn't believe her idea of shagging Collin Ainsworth had led to the discovery of Katherine's secret hideaway in this quaint little valley. That was a stroke of luck. Although she didn't know the woman, Tanya could understand the appeal of the place. It was peaceful, quiet, low-key, a place to get her bearings and figure out her next move. But everyone eventually had to deal with the troubles that came into their lives. Running from Texas and hiding in Wisconsin wasn't a good game plan that had helped Katherine. In the end, she was about to be arrested, although Tanya had to admit she seemed to have had a streak of luck for over thirty years. However, that was about to change.

Tanya locked eyes with her former partner, Hatchet Brousard, who was sitting in the back seat of the car, and a mutual understanding passed between them in a glance. Hatchet had found out last year about the realities of being shot by a seemingly innocent citizen, and she knew his worldview had changed forever. As if in response to an unspoken pact between them, Hatchet spoke first.

"So, what do we know, Chief, about Katherine? Can we expect resistance or gunfire?"

"Good question, Hatchet. From all indications, I don't think she will resist, but life isn't predictable, is it? I wouldn't expect her to come out guns blazing, but you of all people learned about surprises the hard way last year," Tanya responded, her voice tightening as she spoke. "We will approach the cabin as if she were armed and dangerous.

Consider every contingency. Leave nothing to chance."

"Sounds reasonable to me, Chief," Lt. Hepple added. "What about Collin Ainsworth? He around?"

"We don't know that, either, but we will assume she may have someone with her in the cabin," Tanya said. She cleared her throat loudly. "Are we ready, then?"

"As ready as we'll ever be," Hatchet said softly.

"I'll lead," Tanya reminded the men. "Katherine will probably respond more favorably to another woman; she might feel less threatened. You two stay on either side of the cabin door. There may be a back door, so be ready to pursue suspects on foot if needed. That's our plan. Are we clear?"

"Perfectly, ma'am," Hepple said. When Hatchet didn't respond, Tanya caught his eye in the rearview mirror.

"On board, Chief," he said softly.

"All right, let's get this over with," Tanya said, opening her door. They stepped out of the vehicle and walked up the road and then up the steep driveway to the cabin. From the road, the building looked like a typical hunter's shack, someplace that would probably only be used during deer hunting in November. As the three got closer, it was obvious the cabin had been neglected; the logs were faded, and some of the chinking was missing. An old pickup sat in the driveway covered with a light dusting of snow.

Tanya stepped up to the front door, took a deep breath, and knocked loudly. She had an instinctual sense that someone was in the cabin. A few moments later, she heard light footsteps and the door opened. Katherine Waite was smaller than Tanya expected. She appeared nervous. Her eyes were big, and she fidgeted with the zipper of the vest she was wearing.

"Yes?" she said softly. "Who are you?"

"Are you Katherine Waite?" Tanya asked as she flipped open her badge.

"Yes, I am."

"I'm Police Chief Tanya Pedretti of the La Crosse Police Department. I have a warrant for your arrest for your participation in the 1990 bombing at the university in La Crosse, which killed Professor James McClintock. May we come in?" she asked.

"I was expecting you to show up at some point," Katherine said reasonably. "Yes, come in." She stepped to the side of the door, and the three officers entered the cabin. It was surprisingly cozy, despite the used furniture and minimal decorations. A wood fire glowed warmly in the small woodstove, and the rooms were clean and organized. A cup of coffee sat on a second-hand end table, and the TV was droning softly in the background. Katherine volunteered to get coffee for her guests.

Tanya accepted coffee in a Styrofoam cup, but the men refused. As they stood awkwardly gathered in the small living room, Katherine invited them to sit down, but Chief Pedretti was anxious to move on. She turned to Hatchet and Hepple. "Do a quick check to see that there's no one else here." As the men moved through the cabin, she turned back to Katherine and said, "We're not here to socialize, ma'am. We're going to take you to La Crosse, where you'll be incarcerated in the county jail until your trial can be scheduled."

"Yes, I understand," Katherine said. "I'll get my coat and purse."

When Katherine was ready for transport, Tanya snapped

a pair of handcuffs on her wrists and led her down the driveway to the squad car below. Once Katherine was inside the car, Tanya and Hatchet stood outside the vehicle looking at the surrounding blue-gray hills.

"That went well," Hatchet said. "Better than I thought it would."

"Yes, it did go well," Tanya agreed. "But Katherine's life is about to change in ways she knows nothing about."

"That happens when you make stupid decisions."

"That's true," Tanya agreed. "I didn't expect her to be so docile, though. I thought she'd be more feisty, maybe put up a fight."

"Life is full of surprises, huh? Ready to head out?" Hatchet asked.

"Yep. You know the press will descend on us like a screaming eagle, don't you?" Tanya said, glancing at Brousard.

"They always do. That's their job. You can handle it."

"Guess I'll have to."

"Ready then?"

"Out of the frying pan, into the fire," Tanya said.

"You could say that, Chief."

On Saturday morning, after a flurry of instructions from the doctor, Trygve wheeled Sonja out to the curb, opened the passenger door of the pickup, and helped her get in the front seat. He'd brought a blanket along, which he laid over her knees. A cold snap had descended during the night, and the temperature was below zero. Sonja smiled weakly but stared straight ahead. She still had a mild headache, and she was very tired. Every limb seemed to ache, the result of being whipped around inside the vehicle. A nurse took the wheelchair and pushed it back to the hospital entrance while Trygve went around the front of the truck and got in behind the steering wheel. He cranked the heater and helped Sonja buckle her seatbelt.

"It'll be good to get you home," Trygve said. "Coco has been very sad since you've been gone. Sonny and Cher missed you, too. Every time I go to the barn, those mules bellow up a storm wondering where you are. Of course, they miss all the apples and carrots you bring them, which I don't do."

"Yeah, I know how to spoil them. I've missed them, too." Sonja lay her head against the back of the seat and closed her eyes. Trygve looked at her, worried about her demeanor. Since the accident, she'd been so subdued and pale. Her natural effervescence had disappeared, replaced by an unsettling calm and sense of defeat that left Trygve wondering how to connect with the woman he loved. *Wasn't this what I wanted?* he thought. *Didn't I want Sonja to give up her search for her sister? Now I've got what I wanted, but suddenly it doesn't seem fair.*

He drove silently home to Barre Mills and helped Sonja into the house. Settling her on the couch, he covered her with a comforter, turned on the TV, and went into the kitchen to heat up some soup. Coco snuggled in the crook of Sonja's arm licking her face with pent-up excitement and affection. In the corner by the fireplace, the Christmas tree twinkled with silver bulbs and blue lights, and the spruce tree out on the front yard with its brilliant white lights spread a cheerful glow on the deep snow. Despite the beauty of the season, Sonja now understood with new insight how people could be depressed during the happiest time of the year.

Trygve appeared with a TV tray and set a bowl of hot soup in front of Sonja. She took a taste. It was delicious and warmed her insides, but after several spoonfuls, she couldn't keep her eyes open. She lay back on her pillow and fell asleep still clutching her spoon in her hand.

She awoke with a start a couple of hours later. She could hear Trygve sawing and hammering out in his workshop. The word had gotten out in the last few months about his quirky chairs, and he'd been swamped with Christmas orders. He'd worked every evening and during the weekends to finish a couple of chairs that needed final touches before Christmas Day. During Sonja's nap, he took away the soup and laid her cell phone on the end table where she could easily reach it.

When Sonja woke up, she picked up her phone and checked her inbox. Twenty-two messages were waiting for a response, all from her blue-collar friends. Wally Leatherberry at Windows on the World and Scottie Newcomb at Suds and Duds laundromat sent wishes for a speedy recovery. Art Ravenwald, her artist friend who made mobiles, encouraged her to "take it easy, don't be pigheaded, and listen to Trygve for once." Dean Belton called with news of the death of his wife, Mary Margaret, which saddened Sonja, but he wished her well and encouraged her to contact Rolly Gulbrandsen, the detective who had worked on Katherine's case. Stella Westley, her neighbor on the dairy farm down the road, promised to come with a hot dish and coffee cake and "do anything that needs doing." Many of Sonja's cleaning clients had flooded her phone with encouraging messages expressing their love and concern and postponing their cleaning jobs until she was feeling better. She was overwhelmed by the love and attention that came your way when you crashed your car into a crumpled heap during a snowstorm and then lounged on the couch with a headache and some purplish bruises—all because you were careless and stupid. Suddenly distracted driving took on a whole new meaning. While she was reading her messages, Tanya Pedretti called.

"Hi, Tanya," Sonja said softly. Her normal tone of voice hadn't returned yet. Instead, she sounded wispy, wobbly, and weak.

"Hey, kiddo. How's my favorite amateur detective?" Tanya asked.

"Why are you asking? Do you need my help?" she whispered, chuckling. "I might be out of commission for a few days, according to Dr. Holmes, so you can count me out of any investigations."

"And what did Dr. Holmes say?"

"I have a major concussion, which requires complete rest and quiet. No driving, no cleaning jobs for at least two weeks, and I should expect to be dizzy with headaches now and then. I've got bumps and bruises on my limbs that give new meaning to the color purple. Nothing like having excuses delivered on a silver platter so you don't have to go to work."

"I'm sorry you got banged up," Tanya replied. "I read the report: driving too fast for conditions. One thing I know—you're not going to like the part of Doc's formula that says rest. This would be a great time of year to go on a Bahamas cruise, if you were up to it, but you're not. By the way, the pictures of your mangled car on Facebook are pretty impressive. You should look at the comments when you get a chance. The fact you escaped from that wreck without serious injury is a miracle in itself," Tanya said.

"Oh boy, I haven't seen the car yet, but I can just about imagine. I'll have to check it out. I don't remember much about the whole thing except my crumpled hood, but I really hate to think about shopping for a new car. That's always a pain. I'm hoping the garage can fix it."

"Either way, the sticker shock might send you into heart failure," Tanya replied laconically.

"Any news about my sister?" Sonja asked casually. She really wasn't expecting any news; no one had heard any more about Katherine since her disappearance from Fort Worth, although rumors and innuendos about her whereabouts had cropped up on social media. Trygve had wisely recommended that Sonja reconsider the amount of time she was spending trolling social media platforms about her sister's whereabouts.

"Have you talked to Trygve about it?" Tanya asked.

"No. Why?" Sonja asked sharply. "Are you avoiding the subject?"

"No, not at all," Tanya replied cooly. "Just keeping you accountable to the promises you made when we had lunch. Remember what you said?"

There was a moment of prolonged silence. Finally, Sonja spoke. "Yes, I do remember what I said. I promised that my final probe into my sister's disappearance would be my apology to Mrs. McClintock over in Trempealeau, which I was on my way to do when I got smucked on the highway in Onalaska and ended up in the hospital. I'd like to think

I'm getting a little wiser in life, but I'm wondering if my accident is God's way of saying 'Enough is enough.' I don't know, but it makes you stop and think, doesn't it?" Now it was Tanya's turn to be speechless.

"Tanya? Are you still there?" Sonja asked after several moments of unsettling quiet.

"Yes, I'm here," Tanya said softly. She cringed with trepidation when she thought of Sonja's reaction to the news that her long-lost sister was incarcerated in the La Crosse County Jail. She took a deep breath and spoke.

"Actually, I do have some news about your sister, Katherine. We found her hiding out in a small hunting cabin down on Mundsack Road near Genoa. We went down there and took her into custody without incident. She is currently being held in the La Crosse County Jail without bond—obviously she's considered a flight risk. She's awaiting a trial date."

Sonja felt the room recede. Her mind raced at the thought that, at this very moment, her sister was a mere fifteen miles away. She'd waited thirty years for this revelation, and she was stunned with surprise. Just as suddenly, a wave of apprehension washed over her. What was she supposed to say and do now? For so many years she had imagined this moment, and now that it was here, she couldn't respond. Instead, she was frozen with disbelief.

"You really found her?" she finally asked softly.

"We really found her, kiddo," Tanya said gently. "Take your time absorbing the news. If you want to speak to her, you can call the jail. You can visit her in person, too, when you're ready. But like I said, take time to absorb all that has happened. Right now, you're hurting from your accident, and you need to rest. There will be time later to catch up with your sister. She's not going anywhere."

When there was no forthcoming answer from Sonja, Tanya interrupted the silence. "Sorry, but I've got to get back to work. If you have any questions, call me, okay?"

"Sure. I'll call," Sonja whispered hoarsely. She heard Tanya click off. She lay on the couch for several minutes wondering what she should do.

Trygve walked into the living room a few moments later. "You're awake. How are you feeling?" His shirt sleeves were covered with a light layer of sawdust, and Sonja could smell varnish as he stood by the couch and stared down at her. Her complexion was pale, and she seemed especially somber.

"They found Katherine," Sonja said simply while she stared upward at Trygve.

"Yeah, I know," Trygve said.

Her eyes widened in surprise at the guilty expression on her husband's face. "You knew, and you didn't tell me?" she asked.

"I wasn't going to tell you about your sister when you had just wrecked your car, and you were lying in the hospital with serious injuries. I would have gotten around to it eventually, but at that moment the timing didn't seem right. How did you find out about it?"

"Tanya called and told me."

"As was her duty," Trygve said tersely.

"What about your duty as my husband, Tryg?" Sonja fired back.

"Don't even go there, honey," Trygve began. She could

see his frustration by the frown that wrinkled his forehead and the sudden spark in his brown eyes. "I have been with you through thick and thin, through all the ups and downs of this whole convoluted affair with your sister. If you want me to apologize, I will, but it won't change how I feel. You know I'd do anything to ease the pain your sister's disappearance caused for you all these years, but honestly, I'm sick of this whole thing. You've been draggin' this around for the last fifteen years, as long as I've known you. It's time to put this whole affair to rest. I'm tired of it, and so are you, I think. Am I right?"

"She's my sister, Tryg. It's not like I can just dismiss her and forget about her. I love my sister—"

"Despite the fact that she deceived you and went into hiding for over thirty years! Trygve shouted. "Honestly, honey, I don't get it—"

"No, you don't, Tryg. You don't get it," Sonja said loudly. She grimaced when her headache began throbbing again. "You can't just wave this all away with some kind of magic wand and an abracadabra. It has to be sorted out, which might get a little messy, but I'm going to do it whether you like it or not," she said. She sat up suddenly, then lay back down and stuffed a pillow behind her head. Her headache was revving up again.

"How's the headache?" Trygve asked.

"Apparently, yelling is not good for a concussion," she said.

Trygve sat down beside Sonja and grabbed her hand tightly. They sat quietly for a few moments, the tension between them slowly dissipating.

"Are you with me or not?" Sonja finally asked, pouting.

"Do I have a choice?" he asked, bending over and kissing her cheek.

"Not really."

"Okay, then I'm with you. Tell me what you want to do."

CHAPTER 21 • SONJA

You Said a Mouthful

Have you ever been frozen with the kind of indecision that takes over your life so you can't think, or eat, or sleep? Well, believe me, it's no picnic. After the news about Katherine's arrest and incarceration, I struggled to find the meaning behind the whole ordeal: a terrible crime, a fake death, a sister who deserted her family. How could someone make such poor decisions? I didn't understand any of it, and I had very few answers. Making suppositions only muddled the facts, although I'd spent an inordinate amount of time doing that in the last few days. To top it off, I had to call my sister Darlene to break the news about Katherine's arrest.

"Say what? Will you repeat that? I don't think I heard you right," Darlene demanded when I told her about Katherine's arrest, although I knew there was nothing wrong with her hearing.

"They found Katherine in Genoa," I said calmly.

"Genoa, Italy? How the hell did she get there?" Darlene demanded rudely.

"No, no. Genoa, Wisconsin. It's a little fishing village on the banks of the Mississippi."

"What was she doing there?"

"I don't know. All I know is what the police told me. She rented a small hunting cabin on a quiet country road near Genoa, and she was staying there," I said.

"What were her plans?" Darlene demanded.

"I don't know that either," I said.

"Well, what *do* you know?" my sister barked rudely.

"I know I'm going to visit Katherine at the jail and try to cram thirty years of living into a half-hour visit."

"Good luck with that. Her answers may not help you much."

My mind wandered back to Darlene's association (I hesitated to call it friendship) with the lawyer, Sherry MacMann. I'd been dying to ask her about Sherry. Would I get the truth from her? Probably not, but I was through with the safe, predictable things, so I plunged forward.

"I talked to Sherry MacMann recently," I said carefully.

"Whaddya do that for?" Darlene asked, but her voice had lost some of its normal acidity in the last few minutes. She was wary and suspicious, a rare condition I didn't see very often in my brash, cocky sister.

"You suggested it. Remember?" I said calmly.

"Well, I didn't think you'd actually do it."

"You thought wrong."

"Now listen here, baby sister—" Darlene started. I could tell by the tone in her voice she was going to rally a defense for her secret friendship with the aloof lawyer, but I was in no mood for her verbal karate.

"No, don't say a word, Darlene. Just listen for once," I interrupted. "Just this one time, I want you to listen to what *I* have to say. After my conversation with Sherry, I realized you two have enjoyed a clandestine friendship throughout the years since Katherine's disappearance. You used me as your little guinea pig. I can imagine all the fun you must have had keeping me in the dark all these years.

"It was only out of love," Darlene interrupted.

"Spare me. I don't believe a word of it," I snarled. "You've known for a long time that Katherine was alive somewhere, but you kept it from me so you could control me and use me. That was quite the little show you put on. Convincing Sherry to phone me and threaten me so I'd quit digging into Katherine's case. Well, I have news for you, big sister. I'm done being a victim of your double-dealing, double-crossing games." My voice had increased in volume as I spoke, my heart was racing, and I could feel a blush spreading across my cheeks, but Darlene barged in.

"Now that's about the stupidest thing you've ever said," she snapped. "And hurtful, too." I could hear her sniffling, the beginnings of a fake crying jag, which infuriated me even more.

"You wouldn't know hurt unless it walked up to you and slapped you across the face," I said roughly. "I'm going to see Katherine at the jail. You can do what you want, but don't include me in your plans and don't call me." I disconnected and stood in the kitchen breathing hard, frustration and anger washing over me like waves, the phone clutched in my fist. I turned around suddenly, and there was Trygve.

He opened his arms, and I walked into them. "I've

been waiting for you to do that for a long time, baby," he whispered into my ear.

I pulled back and looked at him. "You have?"

"Yes, it's about time you drew a line in the sand with Darlene."

"But what if she never calls me again?" I asked.

"There are worse things in the world."

I smiled at Trygve. I could always count on him for a good dose of common sense and humor. It helped put things into perspective.

"You'll figure it out as you go," he added quietly. He took my face in his big hands and ran his thumb across my cheek. Then he kissed me long and hard. He pulled back and said, "Don't worry. She'll call eventually, but until then, I'm looking forward to some peace and quiet. A few months without Darlene on the other end of the line sounds mighty good to me. How about you?"

"Actually, that sounds really good," I said, and Tryg hugged me and held me close.

Sonja and Trygve spent Christmas Eve in front of their fireplace with Coco, who chewed enthusiastically on a real soup bone Trygve had saved for him. The mules, Sonny and Cher, were given an extra portion of hay, a pail of shelled corn, and a few juicy red apples as a Christmas treat. They brayed with gusto when he left the barn and shut off the lights.

Trygve made cheese fondue and served it with a French baguette torn into chunks. They drank a whole bottle of red wine while they listened to their favorite Nat King Cole album of nostalgic Christmas songs and cuddled on the couch. Later, Tryg grilled steaks and served twice-baked potatoes with a crisp lettuce salad on the side. Around ten o'clock, Trygve handed out the gifts that were under the tree. From Trygve's parents, Sonja received a Norwegian sweater, something she'd always wanted but had hesitated to buy because of the steep price tag.

"Try it on," Trygve said. "I think it's the right size."

Sonja slipped the wool sweater over her head, then admired herself in the living room mirror. "It looks great on you, even though you're not Norwegian," Trygve commented.

"Well, you aren't, either. You're American with Norwegian ancestry," Sonja argued.

"A minor point," he replied, making a wry face.

"But an important one, nonetheless."

They opened other gifts until Trygve leaned under the tree and dug out a very small, brightly-wrapped gift that said simply "To Tryg."

Carefully peeling off the paper, Trygve pried open the long, narrow box. Inside lay two airline tickets to Norway and a weeklong itinerary of a cruise along the Norwegian coastline in June, including a visit to the cousins of his parents. "Holy smokes! That'll break the bank," he said. He leaned over and kissed Sonja. "Thanks, honey, but with my new job, I'm not sure I'll be able to get off that many days."

"You'll only use four days of vacation. We'll leave on a Friday and come home the following Sunday, which gives us nine days. I worked it all out with your boss. One more thing—your parents chipped in a hunk of change to make this happen, so I can't take full credit."

"Well, no matter what, it's a great gift. Thanks, baby," he said. "This trip is going to be great."

Sonja yawned and stretched her arms upward toward the ceiling. "I'm tired. Let's go to bed," she suggested. She stood slowly and walked down the hall toward the bedroom. "Oh, by the way, you need to take me to Middleton on Sunday since I'm not supposed to drive yet."

"Why are we going to Middleton?" Trygve asked.

"There's someone I need to talk to," Sonja explained.

"Does this have something to do with your sister?"

"Yes, but believe me, I'm only fulfilling a promise I made to Tanya. You can't argue with the chief of police, Tryg."

"Well, I could—"

"—but you'd lose," Sonja finished. "We'll leave about nine, okay?"

Trygve saluted crisply. "At your service, ma'am."

"That's more like it," Sonja remarked with a smile.

CHAPTER 22

Silence Is Golden

Sunday morning dawned cold and frosty. Overnight, river fog had moved inland, and the trees and fields were glazed with frost, turning the scenery into a winter wonderland. Trygve and Sonja enjoyed the icy landscape as they drove southeast toward Madison, talking little, their thoughts centered on the newest development in the saga of Sonja's sister.

When they reached Middleton, Sonja directed Trygve to the Care Cove Retirement Center, a sprawling condominium that featured assisted living apartments and a wing dedicated to full-time nursing care for patients with Alzheimer's. Trygve dropped Sonja off at the front entrance, promising to return an hour later to pick her up. He headed to a nearby lumberyard that specialized in exotic woods, which he needed for a specific chair project.

The front desk of the facility was manned by a middle-aged, friendly woman dressed in pink nursing scrubs who greeted Sonja with a smile. "How can I help you?" she asked politely.

"I'm here to see Rolly Gulbrandsen," Sonja replied. The woman referred to a chart on the wall, which showed a floor plan. She ran her finger over the small squares.

"Yes, he's on the second floor, apartment 289. Does he know you're coming?"

"Yes, I called him yesterday," Sonja answered.

"Then you're all cleared to go up. Just sign the guest register here and enjoy your visit."

Sonja groaned inwardly as she walked to the elevator. She wasn't sure what former Detective Gulbrandsen was going to tell her or even what he would remember, but she wanted to pick his brain about her sister's case. All she wanted was someone to confirm the facts about Katherine's drowning that she'd read in the police reports. Then she'd be ready to visit her sister in the La Crosse County Jail. She couldn't deny a second motive in scheduling this visit: Being well armed with the facts was her new best strategy for maintaining her mental health, which lately had fluctuated wildly. Dr. Law, Dr. Tom Nielson, and her friend Tanya had all expressed their concern for her state of mind, and she was determined to take their advice and, as much as humanly possible, put her mind at ease with the facts. But despite her strategy, some days she was buoyed by hope, and other days she felt defeated under a weight of depression and anger.

Sonja knocked on the door of apartment 289. A few moments later, the door opened. A man with short-cropped gray hair and brown eyes peered at her. He was stooped with arthritis, his back hunched from the crippling disease.

"Sonja, I presume?" he said quietly, extending his hand.

"Yes, I'm Sonja Hovland," she said, clasping his hand. "Thanks for seeing me today, Mr. Gulbrandsen."

"You may not thank me once we've talked," Rolly said tartly. "If I were you, I'd reserve judgment until we're done."

"I'll take my chances," Sonja replied. He smiled warmly.

"Come in, please," Rolly said and directed Sonja into a small, cozy living room furnished with a loveseat and two recliners. The television was droning softly in the background, and Rolly turned it off, inviting Sonja to sit down on the loveseat.

"Do you want something to drink? Coffee, tea, or water?" Rolly asked. Sonja shook her head. "Or maybe something stronger?" he teased, his eyes twinkling.

"Oh, no! I don't drink alcohol in the middle of the day," Sonja said.

The old detective sat down opposite Sonja in a recliner and leaned forward, clasping his hands together. "So, let's get right to it then. What is it you'd like to know?" he asked.

"I don't know if you've heard the recent news about my sister. They found her last week living in a small hunting cabin near Genoa," Sonja explained.

"Oh, yes. It made the Madison news," Rolly said, nodding his head vigorously. "I just about fell off my chair when I heard it, but then, I always believed she was alive somewhere. Of course, nobody is interested in what an old, retired detective has to say about a case that's over thirty years old," Rolly said. Then he smiled. "Nobody except you, that is." Although his smile was warm, he had an austere quality about him that Sonja found interesting. She could feel the weight of his analytical mind and his keen sense of curiosity settle on her. He leaned back and crossed his arms over his chest as he observed her, waiting for her to speak. *Still a detective even after all these years*, she thought.

"I'm very interested in what you have to say," Sonja said. "Why did you believe my sister was still alive after all these years had passed? There must have been something about the drowning scene that tipped you off."

"Well, first of all, you have to understand how this case affected the La Crosse community. People were shocked to their core. Nothing else that had happened in the city's history came close to having such a profound effect, except maybe the disappearance of Evelyn Hartley back in the early 1950s and the drowning of several young male college students in the Mississippi in the '90s. The case of the bombing at the university sent shockwaves throughout the state. A lot of parents withdrew their kids from the university because of the violent nature of the crime. You can't blame them. I talked to parents who were afraid the bombing would set off a string of copycat events, although I was pretty sure that wasn't going to happen. Still, I understood their concerns. As is typical of a major criminal case, everyone and their dog thought they knew something about the drowning and the bombing, but in the end, all the theories and speculation eventually butt heads with the cold, hard facts, as it always does."

"I have to be honest here, Mr. Gulbrandsen. I've been struggling with this my whole life," Sonja said soberly.

Rolly nodded, his face an expression of solemnity and understanding. "I believe you, and that's normal. Anyone who confronts the reality of a loved one's violent death or a family member who's gone missing under suspicious circumstances lives with the uncertainty of a very difficult situation. Explanations fail, doubts set in, anger and sadness follow—it can be a vicious cycle, but it goes with the territory," Rolly said. "Tell me what things you've struggled with over the years."

Sonja swallowed hard and began. "My sister was a great athlete. She jogged, swam in Lake Superior, sailed, and kayaked on the water all the time. I couldn't accept that she had drowned. It would have been easier for me to believe she'd been abducted or murdered than to believe she'd drowned. Now all these years later, I've discovered I was right all along. She didn't drown. She faked her own death, and by all indications, she seems to have lived a successful life in Texas, and she almost got away with it."

"Well, she did get away with it for over thirty years, which is a remarkable feat in itself. But as I'm sure you've been told, being a great swimmer is no guarantee when it comes to the currents in the Mississippi," Rolly said. "Let me tell you what we found in the river. You might remember that nobody could find your sister Katherine immediately after the explosion, even though the Ainsworth brothers told the police she'd driven the getaway vehicle. A fisherman found a shoe and a paddle along the shore near Green Island and brought them into the station the day after the bombing. That was the first indication we had about where she'd gone after the crime."

"Well, I was only ten at the time, but since then I've learned more about those immediate hours after the bombing," Sonja explained.

Rolly continued. "The kayak was jammed into the shoreline near Blackhawk Park and was found a couple of days after she disappeared. That same day, the boat patrol found her life vest drifting in open water below Target Lake in the main channel. The life vest was a big issue for me. It didn't make sense that someone who was drowning would remove their life vest. Why would you take off the one thing that could save you and keep you afloat in the river currents? To me, that made no sense at all. That's when I started getting suspicious about the drowning. The fact that she went kayaking at night in April also tipped me off that something wasn't right about the whole thing. It was still pretty cold to be kayaking. Some places close to shore were still frozen over. And since we never recovered a body or parts of a body, I believed that she faked her own death and escaped from the area, although many of my colleagues doubted that a young college girl could plan something like that and get away undetected."

"Was there anything else that triggered your suspicions other than the vest?" Sonja asked.

"Not really. The location of the vest in open water was the one piece of evidence that I questioned from the beginning. I believed she had been wearing the vest, but others argued with me that she could have just had it in the kayak, and when it tipped over, the vest went in the river with the other equipment. It was a valid argument, I guess, but something about the whole thing bothered me. Call it intuition or experience—whatever. As time went by, her disappearance faded from people's memories, and they went back to their daily lives." He stopped speaking briefly and stared through the window at the snow gently falling outside. "Every cop has certain cases that come back to haunt you. Katherine's drowning would come up in conversations with other cops through the years. I never forgot it. When I heard the news that they'd found Katherine, I wasn't really surprised. I'd been expecting her to turn up someday. And she did."

"Oh, I'm so glad I came to talk to you," Sonja said with heartfelt conviction. "For years, I've felt so alone in my belief that Katherine was still alive somewhere, and I've just about driven my husband crazy in my search for the truth. I'm not sure how to navigate the next steps in reconnecting with my sister, but I guess I'll figure that out as I go, too."

"Yes, I'm sure you will," Rolly said. "You seem to have plenty of determination and resilience. I hope things work out for you. Just remember this: You have another opportunity to repair your relationship with your sister. I hope you can forgive her, because when you forgive, you don't change the past. You change the future."

Sonja nodded her head in agreement. "I never thought of it that way, but that's very true." She stood and reached down to shake Rolly's hand. "Thanks so much for clearing up some of my confusion. This has been quite a journey, but I'm thankful I persisted in getting to the bottom of the whole thing."

"I'm glad I could help. At my age, not too many people are interested in what I have to say anymore. Keep in touch, and I hope things turn out well between you and your sister."

Sonja walked to the door of the apartment. She turned and said, "Thanks again, Rolly. What you told me has really helped."

"It was my pleasure. Have a good trip home," he said as he closed the door softly.

Trygve was waiting near the front entrance when Sonja returned to the ground floor of the facility. She climbed into the truck and tucked her purse next to her on the seat.

"Well?" Trygve asked.

Sonja shrugged nonchalantly, but her heart was full and weirdly satisfied after her talk with Rolly. "Let's just say, I'm at peace."

"So this trip was worth the drive?" Trygve questioned.

"Absolutely," Sonja responded.

"Are you going to tell me what the wise old owl said?" Trygve asked.

"Maybe, but I've got to think about it for a while."

"Fair enough. Lunch?"

"Sounds great. Know of a good Chinese place?"

"As a matter of fact, I do," Trygve said.

CHAPTER 23

Ring of Fire

Katherine Waite lay on her cot in cell #10 at the La Crosse County Jail listening to the sounds floating around her. Everything here was open, and noise traveled insidiously, louder than normal, hovering around you, interrupting your thoughts and, more importantly, your sleep. For someone who had lived alone most of her adult life, adjusting to the noise level was difficult, but to complain was unnecessary. She'd put herself here as surely as if she'd walked into the police station and said, "Here I am. Put me in jail." What had possessed her to travel back to Wisconsin and take up residence in such close proximity to her sister Sonja? What had she been thinking?

She realized now that some strange psychological phenomenon must have invaded her brain and drawn her back to her home state, to the very town that had sent her running from the consequences of her actions over thirty years ago. She'd wracked her brain trying to understand her own motives. Was it guilt? Curiosity? Belligerence? A stubborn refusal to acknowledge reality? Was she delusional or just plain stupid? She didn't know, but whatever it was, the experience of incarceration was becoming very real to Katherine. Losing her freedom and the ability to make her own choices had deeply impacted her. Now her focus each day was to simply survive moment to moment—survive the noise, the invasion of privacy, the insults of the other inmates, and the mind-numbing boredom. Just survive.

Christmas had come and gone. Do-gooders from several churches and ministries in town had come around with paltry gifts, singing worn-out Christmas carols, and sharing plates of stale cookies. Katherine supposed they meant well and had good intentions, but to her, it seemed like a slap in the face. She spent Christmas Day reading magazines, drinking coffee, and avoiding interactions with others. Her pallid complexion, serious demeanor, and monosyllabic responses drove away anyone who attempted to have a conversation with her.

It wasn't until late on Christmas night that her defenses began to break down. She realized neither of her sisters was going to come and visit her, and although it saddened her, she refused to let the situation upset her. Since her drive from Texas and her capture, she'd used one of the jail's laptops to trace the whereabouts of Darlene and Sonja. She was surprised to find that Sonja was well-known in the La Crosse area. Her cleaning business around town had a stellar reputation. But more surprising was the reputation she'd gained in the community for her detective skills, especially after a case she'd been involved in last year. A dead dentist discovered in his chair without a mark on his body? It sounded like an authentic conundrum that only professionals could solve, and yet her sister, an amateur upstart, had been instrumental in helping the police capture the culprit who had committed the crime. How was that even possible?

Her other sister, Darlene, had a very different story. She had distinguished herself over the years as well, but not to any degree of excellence or renown. Divorced and fired from her job as a dispatcher at the Lake Elmo Police Department for disseminating official police business to the general public, Dar seemed to struggle with personal relationships and mental health issues. She frequently posted tirades on Facebook about everything from homosexuality to gender dysphoria to government abuse and excess. She was a lightning rod for insults and stinging rebuttals, which she seemed to welcome and even enjoy.

When the lights in the hallway finally dimmed at eleven, and the jail became quieter, Katherine lay down on her cot, rolled toward the wall, and pulled a thin jail-issued blanket over her shoulders. Scenes from childhood Christmas celebrations played on the movie screen of her mind. They had been happy times of family unity with her parents and sisters. Memories of holiday food, especially Swedish kringle, a sparkling Christmas tree decorated with tinsel and lights, an evening church service filled with old familiar Christmas carols, children with bright, eager faces, and gifts lying beneath the tree waiting to be torn open in excitement when they returned home, flooded her mind. Suddenly, without realizing it, she was crying deep, gasping sobs. Exhaustion, regret, and sadness washed over her, and when she finished crying, she fell into a deep sleep.

Several days after the new year, while Sonja recuperated from her accident and enjoyed a hiatus from her cleaning jobs, she prepared to visit her sister Katherine for the first time. She went to her favorite bookstore on Pearl Street and bought a book about crochet, remembering that Katherine had been enthralled with the hobby as a teenager and had made several hats and doilies. She bought some crochet hooks and colorful yarn. Along with the craft items, she included other things like hand lotion, shampoo, a deck of playing cards, a Scrabble game, and a soft velour sweater. She placed all of it into a large bag filled with tissue, and at the last minute, she jammed in a small book of poetry entitled *Dog Show* by U.S. poet laureate Billy Collins.

Although the act of stuffing the items in the bag was therapeutic, she wondered how the gifts would be received by her sister. Ever since Tanya had called and told her about Katherine's capture, Sonja had struggled with a tangle of ambivalent feelings in varying degrees of intensity: anger, disgust, confusion, and yes, even fond remembrance and love. She didn't know how she could still love her sister after all the things she'd done. Sonja remembered the sadness everyone had experienced at the news of her death, and the subsequent revelation of her involvement in a major terrorist crime. She was sure it had contributed to the early demise of her parents. How was she supposed to forgive Katherine for that? She shook her head as these thoughts and others bounced around in her head. Trygve walked into the kitchen while she was finishing up the gift bag.

"Whatcha doin'?" he asked, coming up behind her and looking over her shoulder.

"Just putting together a little gift bag for Katherine,"

Sonja replied. "I bought some stuff I thought she might like to keep herself entertained while she's in jail."

"Bringing gifts is a nice gesture, but what are you going to talk about? Have you figured that out yet, because I think that's more important than this other stuff," he said as he pointed at the bag.

"To be truthful, I have no idea what we'll talk about. I'm sure it'll be awkward at first. Believe me, honey, I have no illusions about this. After all, I haven't seen my sister for over thirty years. How could it *not* be awkward?"

"That's true, I suppose. You want me to drive you over to the jail and wait outside?"

Sonja gave Trygve a shy grin and tilted her head to one side. "No, but thanks for the offer. I'll drive myself into town, so you're off the hook. This is something I have to do myself." She hugged Trygve tightly. "Thank you for sticking with me, Tryg," she whispered in his ear. "I know this hasn't been easy for you." She pulled back and looked into his kind, brown eyes.

"You can say that again."

"I know this hasn't been easy for you," she repeated with a teasing grin. Trygve smiled and kissed her.

"When are you going?" he asked.

"In about five minutes. I should be home by four-thirty or so. If I stay longer, I'll call you, okay?"

"All right. Want me to make something to eat later?"

"Sure," Sonja said.

"Tacos?"

"Yeah, that sounds great, along with some good beer. Wish me luck, Tryg," Sonja said softly.

"You don't need luck, hon, but you need a lot of other

things."

"Like what?" Sonja asked, puzzled by Trygve's comment.

"Like forgiveness, understanding, empathy, grit, courage—"

"I got it, Tryg," Sonja interrupted.

"I hope so."

"There's nothing like high expectations to get your nervous energy pumping. I'll see you later," Sonja said as she leaned down and picked up the gift bag. She walked silently to the garage, climbed into the loaner car from the body shop that was fixing her Subaru, and proceeded down the driveway. When she looked in the rearview mirror, she could see Trygve standing by the living room window watching as she drove away. She wished none of this had happened, but it was something she didn't have any control over. You couldn't turn back the hands of time, could you? You couldn't control fate or other people's choices. All she could do was control her own responses to whatever happened at the jail. She thought again about what Rolly Gulbrandsen had told her: "When you forgive, you don't change the past. You change the future."

"Here's to the future," she whispered as she stepped on the gas.

CHAPTER 24

Wouldn't It Be Nice?

Collette Tierney snuggled closer to Hatchet Brousard. They were watching a movie in Collette's cozy living room after returning from dinner at a new Mexican restaurant called Taco Supremo. The lights were turned low, and they each sipped a delicious glass of wine from a local vineyard. Collette marveled at the relationship that had developed between them. For two people who'd thought they were self-sufficient and comfortable in their single lives, things had certainly exploded like a bolt out of the blue into a sizzling romance.

"Remember that first night we had pizza together back in September?" Collette asked softly.

Hatchet turned to her, and his eyes softened. "Oh, yeah. How could I forget? I don't remember anything about the pizza. I just spent my time feasting my eyes on your beauty."

Even though the phrase was a worn-out cliché, she knew Hatchet was sincere. Collette raised her eyebrows. "My take was a little different. You seemed to be so in control, such a gentleman, all business."

"And now I'm not?" he asked, kissing her tenderly.

"No, now you're not. Now I know what's under the surface of all that tough exterior. And you should really let others see your vulnerability more often. It's very winsome, you know."

"That's something most men—especially cops—aren't willing to do," Hatchet said.

"Well, that's fine, I guess," Collette continued, "as long as you keep showing it to me."

They kissed warmly.

"Heard any more about Katherine Waite?" Collette asked.

"She went to jail without a whimper. I wouldn't have believed it if I hadn't seen it myself. Hiding out in that little cabin down in that peaceful valley near Genoa was not where I thought she'd land. I still can't understand what pulled her back to a place where her chances of being discovered were pretty good. The chief was surprised at how submissive she was during the whole process," Hatchet said, "but that's probably how she managed to elude law enforcement for so long. She kept her nose clean and stayed true to her invented persona. Apparently, she never hinted that she had a family here in Wisconsin. The people who knew her at the plant only knew her in the context of the workplace. She lived an extremely secretive, private life. That's hard to pull off for thirty-some years."

Collette nodded in agreement. "I wonder how Sonja's doing with all this," she said. "I sent her a message after her accident, but I never heard back from her, which is unusual. Underneath all her bravado, Sonja is a very sensitive person. This must be terribly difficult for her to process."

"Anybody, bravado or not, would have trouble with a situation like this. Brady, my friend who's a jailer, says Katherine is very quiet, keeps to herself, and doesn't seem to want to develop any relationships with other people. Sonja might find her sister harder to connect with than she thought."

"Maybe the real world is a little too real for Katherine. It looks like her history has finally caught up with her. Know what I mean?" Collette asked.

"Yeah, I do know what you mean," Hatchet responded with a sigh. "That's not unlike me before I met you."

"How so?"

"Ever since my failed relationship with Tanya way back when we were in college, I kinda shut myself off to the possibilities that existed out there for me. I wasn't interested in anyone or anything that reminded me of my failures. But then you coaxed me out of my cave, so to speak, and I began to see that good things could still happen to a forty-year-old injured cop who was trying to find his way back to some kind of normal."

"I did that?" Collette said, laying her hand across her chest. "Are you sure?"

"Yeah, you did that, baby, and I love you for it."

"Not a problem. Glad I could help," Collette said with a smile. "Anytime."

THE MIDDLE OF JANUARY

Sonja arrived in the parking lot of the La Crosse County Jail on Fourth Street, and for a few moments she sat in the car trying to muster up her courage to go into the building.

The gift bag sat in the seat beside her, a bag that represented promise and comfort, hope and joy. But Sonja was having serious misgivings about visiting her sister. Breaking the ice to establish a line of communication after a period of thirty-five years of silence was much harder than she had anticipated. It would be difficult and awkward. Her stomach rumbled with distress, and she clutched the car keys tightly in her hand. Grabbing her purse and the gift bag, Sonja stepped out of the car. Her boots clumped on the cold, hard pavement as she made her way to the entrance. It was bitterly cold, and her breath formed little clouds of condensation.

She pulled the door open and walked in. Seated behind a glass enclosure, a jail attendant looked up from the book he was reading when she approached the window.

"Can I help you?" he asked.

"I'm here to see Katherine Waite," she said.

"I'll need to see some ID. Do you have a Securus account?"

"Yes, I do. I registered online earlier," Sonja explained.

"Then a driver's license would be sufficient. I can just check your account and verify your identity from there," the attendant explained.

Sonja dug in her purse and retrieved her driver's license. She handed it over, and once the attendant verified her identity, he gave it back to her. "Can I see my sister now?" she asked.

"Just have a seat, and I'll call you when we have everything ready," he said, pointing her to a chair in the small waiting area. Fifteen minutes later, the attendant came back to the window and called Sonja over. "Okay, we're ready. Just come in through this door."

The door buzzed, and Sonja walked through it.

"What's in the bag?" the attendant asked.

"Just some things I thought my sister might enjoy."

The attendant shook his head. "All packages need to go through ICare to be delivered to the prisoner. You'll have to leave the package here, but she'll get it on Friday. We have to follow security protocol, ma'am."

"That's fine. I'll just leave it with you," Sonja said.

When the security procedures were over, he led the way to the elevator, where they rode up to the second floor. Stepping out of the elevator, Sonja followed the man down a long hallway. They walked to the end and turned right down another hallway until they stopped in front of a solid door with an observation port. When the door opened, a jail attendant stood inside against the wall, and a small, petite woman sat on one side of a long table. She looked up expectantly when Sonja walked in. Suddenly the moment had arrived—the moment when Sonja realized her sister looked like her sister from long ago. She stared at the woman with the same coarse brown hair now streaked with gray and cut in a simple wedge style, the light hazel eyes that looked like they'd seen a ghost, the tiny nose and ears, the compact, athletic body she'd had when they were kids. She looked familiar, so familiar that Sonja began to cry, which set off tears in Katherine. The two sisters regarded each other as the years rushed by in a flurry of memories.

For several moments, words were not needed. The tears and the clasping of hands said it all. Finally, they both spoke at once, which broke the tension, and they began laughing at the incongruity of this bizarre moment.

"You go first," Sonja said. "You're the oldest."

"Don't remind me," she said grinning. "You always were a stickler for details. Tell me about your life."

"That might take a while."

"I've got nothin' but time," Katherine said.

Sonja dipped her head in a shy gesture and launched into a recollection of her life: attending college in La Crosse, starting her cleaning business, meeting and marrying Trygve, losing three babies. Finally, after half an hour, she ran out of things to say.

"Sounds interesting," Katherine said.

"Now it's your turn," Sonja said. "What about you? Tell me what you've been doing."

"After I left La Crosse, I ended up in Fort Worth, Texas. I bummed around for a few days getting my bearings, then I landed a job at Innovative Fabrications, and the next thirty-five years is history . . . up until the shooting in September. Everything changed that day. My choices caught up with me."

"But up until then, you had a good life, right?" Sonja asked.

Katherine shrugged her shoulders. "Depends on how you define a good life. I had all the material possessions I needed to live comfortably, but I had to learn to go it alone, to trust no one for fear I'd be discovered and be arrested. That doesn't lend itself to feelings of security and confidence."

"You were always looking over your shoulder?"

"That's one way to put it. But not anymore. Now I have to face what I tried to run away from thirty-five years ago."

With that statement, the conversation seemed to dry up and blow away. Sonja sensed that Katherine was overwhelmed by the exchange about the past they'd had.

Telling their stories had left both women emotionally exhausted; it seemed they had reached the end of the visit. Whatever connection they'd made now was over for the time being.

Sonja stood abruptly, stretching her legs. "I think it's time for me to vamoose," she said, "but I'll be back again in a few days, and we can talk some more then."

"Right. That sounds good. I need time to process everything you've told me," Katherine said. "Thanks for coming."

The two women clasped hands briefly, Sonja turned and left the room, and Katherine was taken back to her cell. Later that week, as Katherine lay on her cot reading the poetry book Sonja had brought her, she wondered how the conflict and inconsistency in her life would be resolved. Her trial wasn't on the court schedule yet, and she was already concerned about the possible outcomes that might come from a lengthy trial. She wasn't naïve. She knew a lengthy prison sentence awaited her, but Sonja's visit had encouraged her, if only for a moment. At least one of her sisters wasn't hanging her out to dry after the way she had disgraced the family name by being involved in a major terrorist event. That was admirable. Katherine had always known that Sonja was gutsy and brave. If anyone was willing to take a chance on her, it was Sonja. She wondered if Darlene knew she was in jail. Katherine sighed heavily. So many unanswered questions. She went back to reading another poem by Billy Collins from a collection of poems called *Dog Show*, and she thought it spoke rather poignantly about her current situation.

In the poem, the dog is portrayed as the guardian of the

farm, always at his post, protecting against intruders who may have evil intentions. That's what she'd become over the years, a guardian of her secret. She read the last few stanzas again:

> Is it madness, this inability to distinguish
> Between friend or foe, or is it wise
> If you can't tell one from another,
> To run barking madly after everyone
> Simply to be on the safe side?
>
> Whatever the case, it's a kind of job
> And you're free to do it all year round.
> And in return, this guardian of family
> And farm, roosters and hens,
> Is rewarded with kibble and scraps
> And a porch to sleep on when it rains.
> And best of all, he is given a name
> That is his and his alone,
> Enough to turn his head and bring him home.

Katherine thought about the phrase "to distinguish between friend and foe." She seemed to struggle with that concept, probably because she'd kept everyone at arm's length for so many years. She was definitely out of practice when it came to determining whether someone was a friend or an enemy. But she smiled at the last few phrases of the poem: "he is given a name" and "bring him home." She had come full circle; she once again possessed her real name, Katherine Waite, and she was home, although she didn't have a porch to sleep on—yet.

CHAPTER 25

Fundamental Things Apply as Time Goes By

JUNE

It was a beautiful summer day in June with plenty of warm sunshine, a hazy blue sky, and the smell of freshly mown grass lingering in the air. Sonja stood in the doorway of the barn watching Sonny and Cher stretching their necks under the wooden fence for mouthfuls of tender grass just beyond the corral. The flock of chickens pecked nervously at the potato and carrot peelings and eggshells Sonja had scattered on the ground for them this morning. Coco sat obediently at Sonja's feet and watched the activities of the farm animals with dispassionate boredom.

Trygve was busy maneuvering his tractor in the far pasture, raising and lowering the bucket, scraping dirt from a ditch into a shallow swale that had developed over winter. Sonja smiled. Trygve loved his tractor time. She doubted that he needed a tractor. After all, they only owned forty acres, but the urge to farm and do farming things was strong, and she supposed if it made her husband happy, then who was she to question his motives?

She walked slowly across the barnyard toward the back of the house. Trygve had decided to replace their wooden deck, expand its size, and put a lattice roof over it for more protection from the sun. He'd ripped off all the old material and replaced the four-by-four posts and bracing. Now he would start putting on the new boards. Coco snuffled loudly and sniffed the pile of lumber for the new deck. Sonja entered the door to the garage and walked into the kitchen. Her phone, which was lying on the counter, was ringing.

"Sonja Hovland. May I help you?" she answered.

"Sonja, Tanya here. Are you ready for more of your sister's trial today?" Katherine's trial was in its second week, and today there would be more testimony about the thirty-five-year-old crime.

"Well, it depends on what you mean by ready," Sonja said. "Ready for the truth? I hope that's what I'll hear, but I guess I'll keep an open mind about Katherine's involvement in the bombing. Hopefully she wasn't in on the planning of it, although she would probably never admit it if she was."

"How have your visits been with her?" Tanya asked.

"We have a long way to go in making an emotional connection. We've exchanged a lot of facts, but the depth of our conversations usually just skims the surface. Maybe things will change over time, but I'm beginning to think Katherine has walled herself off and she's happy in her insulated world. She's having a hard time connecting with me."

"That's not too encouraging," Tanya said sympathetically. "How can I help?"

"I don't know that you can," Sonja said. "Who's testifying today? Do you know?"

"The latest is that the two officers from Fort Worth will be giving their testimonies, although I don't know what they could tell us that we don't already know. Of course, it would probably be new information for the jurors. I've been asked to testify about her capture. And the scuttlebutt around the law enforcement center is that Collin Ainsworth is set to appear and give his rendition of the events leading up to and including the day of the bombing. That might prove interesting."

"Frankly, none of this fascinates me, if you want to know the truth. In fact, I'll be glad when this is over, and the judge makes her final decision," Sonja said with a bitter tinge in her voice. "Maybe then Katherine and I can get a footing in our relationship and move on to new territory."

"It will be difficult no matter what happens, but you've handled yourself well, Sonja. Is Trygve coming with you today?"

"Yes, he's planning on it."

"Good. I'll see you there," Tanya said, and she hung up.

The trial of Katherine Waite caused a major stir in the media, both locally and nationally. After Katherine had been captured, a special report aired on a La Crosse television station which reiterated the gory details of the bombing event at the university. A national outlet had picked up the report and re-broadcast it, which caused a considerable stir in the nation's memory. A reporter called it "one of the first domestic terrorist events in United States history," which, in Sonja's opinion, was a disgusting attempt to grab the spotlight and exaggerate the truth.

Unfortunately, the reporter's analysis of the event found an audience, and Sonja, Trygve, and Darlene had been thrust into the limelight for all the wrong reasons. Darlene seemed to relish the attention as only a narcissist could, while Sonja and Trygve maintained a silent, dignified demeanor, which seemed to encourage wild speculation on social media about their relationship with Katherine and the dynamics of their family. Every part of it sickened Sonja. Regret, loss, and frustration dominated her thoughts until, in desperation, she'd lifted a prayer heavenward. Then, and only then, did the tension ease.

After her conversation with Tanya, she spent time carefully selecting her clothes for the trial. She chose a pair of navy dress slacks, a crisp white blouse with a muted scarf around the neck, pearl earrings, and a conservative navy blazer. She spent extra time on her makeup and hair. When Trygve came in from his tractor work, he whistled appreciatively.

"You look great, honey," he said as he kissed her cheek.

"Flattery will get you everywhere," Sonja said, although joking about the trial felt like a betrayal. "I might enjoy this if my sister's future wasn't on the line," she said sourly.

"Actions have consequences," Trygve said. When he looked over at Sonja, she stared at him, a frown crinkling her forehead.

"Just the truth and nothing but the truth," he concluded sheepishly, holding up his hands.

"We need to leave by nine-thirty. Will you be ready by then?" Sonja asked briskly.

"Absolutely. I'll shower right now and get ready," Trygve said, picking up on his wife's solemn attitude.

A few minutes after nine, Trygve and Sonja climbed into the Subaru and drove into La Crosse to the courthouse on Vine Street. The sun glinted from the large windows on the block-like structure, and Sonja noticed a crowd of reporters that had gathered in the lobby. They managed to avoid the press by using a side service door, and they stepped into the elevator. After going through the security screening, they found a place in the gallery among the crowd that had gathered. Tanya came in a few minutes later and leaned across a row of chairs. She was dressed in a beige pencil skirt, a black shell, and beige sandals. Her arms glowed with the beginnings of a tan, and her makeup and hair were flawless. *She looks happy,* thought Sonja. *Things must be better with Roy.*

"How are you doing?" she asked.

"We're fine," Trygve said, speaking for his wife. "We're heading to Norway at the end of June. Hopefully all of this will be over by then."

"It needs to be over," Sonja said gruffly.

"Hang in there," Tanya encouraged. "Today will probably be the end of the testimonies, the evidence has been presented, and then the jury will deliberate. The toughest day will be her sentencing, but let's take things as they come." She reached over and squeezed Sonja's hand, then found a seat in one of the front rows closest to the defendant's table. Fifteen minutes later, Katherine was escorted into the courtroom. She looked pale and subdued sitting beside the district attorney.

Judge Sylvia Benson entered the courtroom, and the proceeding began. After several testimonies, including the two Fort Worth detectives who'd accurately identified

Kitty Currant as the missing Katherine Waite, Collin Ainsworth was called to the stand. Sonja was taken aback at his appearance. He had a swarthy complexion and was dangerously handsome with dark curly hair, brown, luminous eyes, and full lips. However, even good looks couldn't hide the effects of his prolonged incarceration. He had a hunted look, his eyes wandering furtively around the courtroom. The only time he seemed calm was when he looked at Katherine, who smiled at him shyly.

The prosecuting attorney led Collin through the planning and execution of the bombing, reviewing the details for the jury. When asked if Katherine had helped in the planning of the event, he answered no; she had only driven the van in which the two Ainsworth brothers had escaped from the scene. Once they returned to their apartment, Katherine had vanished, and he hadn't seen her again until she returned to the Bad Axe Valley several months ago, when he had spent the night with her at the hunting cabin.

Sonja couldn't adequately describe the relief she felt when the judge gave her final instructions to the jury. Katherine had decided not to testify, waiting instead for an opportunity to speak at her sentencing, where she would offer an apology to the McClintock family. A brief glance and hesitant smile from Katherine were the last impressions Sonja kept in her mind as the jury was escorted from the courtroom to a room where they would begin their deliberations.

Tanya waited for Trygve and Sonja to gather up their things, and they retreated to a small coffee shop across the street from the courthouse until the jury came back with a verdict. Sonja was too keyed up to have anything other than water, but Trygve had a piece of cherry pie and a cup of coffee.

"What did you think of Collin's testimony?" Trygve asked Tanya.

"Straightforward and to the point. He didn't embellish anything. It was effective, I thought," Tanya replied, "and honest."

"Well, I'm glad he didn't embellish his description of his night at the cabin with Katherine," Sonja spouted suddenly. "All that would do is add to the mystique of their star-crossed love affair."

Trygve gently wrapped his arm around Sonja and pulled her close. "It'll be over pretty soon, honey. I know it's tough to hear all this."

Sonja moaned. "You have no idea what it's like until it happens to you."

Fifteen minutes later, Tanya looked at her phone. "They're back with a verdict. Let's get over there," she said.

They crossed the street in a hurry and barely got a seat before the jury filed into the courtroom. When everyone had settled down, Judge Benson addressed the jury.

"What say you to the charge of fleeing the state to avoid a warrant for arrest?"

"Guilty."

"For the charge of domestic terrorism, U.S. Code 2331, what say you?

"Guilty."

Judge Benson paused a moment at the solemnity of the occasion. "The prisoner will be remanded to the La Crosse

County Jail until the time of sentencing, which will be determined at a later date. The court thanks the jury for their service. We are adjourned."

In the weeks that followed Katherine's conviction, Sonja began preparing for their trip to Norway, scheduled for later in June. They would depart from Rochester and fly to Oslo. Their itinerary included a few days in the capital city and then a cruise along the coastline from Bergen to Trondheim, where they would experience the majestic coastline of the Geirangerfjord. Trygve was as excited as Sonja had ever seen him. She assumed his excitement came from the chance to escape the constant attention of social media and the fallout from Katherine's now infamous lost years and misadventures in crime.

"Are you looking forward to our trip?" Sonja asked one evening as they walked along the road.

"Oh, yes. I can't wait to see the places my parents have talked about so much. They've been to Norway five times, you know."

"Yes, I know that. They were disappointed that we weren't staying longer, but I explained we had to get back to our jobs," Sonja said.

The evening was beautiful. The sun was beginning to set behind the towering pine trees on the hillsides, and the temperature was warm with the scent of summer in the air. Their neighbor, Tom Stettler, who owned a beautiful dairy farm next door, was just letting his cows out to pasture after the evening milking, and he waved a friendly greeting. When they got home, they would play a game of Scrabble. Sonja fully expected Trygve would trounce her as usual, although she was sure that some of the words he used were made up on the fly to try and impress her. When she challenged him, and they looked up the word in the dictionary, he pouted when he discovered it did not exist.

"What are you going to do about Katherine's sentencing?" Trygve asked. "Are you going to that? It's Thursday, you know."

"Yes, I'll go. I've been with her through the trial; it wouldn't be right to cop out on her now, especially when the sentence is passed down. I just wish I knew what to expect," Sonja said. "That might be a tough day."

"Do you want me to be there?" asked Trygve.

"No, you don't have to be. Tanya will go with me."

"Ready for a game of Scrabble?"

"Bring it on, baby," Sonja said.

CHAPTER 26

The Love Boat

The weather along the northern coast of Norway had been cloudy and cold, but this morning the sun was shining brightly, and the sky that had been scudded with patchy fog and low gray clouds yesterday had disappeared, replaced by a luminous blue sky. The Norwegian cruise liner they boarded yesterday was luxurious, complete with all the amenities that made you feel special and well-cared for.

Sonja lay in Trygve's arms in their cabin watching the scenery glide past their large window. This trip had given her ample time to review all that had happened in the last six months. Her investigation into her sister's death had been eye-opening, but nothing had prepared her for the surprising conclusion of finding her sister alive, just as she had always suspected. She couldn't believe she had weathered the storm as well as she had, but without Trygve beside her, she would have been overwhelmed by the surprising turns and detours of the case. As for Tryg, he was rejoicing that the mystery of Katherine Waite's drowning and subsequent discovery of her secret life in Fort Worth, Texas, had finally come to a resounding conclusion.

Trygve stirred in the bed beside her. Sonja raised her head and gently kissed her husband's lips.

"Mornin', love," she said.

"Mornin'. Is there any coffee?" he asked, yawning widely.

"I can make some." Sonja climbed out of bed and grabbed her bathrobe off the back of the chair while Trygve sat up against the headboard of the bed. She slipped the packet of coffee grounds into the machine, poured water into the reservoir, and flipped it on. Instantly the room filled with the invigorating scent of fresh-brewed coffee. Their cabin was spacious, with a gleaming bathroom, a small sitting area with two stuffed chairs and a coffee table, and their king-sized bed.

"This is a nice change of scenery, wouldn't you say?" he asked, looking at the steep, rocky hillsides in the distance that bordered the blue water of the fjord.

"It's wonderful, honey. This trip is just what I needed to recover from the mess Katherine got herself into. How can people screw up their lives so bad?" she asked as she brought Trygve a cup of coffee.

"It's easy if you make poor choices, or have an impulsive nature, but what I want to know is how are you feeling about everything now, sweetheart?" Trygve asked. His compassion and concern for her lifted Sonja's spirit like nothing else.

"I'm recovering slowly, trying to process everything, but that day in court when the judge handed down her sentence was a real nail-biter. After the McClintock family spoke about their loss, I thought the judge would throw the book at Katherine."

"From what you told me, no one was more surprised by the sentence than Katherine," Tryg commented languidly,

"Who would have ever thought she'd only get three years?" Sonja commented, nodding her head. "Wonders never cease, but I'm also sure Katherine's very heartfelt apology helped. When she asked the family to forgive her for what had happened, there wasn't a dry eye in the courtroom, me included."

"I'm sure her spotless record in Texas, her reliable employment at IF, and the fact she disarmed an active shooter during a shooting at the plant all helped, huh?"

"Sure did. The judge said that due to her flawless employment record and her courage in disarming an active shooter during a highly charged, emotional situation, lives were saved due to her heroic actions, so Judge Benson reduced her sentence. That was pretty amazing."

"Well, it helped that she never even had so much as a traffic ticket in over thirty years," Tryg said, "but I just want you to remember something, Sonja."

"Yeah. What's that?"

"Your sister is flawed like all of us and made some bad decisions, but she's not a criminal at heart," Trygve stated. "She was young and foolish, but to be fair, we've all made some bad choices. It's just that the guys she got hooked up with were a couple of radicalized people who had an agenda they couldn't let go of. They acted impulsively on their ideals, and unfortunately, they killed someone in the process. Katherine, though, said she had nothing to do with the planning of the bombing, and the judge must have believed her and decided her self-imposed sentence of exile in Texas fulfilled part of her punishment.

"Yeah, she basically said that when she handed down her decision." Sonja's shoulders slumped when she thought of the consequences her sister paid for one foolish choice. "Just think of all the stuff she missed over the years that she can never recover: our parents' funerals, time spent with her sisters, our wedding, all of her friends she left behind . . . lots of stuff that's now water over the dam."

"Right, but just remember she can rebuild some of what she's lost. You've started that already by renewing a relationship with her," Trygve reminded her.

"Yeah, I guess I did, didn't I?" Sonja said with a sigh.

Trygve patted the bed. "Come here, honey," he said.

Sonja set her coffee cup down and slid under the blankets beside Trygve. "I just have one request," he said, wrapping her in his arms and drawing her close.

"What's that?"

He kissed her long and deeply. "For the next three days, there's no talk about your sister. It's just me," he kissed her again, "and you," more kisses, "on a boat in the most beautiful place in the world."

"I can live with that," Sonja said as she kissed Trygve again.

THE END

ABOUT THE AUTHOR

Sue Berg is a Wisconsin native and a cheerleader for the Midwestern way of life. The beauty of Wisconsin, the authenticity of its people, and the rural way of life are all ideals she incorporates into her novels. Since retiring from a teaching career that spanned thirty-two years, Sue has pursued writing full-time and has completed six novels in the award-winning Jim Higgins Driftless Mystery Series set in the coulees and bluffs of La Crosse, Wisconsin and *Death at the Dentist*, the first novel in The Dirty Business Mystery Series, which features housecleaner, Sonja Hovland and her blue-collar cohorts.

Sue resides in the beautiful Driftless Area near Viroqua, Wisconsin with her husband, Alan. She enjoys gardening, quilting, writing, and camping on the Mississippi River with her family.

ENJOYED DEATH AT THE UNIVERSITY?

We think you'll also like the Jim Higgins Driftless Mystery Series!

The Driftless Mystery Series set in the beautiful Driftless region of the Upper Midwest does not disappoint. With complex characters, intriguing plots, and surprising twists and turns, this series will delight you with its ability to entertain while upholding the values we all treasure; love, faith, loyalty, and family. It is destined to become a beloved and enduring legacy to the people and culture in this unique part of the country.